LOUISE MUMFORD was born and lives in South Wales. From a young age she loved books and would make up stories based on her favourite characters, so it was only natural that she studied English Literature at university and it was a delight to graduate with first-class honours. As a teacher she tried to pass on her love of reading to her students (and discovered that the secret to successful teaching is . . . stickers! She is aware that that is, essentially, bribery.)

In the summer of 2019 Louise experienced a once-in-a-lifetime moment: she was discovered as a new writer by her publisher at the Primadonna Festival. Everything has been a bit of a whirlwind since then.

Louise lives in Cardiff with her husband and spends her time trying to get down on paper all the marvellous and frightening things that happen in her head.

Also by Louise Mumford

Sleepless

THE SAFE HOUSE

Louise Mumford

ONE PLACE. MANY STORIES

HQ
An imprint of HarperCollins*Publishers* Ltd
1 London Bridge Street
London SE1 9GF

www.harpercollins.co.uk

HarperCollins*Publishers*
1st Floor, Watermarque Building, Ringsend Road
Dublin 4, Ireland

This paperback edition 2022

1
First published in Great Britain by
HQ, an imprint of HarperCollins*Publishers* Ltd 2022

ISBN: 9780008480882

MIX
Paper from
responsible sources
FSC® C007454

To Jason, always.

Chapter 1

Sixteen years earlier

There was a killer prowling around their terraced house, Esther's mother told her. It pressed itself against their windows, slithered over the bricks and licked at the door-knocker.

The only thing to do was escape.

'We are going to go far away and live amongst the trees. Would you like that? The trees?' Mother asked, wrapping a scarf around five-year-old Esther's mouth and nose so she couldn't have answered even if she had wanted to.

Esther had no opinion on trees. She had opinions about the best food to eat for dinner, the best colour in the universe and who Mr Wiffles, her toy whale, had fallen out with that day. But trees? She saw a few scraggly ones from her bedroom window. They moved in the wind and shook their branches like they were laughing at her.

Maybe they were.

But, tonight, all Esther could see were the flames.

'You're going to have to carry some things. The rest we'll leave behind.' Her mother pulled Esther's arms through the rucksack, which she had picked all by herself. It had whales on it too.

She could have helped hoist the bag onto her own shoulders, but she remained a dead weight. She wanted to stay here, at home. Even with the killer. Home had her bedroom with its deep-sea diver wallpaper and the bit of carpet that pulled up to reveal a hiding space under the floorboards. There was going to be no carpet in the new house; all the floors were going to be smooth, dust-free and easy to clean, so Mother said.

That was Esther's fault.

'But, Dad—' Her father had raced off into the night, Mother had told her, gone to help, straight into the heart of the fiery monster that lay beyond their living-room window.

'Your father will follow us; he promised. Right. We're going to open the door now. Then it's straight to the car. But you can't take the scarf off even when you're in there. Clear?'

Esther's fault.

'The new house is so much safer for you, Pips. I should have done this years ago.' Because the killer outside, it wanted her particularly. The new house would protect her. It was a fortress, built to keep out the enemy. Except the enemy wasn't a horde of people with guns and bombs, it wasn't a nuclear blast, or flood or even the fire outside.

It was the air.

'Got it?' her mother asked and Esther's hand instinctively went to her pocket where she kept her inhaler, even though she didn't need to check – it was always there.

Her mother handed her the goggles and she put them on. Esther liked them at least: it made her feel like the divers on her wallpaper in the room that she didn't want to leave.

She wasn't ready to dive.

But it was over in seconds. Her mother pulled her, and, caught in her current, she bobbed along in her wake. Outside, their world had changed.

2

There was smoke, of course. But there had always been smoke. Esther felt the grip of that hand that squeezed her chest and she wheezed, reaching for the comforting shape of her inhaler, each breath something that threatened to squeeze out all the air from her body.

The sky was no longer black but a fiery, cloudy orange. Her mother bundled her into the back of the car, belted her into her child seat and started the engine at the same time as clicking her own belt into place. It was hard to turn her head in the scarf, but Esther did her best, trying to look back one last time at the small house that had been theirs.

And then, briefly, she really was under the sea, except the sea was made of faces, hands and fumes and the car swam through it all.

But soon that passed too. Hours sped by until dawn lightened the night sky. Concrete turned to wasteland and then bloomed green. Well, green*er*. Esther slept through much of the journey.

The roads finally ended. They bumped and jolted over a dirt track. Esther ran a finger around the edge of her scarf, her skin itchy and hot, but she wasn't brave enough to inch the material back and let in some cool air because the killer was in the car with her.

It kept her company all the way to the House.

As soon as Esther saw it, she knew it needed that capital H. They had to leave the car and walk the last part, her mother scooping her up and running for most of the way. They could leave their home and everything they knew behind but that wouldn't save them – save *her* and her weak little lungs that couldn't even do their one job properly. Things had gone too far, her mother told her. The air was too poisoned, wherever they went. Except for one place, and one place only.

Finally, she stood before it, clutching her mother's hand. 'Our hideaway.' Her mother dragged her closer. Set into the hill with earth making up most of its walls and roof, the front of it was a blank concrete face with two narrow windows.

'To keep you safe, Pips.' Her mother pulled her forward, into the shadow of the House. 'Like you're a toy, hmm? A special one. All snug in your packaging.'

But Esther had opened lots of those toys, the figure within pressed face first against the plastic and every time she'd almost heard each one gasp in relief as she freed them. Snug was not a new word to Esther, but that day, standing in front of the House, it did not mean cosy and protected.

It meant trapped.

* * *

Just her and her mother in the House in the hill. A prayer each day:

'To what do we give thanks?'

'The House.'

'What protects the air we breathe?'

'The House.'

'What gives us plants and water and power and comfort?'

'The House.'

'What keeps us safe?'

'The House.'

Princesses in their towers always pined for their escape in the fairy tales her mother used to read to her and for a long time she had not understood why. Out There was a smog-filled thicket of thorns waiting to wrap around her throat.

There was nothing for her there, her mother said. The House was her world, and she would never need to leave it again.

And that is how it was for the next sixteen years.

Chapter 2

A demon lived in Esther's chest.

It squeezed her lungs and she heard that too-familiar wheeze. Water dripped down her bedside cupboard from the glass she had knocked over and she thought to herself that she would need to wipe that up before Mother saw it, but then her windpipe collapsed to a thin straw and no matter how hard she tried to suck in a breath, she couldn't get enough air.

Panic bubbled.

She knew that all she had to do was stagger or crawl over to the inhaler somewhere on her dressing table and, in a few puffs, a blessed ease would spread through her chest. She'd done it before; she could do it again.

Breathe.

Breathe.

This was why she did not leave the House. The air was cleaner here amongst the trees in their hillside bunker, but cleaner did not mean *clean*. Not for her. Not anymore. The demon in her chest spent much of its time dozing because of the carefully filtered air that was pumped around the House. As she got older, Esther appreciated the time and planning that had gone into their home, everything from the backup filtration system run by a generator to the tubs that grew fresh vegetables and the water supply piped from a nearby well.

The House kept her demon drowsy. Out There, it would wake up.

The concept of Out There was quite a hazy one, Esther had to admit, built on the old films she watched, none of them dated beyond the millennium. She knew the world had moved on since then. The thing was, she also knew she would never be able to move on into it, not now, with its polluted skies that would make her demon roar into life with glee.

Stumbling, she gripped on to her bedspread, bunching it into her fist, the whole thing sliding off, dragging Mr Wiffles with it until he was almost touching her nose. Then, somehow, she was on the floor, but that was okay because she could pull herself up to the table and grab it if everything would stop spinning and the straw that passed for her windpipe would loosen up a little. There was nothing to fear.

Oh, but there was. The demon pressed down on her, squatted on her chest, put its clammy lips around her windpipe and then bit down hard.

She heard birdsong. Fake. Esther's mother sometimes played ambient noise to stop the silence taking hold. The birds had been some of the first to go, she'd told her, even in the countryside, away from the suppurating heart of the city, though there were breeding programmes to protect what was left. In captivity of course. The skies were no place for them now, though Esther had seen shapes in the distance every so often, wheeling and graceful smudges in the sky. There were still people Out There. Esther knew it wasn't some sort of B-movie apocalyptic wasteland beyond their door because people were like parasites, her mother told her – they survived anything, even poisoning their own air. It was the poor innocent creatures that suffered the worst: the animals, the children. Cities limped on, as did the people, their lungs blackening with each breath.

That was why Mother had built this place for her.

The House purred. It had better lungs than Esther: the beautifully engineered air-conditioning and filtration system that kept the air inside at optimum purity. And it had roots: a series of storage tunnels underneath that held everything that two people might ever need.

Esther swung out her arm and swiped for the inhaler, her hand grasping nothing. It was not on her dressing table. She needed to think. Where had she put it, before she went to bed the night before? But thinking was becoming difficult.

It was in those moments that she was closest to her father.

A hero, her mother told her. A man who had lost his own life saving others.

Her mental picture of him had, over the years, shrunk to photograph size, bordered white. A man forever stilled in a dozen or so poses, next to a tree, holding a hat, pushing the hair out of his face. Esther couldn't remember what that hair smelled like, or whether the skin on his hand was rough or smooth, or what he looked like when he wasn't frozen in a smile.

She might not have known those things about her father but she knew how he must have felt as he died saving those other people from a fire that then killed him, choking for a breath that wouldn't come. Frankly, as mementoes went, she would have preferred a pocket watch or something.

She sat on the floor by her bed, Mr Wiffles eyeing her from her blue bedspread, chosen when she was a child because she had wanted it to be his sea.

'I ... I ...' she tried out the words.

The cuddly whale gazed back at her, unblinking, his stitching a little looser now than it was sixteen years ago. Like everyone's.

'My inhaler ...' she tried again.

'Well, how am I meant to see that from here?' she grumbled for him in her head. *'I've been lying on this bedspread for the best part of a week now and all I've had a chance to see is your sock drawer.'*

She had to admit, Mr Wiffles had become more bad-tempered with age.

Then she heard it, the blessed clacking sound that signalled rescue.

'Esther?' A familiar voice. Her mother. 'I'm here, I'm here – breathe …'

Esther hauled herself up like an old person as she took a puff, slumping around the dressing table leg as relief hit. Her breathing slowed and she pushed her hair away from her sweaty forehead.

'Thanks …' Esther said, her voice hoarse. 'I nearly had it …'

There was a cool hand on her cheek as her mother's face loomed into view. 'It was on the floor by your bedside table. Lucky you have me, eh?'

'Yes.'

She was. Every day Esther reminded herself how grateful she was to her mother, for this filtered air, for the House. Each breath made the demon in her chest smaller and sleepier until she could kid herself that it didn't exist at all.

'Ready?' Her mother helped her up.

Esther was.

Chapter 3

'Happy birthday, Pips!'

Mother appeared with the time-honoured slice of fig and cranberry loaf topped with a birthday candle that had done sterling service for the past sixteen years because it had never once been lit.

Birthday Breakfast was sacrosanct. Mother even wore her least shabby cardigan, though she never went so far as to change out of her stained work trousers and battered leather slippers. There was the special loaf, as dark as fruitcake. Bread and cakes required flour, which they only had in a limited supply, so this was a treat, served with jam and the best tea, its leaves slowly uncurling like feathery fingers in the infuser.

This birthday was a special one.

'Tiara!' Mother said, her own already in place, balanced precariously in the wire nest of her hair, its pink plastic jewels only slightly scuffed.

Esther could have tried a weak protest, but the tiara was ready in her jeans pocket and she stuffed it on, feeling its little comb claws grip into her hair. She would never be too old for the birthday tiara, even if it had originally been designed for a five-year-old and was now too small, as if she had drunk an *Alice in Wonderland* potion and not her cup of morning tea.

'Twenty-one years old,' Mother said, cutting the loaf as they sat at the tiny breakfast bar in their kitchen.

Twenty-one. A magic number. Esther expected great things from twenty-one because that was coming of age. Not eighteen, still stuck in the hormonal, sulky teens, no, twenty-one was an adult, a grown-up ... an equal.

A grown-up with a question, or rather a birthday request.

Above them the skylight was a bright circle of white sky in the middle of the low ceiling and, below it, the stairwell was its dark shadow leading down to the storerooms, their basic gym, indoor garden and the front door. The concrete walls were painted a soothing green like the grass Esther could see moving beyond her bedroom window, but the paint was fading in places; the grey underneath beginning to show through.

In her imagination, the House was a boil under the skin of the hill. Mother told her that approaching it from behind, walking along the top of the hill, all someone would see was a gentle bulge and the privacy-tinted, extra-tough glass of the skylight, the sign that people lurked under their feet. Only from the front would they see the austere concrete façade looming over them and the hill sloping down from either side.

Esther reached for a slice of fig loaf.

'Wait!' Mother moved the plate away and then put her hands, palms up, on the countertop. 'To what do we give thanks?'

Esther turned her own hands over and bowed her head. 'The House.'

'What protects the air we breathe?'

'The House.'

'What gives us plants and water and power and comfort?'

'The House.'

'What keeps us safe?'

'The House.'

The House was their God and it was one who needed constant soothing in order to stop their worst fear: something going wrong.

The generator, the air conditioning, themselves, bones and blood and infection. So far, their worship had worked. Mother made sure they carefully maintained themselves, like two cars from a reputable garage, but most importantly, they maintained the House.

After breakfast there was routine, birthday or no.

Routine was key. Jelly cube chunks of time could dissolve too quickly if they weren't careful. Whole hours could be lost staring at the inside of a wrist, the bit where blue veins close to the surface were like a sunken map pointing to treasure that would never be found. Routine stopped this. It took time and chopped it up into manageable mouthfuls, never too much in one go, never enough to choke.

The Checklist directed their days. First was the garden.

The garden was the biggest room on the ground floor and had never felt the rays of the sun. It was windowless, with tables arranged under LED lamps, and on those tables were the tubs in which grew tomatoes, peppers, cucumbers, lettuces and whatever else they fancied eating, each one at a different stage of growing. Mother had studied do-it-yourself hydroponics before they moved and had made the containers herself. The plants in their cups were placed into holes in the tub lid with their roots dangling down ready to be sprayed with water by the pipes set underneath.

Each plant was slightly different in the curl of its leaves and the thickness of the stem and Esther liked to see the clean white tangle of roots when she lifted each one in its little pot. The tendrils were the plant's brain matter, damp and fresh, reaching down to the water. Once, as a child, she had wanted to name all the vegetables as they grew but Mother had forbidden it as soon as Esther had started refusing to eat her vegetable friends.

'Sunbathing season yet?' Mother asked.

'Well, it is spring – y'know. It's getting warmer; gotta get my vitamin D …' Esther smiled.

Sunbathing season had started when she had been a child and

she had never quite given it up. So, on some days she collected a book and the creaky old folding chair and set it up close to the plant tubs, plonking Mother's straw hat on her head in order to pretend she was on a beach or in the grounds of a fabulous hotel, the kind with poolside loungers and cocktails that appeared as if by magic. Next to her she plugged in their UV lamp, the one designed to help people who got depressed in the dark winter months, and she imagined it was an exotic sun with rays that would never tan her skin, nor burn it either.

It was the smell that brought her here. The filtered air and her weak lungs meant that most of the House was as scent-less as they could make it, but here no one could stop the rich, almost spiced aroma of the tomatoes. Mother called it grassy, but Esther could no longer remember what grass smelled like to be able to agree with her.

They continued to delicately check each plant for root rot, the birthday request on the tip of Esther's tongue, but she could see that her mother was concentrating, her hands deft and quick, frowning as she adjusted her glasses. Now was not the right moment – and this birthday request had been asked before, on every birthday for the last four years. Each time it had been denied. The moment had to be not just right but perfect.

Esther could have asked her when they moved on from the garden to the next chore on the Checklist. On the ground floor of the House was the gym, a small room where a set of weights, some yoga mats, a poster with exercises drawn on it, a mirror and a running machine could be found. Lately its belt had begun to flap like a leathery tongue with every thud and so they worked together to patch it.

'The old girl has some more years in her yet.' Mother gave the edge of the machine a pat.

It was a sign, the mention of the word "year" – this was the time, Esther knew. She opened her mouth to speak, the question choking her as much as her asthma did, but then her mother gave a yelp and shook out her hand. 'Tough old girl too – shit!' Blood welled in her palm and she dropped the scissors she had been using.

In the time it took to help her mother wash out the cut, discover it wasn't as deep as they feared, wrap a piece of linen around her hand and get back to the machine, they were late completing the Checklist and Mother's lips had set in a tightly pressed line, her glasses pushed back onto her head in a distracted fashion.

Not a perfect moment at all. But that was okay – Esther had all evening and she could wait. She was good at that.

Chapter 4

Evening found the two of them together and the question Esther still hadn't asked sat with them, patiently waiting its turn.

She read, choosing a book from the glass-fronted bookcases that took up most of one wall. According to Mother, books were both essential but also a hazard for Esther's wheezy chest, which was why they were safely behind glass where the dust could not settle in between their soft pages.

Mother continued with whatever fantastical creature she was whittling out of scraps of wood, shaving fat curls from something that began as a lump but then grew wings, or horns, scales and claws. The little creatures lurked in every available space, their eyes watching from shadowy corners.

Esther knew their choice of entertainment would be viewed as simple by the people who lived Out There. An invisible net of electric signals covered the globe, Esther's mother told her, a net that connected everyone, allowed a person to read books on a screen and buy clothes, watch films or find out any piece of information. Their wall of bookcases hardly measured up in comparison but Mother did not want the electric net to wrap around them here in their home because those signals did something to people's brains and eyes; it hypnotised them like a snake so they lost hours watching pointless videos and arguing with people they had never met. Esther and her mother did not watch television, except for old films, and there was no newspaper delivery service to the back of beyond. Anyway, as Mother frequently said, they didn't need to know about Out There. It didn't concern them.

'Twenty-one years old,' Mother said again, holding out Esther's present, her lips twitching into a smile.

This was the Birthday Guessing. Another ritual. Esther unwrapped the tea towel and held up the wooden figure.

'A hippo?' she tried.

Mother shook her head, chuckling. 'No, the head just got away with me.'

Esther studied the creature in her hand. 'A sheep?'

'Nope. Couldn't get the bum right. Give up?'

Esther always did every year. Mother didn't let it stop her, but she was terrible at carving.

'It's an elephant!'

Esther studied it. 'Where's its trunk?'

'Ah, well, the trunk fell off in a sad accident a few weeks ago.'

They laughed. Mother's eyes were soft in the candlelight they used most evenings, not to save power, but because she liked the gentle, flickering glow.

'Thank you.'

Esther would add it to all the others on her windowsill. But it wasn't the present she'd wanted. Her laugh ended in a sigh. Twenty-one years old. She glanced at Mother.

Mother began carving something new, slicing the wood viciously as if removing a canker in rotten fruit. 'Pips?'

Pips – short for Pipsqueak. Something small and inconsequential, not done growing. But she had. She was twenty-one years old, her growing was done and, though the small wooden not-elephant was sweet, that was not what she wanted.

'You told me that when I turned twenty-one—'

'No,' Mother said. The word pinched Esther's heart. Mother

put her whittling knife down and rubbed at her eyes. 'You're not coming with me—'

'But I'm—'

'Twenty-one. I know. But you're not coming with me on the Yearly—'

'But you—'

'No. I have never promised and it doesn't matter how old you are. It's not safe.'

Their once-a-year supply trip, the day when Mother took their van and disappeared from sunrise to sundown, away into the Out There to buy all the things that could not be grown, patched, fixed or ignored. They had enough food to last for decades, the kind of dehydrated stuff that never tasted of the ingredients meant to be in it, powdered things, tins and packets piled high in the tunnels, but every year Mother stocked up on a year's worth of edibles that could not last a decade, like pasta, flour, rice and, more importantly to Esther, the treats that only lasted one glorious week: fresh milk, fruit and meat.

They had been having a variation of this argument for the past four years.

'I would wear my mask and goggles; I would stay in the van. I just want to—'

'No.'

Want. The word filled Esther up and it pushed at her lips, making her temples throb.

'So that's an end to it.' Mother put down the knife. 'How about a nettle tea before bed?'

The tea was a powdery, dank liquid that cooled too quickly and left an aftertaste. One day Esther would say no, but Mother was already straining the dried leaves and, anyway, it was good for … Esther wasn't quite sure what it was good for but it tasted awful enough to be good for a lot of things. Letting her eyes wander to the open door of her bedroom and beyond that, to the black rectangle of glass, Esther saw only her own face reflected back at her.

16

'I only ever want to keep you safe.' Mother put a small ceramic cup on the arm of Esther's chair, stopping to pat her shoulder before returning to her seat and her latest wooden beast.

Safety for Esther meant the clean, filtered air of the House, which kept her chest demon drowsy and gentle. It had meant Mother uprooting her whole life to live in the trees under the hill, leaving behind any friends or family. It meant quiet, ordered, peaceful hours that could be ticked off as easily as those chores on the Checklist. Safety meant all of that, for as long as she lived ... and that could be a very long time.

Candlelight flickered, and, as she drank the tea, Esther felt her eyelids droop.

Here was her final opportunity to argue her case. She was old enough and wise enough to be useful, to help, to take some of the burden from Mother's shoulders – and if her being useful and being helpful meant that she got to experience a little of the world Out There then that would perhaps stop the feeling she had when she woke up in the morning, like someone had taken their fingernails to the chalkboard of her brain.

Each blink became longer and longer.

Slice, slice went the little carving knife.

Esther stayed silent.

And in the night, when Esther half-woke from a leaden sleep, she thought she heard from Mother's bedroom next to her a faint, familiar, muffled sound.

Crying.

Chapter 5

It was no surprise when Esther woke up in front of the door.

For a second she thought she could hear a faint shuffling sound behind her. A dry sigh.

She had to be quick. Pushing herself up from the concrete floor, she sat and swiped at the dirt on her pyjamas. This had been happening for a few months now and, so far, Esther had been lucky. Each time, before Mother woke, she had managed to get upstairs and back into bed, ready to appear, yawning theatrically, as soon as she heard any noise in the kitchen.

She did not want to worry Mother.

'Pips?'

Too late.

Mother stood at the top of the stairs that led to the living room and bedrooms. 'What are you doing down there? Are you okay? What happened?' She ran down the steps and took Esther by the arm before she could even try to stand up by herself. 'I thought you'd collapsed.'

'I'm fine, I'm fine. I think I must have walked here in my sleep, that's all—'

'What? Sleepwalking? Down here? But you could hurt yourself—'

'I'm fine!'

'God – you could open the door!'

'But I haven't – see? Still closed. Still locked. I'm sure it's just a one-off thing. I feel great.'

'Come upstairs – let me see you in the light ...'

Before following her mother, Esther turned to the dark mouth of the tunnel stretching away from the storeroom. Originally the House had been planned as a Cold War bunker though that war had defrosted by the time the place had been built. The tunnel had been meant for ammunition stores but had never been properly finished. It still had a bare earth floor and was a long corridor with stubby offshoots like deep pores where Mother stored everything she thought they might one day need.

This was a place Esther rarely went. It had never been her playroom as a child. She had never scampered there, imagining it was a mummy's tomb, a secret passageway, a cave, a dragon's lair. Mother had never had to warn her to be careful, had never had to explain how those metal shelving units could be toppled if climbed upon, how the wicked edges on the machinery could slice into unsuspecting flesh. Maybe it was because of its earth floor, too grave-like; maybe it was the scratching she could hear under her feet, which she knew was caused by nearby small animals but still made the back of her neck prickle; maybe it was the cold, or the gloom ... Whatever it was, Esther had stayed away.

Reaching behind herself to the massive front door, she placed her hand onto chill metal and then she brushed her fingers over a handle only Mother turned. Beyond it was their rudimentary airlock and then the final door, the one that led to sky and grass and wind.

And, of course, air.

But there was no time to linger. Barefoot, she ran, up the stairs and into her bedroom, wriggling free from Mother trying to take her temperature. She put on the clothes she thought would be suitable for Out There – because that was where she intended to go that day. Trainers to move quickly, her least shabby T-shirt and the jeans with only minimal fraying.

'Pips?' As Esther crossed to the kitchen, Mother belted her cardigan around a pair of pyjamas that once had been printed with stars. 'There you are, my little night owl, up far too early this morning.'

Esther gave the customary soft hooting sound. She was the owl and Mother the early bird. Mother hooted back as Esther grabbed a glass and ran the tap, the trembling in her voice masked by the sound of the running water. 'I'm going.'

There was silence.

'Did you hear me? I said I'm—'

'I heard.'

More silence.

'I—'

'I—I—I!' Mother slammed the rucksack she had picked up from the sofa onto the floor. 'That's all I hear! That's all you think about! But me? I don't have the luxury of only ever thinking about myself. I have to think about you! Which is what I do, every bloody minute of every bloody day!' She snatched the rucksack up from the floor. 'I'm trying to protect you, because I've seen with my own eyes what that filthy, poisoned air does to you – I've watched you nearly die – but ...' She gave a muffled half-scream of frustration and Esther flinched. She tried to think how to explain it, this gnawing feeling in the middle of her that wanted out, that wanted to see something, anything other than these bunker walls and the never-changing trees beyond her bedroom window. Nothing came out of her mouth.

'But you know what? I'm done.' Mother marched over to Esther and pushed the rucksack into her stomach, the middle of it flopping over her arm like a deflated baby. 'Done. Off you go. If you want to go on the Yearly so badly then do so. But you'll go on your own. In fact – it will make a nice change. I think I'll

20

put my feet up for the day, relax, have a chat with the plants, whatever the hell it is you do whilst I'm gone.'

The bag in Esther's arms seemed to weigh much more than empty cloth should have. Mother sat down and turned her face away, wrenching her slippers off without even looking at them. This was silly, Esther told herself. Her mother was being silly. There was no way Esther could do the Yearly on her own – she didn't even know where to start.

'There's the list. Off you go.' Her mother threw a piece of paper in Esther's direction and she watched it float to the floor, slowly, slowly, not a feather because feathers were attached to birds and they could fly; they knew where home was even if they were far away from it. Esther didn't even know where the van was, the one hidden beyond the treeline, kept running only for this once-a-year purpose.

But she could walk.

The nearest town couldn't be that far away, could it? She would simply have to walk there. Squaring her shoulders, she picked up the list and took a breath before heading down the stairs, reaching the first front door.

Turning the handle caused a series of clunking noises that made the door shudder as it began to roll away. It should have been harder to open, Esther thought. She should have had to have put all her weight into it, but it yielded smoothly enough. It revealed a small porch area. A simple idea. Two doors that never opened at the same time, creating a safe space in between. There was even a special filtration system specifically for the porch that would clean and sanitise the air if needed – though they had never used that part. Yet.

Two whole suits hung, like limp people being punished for their crimes. They were overalls, nothing special, the kind of thing that buttoned up to the neck. The mask was the important bit, Mother said. They had recently upgraded: a slim glass strip that stretched from nose to chin with two parts that looked like mini aeroplane engines under each ear. The idea was that there no longer needed to be a seal around the edge; instead air was sucked in, purified via filters and any contaminated air was fanned away. No more fogged lenses and seal sweat. There were also goggles and a hood to be on the safe side.

'It would take you nearly the whole day to walk to anything, you know,' Mother's voice floated down to her. 'And that's just a petrol station and a general shop. To get supplies at the DIY store you would have to go much further.'

Her overall hung in front of her, empty and waiting for a person to fill it out – someone who knew what they were doing. Thoughts spun at her and away but it was the list that did it in the end. She stared at the words and realised she didn't even know what half of those objects were, or where to get them. The paper crumpled easily in her hand.

Esther clenched her other fist, feeling the sharp edges of her nails dig into her palms. She could have carried it on a bit more, the pretence, the foolery that she was a functioning human being who knew how to leave the house and get some tinned food and spare parts, but instead she sank to the floor and let her forehead rest against the cool metal door frame.

A shadowed figure appeared at the top of the stairs. 'Are we done?'

Within the hour Mother was ready. She liked to make it there and back in one day, which meant for an eye-wateringly early start. Outside, a faint pink haze had begun to nudge night out of the sky. Perhaps that was what made her mother paler this morning, Esther thought, eyes sunken in bruised shadows, lips bloodless and cracked. Older.

The thought was not new, but each time it came as a razor, something that drew blood: what if Mother did not come back? What if something happened to her out there? What if she decided that enough was enough and she wanted to escape? What if the car careened out of control? What if, what if, what if …

Lately a new what-if had slithered its way into her brain.

What if, one day, Esther woke up and shuffled into the kitchen, still in her pyjamas, her only thought that of the kettle and the new loaf they'd baked last night, to find Mother cold and stiff in her chair, eyes open but never to see again?

What would Esther do then?

Mother shoved her out of the porch and closed the inner door. Metal clanged back into place, biting off any other words and leaving Esther alone in the waiting shadows.

Chapter 6

Time passed in the dark. Esther sat.

Next to the door was the shotgun. As soon as Esther had been old enough there had been lessons.

'Target,' Mother had said, showing Esther the cartoon face she'd drawn with big eyes and a clown mouth before pinning it onto the concrete dead end of the tunnel.

Things Esther had discovered: gunshot was loud; kickback could hurt a shoulder; no matter how much you tried to breathe out calmly you never quite hit your target.

Face hot, arm trembling, she had breathed and concentrated and shook out her hand, clenching and unclenching her fingers, every day for months until the gun felt like an extension of her arm, until her breathing calmed almost as soon as she raised the muzzle, until she could simply sense when to pull the trigger and when she did – dead shot. Most times.

'Show me,' Mother had said every so often, resting her head back against the sofa, her eyes watchful.

So Esther had. She would unload and check the gun, already cleaned and primed, *always* cleaned and primed, and then she would reload, snapping it all into place with deft, practised movements.

'What keeps us safe?'

'The House.'

Mother had smiled. 'And the bloody gun.'

In the end thirst made Esther get up off the floor.

The Checklist and chores had to be done first, but then the day was hers to do with as she pleased. Usually she danced to old music CDs, cooked something weird for dinner with the ingredients she chose by closing her eyes and pointing to random tins in the cupboard, and watched back-to-back films on DVD that she had seen a thousand times before.

This time she did not want to dance, or cook, or watch a film.

Esther pressed her forehead against the glass of her bedroom window and thought of nuns. Nuns did penance, their fingers working delicately over rosary beads, praying for their souls, anyone's souls, for the world. Sometimes it felt to Esther as if she was the penance and that Out There healed itself a little more after each of her careful rosary days.

'Bollocks,' Mr Wiffles said, swimming on her bedside table. *'You're not a nun. Nothing you do makes any difference to what goes on Out There.'*

A nun probably wouldn't have wallpaper with cartoon fish on it, Esther considered. Redecoration was not a priority, according to Mother, though, of late, she had begun to bring back little taster pots of paint from her once-a-year trip. So far, Esther had managed to paint one entire bedroom wall in a not exactly matching colour but at least one that was plain and had no cute-eyed creatures on it. Luckily their duvet covers were so faded and threadbare by now they couldn't see what the original patterns had been and she had picked off all the stickers from her dressing table. The one shelf on her wall was empty, testament to the great doll and toy massacre of two years ago when she had swept them all into an old hydroponics tub and lugged them down to the tunnels. Mr Wiffles had been the only survivor.

She wandered out into the living room. On the wall was a

small air quality monitor, a half-moon of colour: green to yellow to amber to red with a needle that never moved but lay dead and defeated in the wedge of green. Green for go. Green for safe. Never anything but green. Esther's eyes flicked to it anyway.

The other window lay on the floor. She changed it monthly, a big square piece of paper. It had started as an art project when they had first moved in, but had quickly become a fixture, the large painted sheet taking pride of place on the wall over the sofa. 'See, Pips? We can have whatever view we want,' Mother had said. This month she had planned a return to her favourite under-the-sea theme and had been thinking about fixing a little ledge into it so Mr Wiffles could have a pretend swim.

The big blank square was a white void.

She did not want to paint.

Wandering again, she ended up in Mother's room. Neat bed, neat bedside table, clothes neatly folded on the nearby chair. The only signs of a personality were the misshapen wooden creatures peeking out from odd corners.

They watched Esther open the wardrobe as the familiar scent of lavender wafted out from Mother's home-made essential oil perfume. The clothes within were a mix of drab greys and browns, a few patched pairs of jeans, some T-shirts in the exact same hue of vomit green and a couple of jumpers that had clearly lost the battle with the washing machine. There was nothing exciting amongst them.

Except for the dress.

The dress was an emerald velvet, which shone like sleek fur in the light. It was the colour of precious stones in expensive rings, or of a lush forest canopy somewhere exotic. It was the kind of dress someone wore to a cocktail party in a smart London venue where similarly dressed people laughed softly and chinked glasses. It had no place in Mother's wardrobe.

But there it was.

Of course, Esther had asked about it. 'Foolish sentiment,'

26

Mother had said. 'Guess I couldn't bring myself to leave it behind. I married your father in that dress, chose green because I always hated the idea of looking like a white frilly toilet roll cover on my wedding day.' Esther had never seen a photo.

It slipped on so easily. The hemline fell flatteringly mid-calf, the skirt flaring out in a way that made Esther feel as if she was in a 1950s film. The only mirror in the House was a small square above the bathroom sink and she would have had to climb onto a chair to see the bottom half but she didn't need to – she already knew how she looked; she'd done this before.

She looked like someone else.

But the dress fitted poorly and the neckline scratched her skin. What would her mother think, catching her playing dress-up like a kid? That was no way to convince her that she was ready for the Out There – and convince her Esther would. In fact, she had a better plan, she thought, wrenching the dress off and shoving it back onto its hanger before returning to the living room to tidy away her coffee mug. She had tried to do too much all at once by saying she would go on the Yearly. No, baby steps were needed. A walk perhaps. Yes. A quick stroll around the House, suited up, masked. It would be a start.

Definitely. A really good start.

After a cup of tea. And maybe a snack, to keep her strength up. And when the tea had been drunk and the snack eaten, she sat and told herself she was just about to get going and that she simply needed a minute. The minute stretched.

A shadow flitted over the skylight.

Esther froze. Clouds scudded over the sky and caused shadows all the time. This had not been a cloud. Too fast. A flicker. A scuttle.

She looked up. It was a circle of sky – that was all – in its own little periscope tunnel. She knew the glass was toughened and tinted on the outside, so anyone stumbling across it on the hill would think it merely a drain cover.

No one had ever stumbled across it.

She put the mug down with trembling fingers, as slowly as she could, almost believing that if she made a too sudden movement she would somehow draw attention to herself.

Flicker.

Esther moved away from the skylight even though she knew she was being silly. It was just a storm cloud in the sky, an animal, any number of easily explained and completely harmless things.

Esther took a few more steps backwards, telling herself she couldn't be seen because of the privacy glass, that there was no one there anyway, that shadows flickered across the skylight all the time and it was completely normal.

A loud thud came from the direction of her bedroom.

Chapter 7

It wasn't just a thud. It was a thud, a scramble and then a slither.

'*What the bloody hell was that?*' Mr Wiffles said.

Esther stopped in the bedroom doorway, her stomach tingling with shock. There on the glass was the ghost outline of a bird, beak in profile, wings outstretched as if coming in to envelop her in a feathery hug.

Just a bird.

She replayed the sound in her mind. The muffled thump of its head against the glass, the beak sharply tapping like a spectral fingernail wanting to be invited in.

To Esther, birds were small black shapes wheeling through the sky, tiny blobs seen at a distance, never near the House, never close enough to see properly.

Heart thumping, she edged to the window. At first, she couldn't see anything, just the patchy long grass that formed a green sea around the front of the House. Perhaps the bird had already flown away, Esther thought, and all she would have left would be its glass ghost on her window.

There would be nothing to see.

In the end she almost had to press her face up against the window and twist her neck before she caught a glimpse. A smallish, brown, speckled thing; perhaps a sparrow, though Esther wasn't sure as she'd never really learnt the species of birds. Why bother when they were so few?

It was still.

For a moment she thought it was dead. It was sat as if roosting, its little wings folded on its back and its eyes were closed. For some reason, the idea of a bird she couldn't even name being dead made Esther's eyes sting. Then she noticed the heave of its chest, perhaps the only sign that something was wrong. Why didn't the bird fly away?

A rush of heat flushed from the nape of her neck all the way down to the small of her back. She tapped the window gently and the bird's eyes flicked in her direction and then away again, panicked. It tried to move, its wings rising listlessly, but all it could manage was a hop-stumble a few inches away. She couldn't work out whether it was the legs or wings that were to blame.

She knew what Mother would have done. Mother would have told her to stay where she was, that it was too dangerous to go Out There for a bird that was too stupid to distinguish between glass and air. Mother would have told her to wait until she got home.

Mother told her a lot of things.

Her steps took her down the spiral staircase that punched through the heart of the building, and then, once more, there she was, standing in front of the airlock just as she had been when she had woken up that morning, except this time there was no echo of a shuffle behind her, no papery sigh from a dream she could no longer remember.

Door. Handle. Esther concentrated on doing, not thinking. She wouldn't have to go far. A few steps, suited up with a mask on, a few steps to show Mother that she could deal with things too, that she could make decisions on her own, that she could help.

The world tilted and shimmered as she put one foot into the suit followed by the other, then over the shoulders it went. Even when she sank to her knees and took a few deep calm breaths, not wanting to wake the demon, she knew everything was fine. She was going out for a few minutes – that was all – to see if she could help a fellow creature in distress. That was what people did. Adults.

She should have done this years ago.

Legs feeling weak, she hauled herself up and reached for the mask.

The important thing.

It clicked into place and the little fans on either side of her jaw whirred into action. She was a diver once more, though without an oxygen tank strapped to her back. As her heart hammered, her demon opened one sleepy eye.

No.

Wait.

Calm.

All she had to do was scoop up the bird and bring it inside. She had placed an old box by the door that looked the right temporary home for it.

Another breath.

Mother had chosen this place because the air was the safest it could be and she also had her mask, whirring away over her nose. She would be fine. Baby steps.

Another deep breath, then she grasped the handle and pulled the heavy door across.

Chapter 8

Esther stared through an open door.

The strip of metal on the ground marking inside from Out There was a wall too high to climb, a sea Esther shouldn't swim, a desert that would burn out her lungs.

All she had to do was take a step. Just one.

It was too bright.

The glare scoured her eyeballs and made Esther squint as the demon in her chest opened a lazy eye and she heard the wheeze in her breath. Disorientated for a second, she put out a gloved hand against the door frame to steady her and stayed like that for a while, aware of the inhaler in her pocket, carefully breathing her chest demon back to sleep.

The bird wasn't far away. It must have moved a little in the time it had taken Esther to open the door. Esther reconsidered. She wouldn't actually need to walk out there to reach it – all she would have to do is stretch across to it on hands and knees, the lower half of her body safely in the House. Compromise.

She was a mole, blinking in the daylight. Moles weren't blind, Esther recalled as she willed herself to take another step, but they used movement and scent sensors on their nose to get around

32

and find prey. Perhaps, in another twenty years she would snuffle a path through the House in the same way.

On the outside wall next to the front door was a small keypad, Esther noticed. Nothing as common as a key for this House; no, it required numbers in a set pattern like a spell to get back in, a spell she did not know. The door would have to remain open, even if she ever got up the courage to walk to the bird, otherwise she would lock herself out.

The bird wriggled uncomfortably, flicking its gaze across to her and away again in that panicked rhythm. But it didn't move. There was definitely no disease, no sores around the beak, or mangy feathers, or weeping eyes.

Mesmerised, she wanted to stroke it. How come it looked so healthy? How had it survived so well? It was even smaller than it had looked from the window, and the caramel brown markings on its feathers reminded her of a fawn. It was one of those fidgety birds that should have been bobbing its head about and hopping from side to side, searching for the next meal, or mate.

It would die without her.

Immobile, it would freeze in the night, or be eaten by something else, whatever predator was left in these woods.

Esther imagined how she would save it. She would cup it gently between her gloved hands and carry it inside, into its waiting box. She would drip water from a syringe into its beak and feed it worms, no not worms; she'd have to go outside for those – seeds, she'd feed it seeds, from the pantry jars and hide it from Mother, until it was well and then she would show her what she'd done, the life she'd saved, the responsibility she'd taken on, how thoughtful and careful she was.

The trees rustled their branches together and the grass flattened. The bird flicked another glance at her as she crouched, the lower half of her body safely behind that narrow metal strip that formed the threshold.

'Hello, bird,' she said, her words briefly steaming up the inside of her mask. 'My name is Esther and you flew into my window.'

Flick. Bird glance.

'I don't come outside much. Well, I never come outside. The last time I was out here I was five.'

She remembered coming in through this front door for the first time, gripping Mother's hand as she was pulled through and into the quiet. It settled over them like a blanket too tightly tucked. Their old home had whistled and banged; footsteps had thudded and taps had dripped; the traffic had purred outside.

Eventually she had got used to the silence.

'I think you're hurt, bird.'

Flick.

'Do you have family? Are there other birds waiting for you somewhere?'

And where was that 'somewhere'? Mother had told her that, long-term, the air was dangerous for every living thing. When she imagined people Out There, she imagined them hollow-eyed, grey of pallor with a constant dry cough. So how come this bird was here, healthy enough, energetic enough to hurl itself happily into what it had thought was the sky?

Was Mother ... *wrong*?

There was only the laboured rise and fall of its little bird chest to suggest the thing was still alive.

'Bird?'

If it died out there then for weeks, months afterwards she would have to watch its slow decay from her bedroom window: feather to flesh to flaking bone. She would make herself watch it – as punishment for her weakness.

'Bird?'

But there was no more eye flicking.

All she had to do was crawl forward a bit. She could do it, she had to, because if she couldn't actually leave the House then going on the Yearly with Mother would be pretty difficult.

34

She was safe. She was suited. She had the mask and her demon was asleep.

Then she heard it.

It took her a moment to realise what it was. But there carried on the wind that made the grass sway and the trees wave, it came again.

A voice.

A man's voice.

A man stood where no man should be. He was far enough away that she could not see his face properly but also much too close and a part of her brain told her that made sense because he'd come down from the roof, their roof, the top of their hill. Whilst she had been putting on her suit, he had run down the side of the House, after peering into their periscope skylight, and then he had circled around her so that now he was halfway between the House and the trees. Now there was an open door for him.

She stood and grabbed the handle, knowing the door would lock automatically from the inside, as soon as it was closed.

'Hello?' he called.

He probably thought he was dressed for the terrain and weather. It was spring but his coat wasn't thick enough for the cold here, the padding lightweight and cheap, nothing like the thickness of Mother's. And his boots were thin-soled things with probably no grip. She couldn't get a handle on his face though, to look at his eyes and try to work out the person behind them. Just blurred tanned skin and curly brown hair.

His next words were carried on the wind and fractured like a bird's wing: 'Esther Allbright? Can you help me?'

Can you help me?

A question directed to her and only her by the first new person she had seen in sixteen years. Then it hit her. He knew her name. The weight of it rooted her to the spot, her fingers tight on the door handle, heart loud in her ears and her legs hollow china.

She slammed the door closed.

Chapter 9

He had known her name.

Names had power – that was what the fairy tales had taught Esther. Like Rumpelstiltskin. The miller's daughter would have had her baby taken by Rumpelstiltskin if she hadn't found out his name and this had made him so angry he had stomped down hard enough to trap himself waist-deep in the earth until he eventually tore his own body in two.

Names could kill.

The stairs. Esther wrenched off her mask and ran up them, needing to get away from the door, the metal threshold and the man beyond who held her name so easily on his tongue.

Stumbling on the top step she nearly sprawled onto the floor of the living room but steadied herself and, without thinking about it, raced into Mother's bedroom where she came to an awkward halt. Of course she knew this was not what she was supposed to be doing.

A strange man knew her name.

But there was no reason to think he wanted to hurt either of them, she argued with herself. It would be like wanting to hurt the shy little creatures that scampered away in the woods. Esther sat on the bed. But people did, didn't they? They hunted those shy little creatures because they could, because it was fun to hurt things that couldn't hurt you back. To cause fear.

That was when the thudding began.

Esther knew it was him, knocking on the metal door but the sound of it here, in a place usually so silent made her crouch and cower. The door would hold. He was just a man. He couldn't get in.

Thud, thud.

The sound reverberated into her brain and she thought of Rumpelstiltskin stomping away in fury, slamming his foot down with unnatural force. Each thud was the stamp of a foot, except it should have been her stamping her feet, enraged at losing her name to the monster at her door.

Thud.

'Esther Allbright?'

Instinctively she scuttled backwards on the bed, bringing her knees up to her chest and accidentally swiping the things from Mother's bedside table with her foot.

A large wooden carving of something that looked like a melted bear fell to the floor and broke open along a seam Esther had never noticed before. She remembered Mother whittling it years ago – 'a little night-time guardian is what I need' – and since then he'd stared a bit cross-eyed over her bed whilst she slept.

Esther had never realised that it twisted open.

She'd never realised that it was hollow.

Or seen what was inside.

Pills.

Thud.

Mother did not suffer from high or low blood pressure, or cholesterol. She didn't have heart disease, or diabetes. She hardly ever got a headache or a cold. The pills were glossy capsules and there were a hundred reasons why she would have had them hidden by her bed. They were perhaps indigestion tablets, or laxatives. They could be anything.

But why hide them?

With shaking hands, Esther scooped them up and stuffed them back into the bear, keeping a few in her pocket before fitting the two halves of the carving together again. So easily done. She could almost believe that there was nothing inside it, that it was just a silly wooden carving like all the others scattered around the place.

Thud.

Dying birds, shouting men, pills in the pit of bears' stomachs – it was all too much. Esther pulled the covers over her head and waited for the noise to stop.

* * *

Time, elastic with fear, stretched and then snapped back.

Silence. Esther stared at the stitching on the underside of her mother's bedspread.

'Get up out of that bed, girl!' She couldn't see Mr Wiffles, but she could hear him shouting from her room.

'I just need a moment.'

'What do you think those pills are for, hmm? Come on, think, girl, use the old brain cells, I know you've got 'em!'

Medication for an illness: that's what they were, though Esther hadn't known her mother was sick. The man calling her name and now this, the broken bear and the contents of its stomach, these things felt like they were adding up, a horrific sum. It felt like they were leading somewhere …

Esther should have spent more time thinking, she realised, continuing to stare at the stitching. She had been an insect in a cocoon, safely hidden from the Out There, but all cocoons have to be broken eventually; all baby insects have to haul their fragile bodies out of the mucus and slime and …

What?

What happened to them then? If the nature documentaries were anything to go by then those insects were quickly snapped up by a long sticky tongue. They were dinner.

'*Come on, girl – UP!*' came Mr Wiffles' voice again.

So she did. She dragged herself out from under the covers, wondering if the man had given up, if – when she went to the window – she would see him at the door, still like a statue, waiting for her. Her Rumpelstiltskin.

But that wasn't what she saw when she gripped the windowsill and forced herself to look.

What she saw was Mother.

Chapter 10

Bent double, moving slow.

Esther watched the figure bundled up in a coat, which she knew had a tattered lining, in boots whose leather was as soft as a tongue and it could have been any time in the last sixteen years: Esther at the window, watching, Mother Out There.

She rolled a tyre in front of her.

The man was gone.

Had a whole day passed whilst she had cowered under the covers waiting for the man to give up banging on their door? Then she noticed: that was no new tyre. The sky was morning-bright and the papery-thin quality of dusk was still a full day away. It was too early.

This day, a day that had hardly changed in all those years, had suddenly shattered into sharp edges. Esther put a palm on the glass and tried to slow her breathing.

There was no denying what she had seen. A man. She had to tell Mother.

Everything.

Mother zigzagged across the grass to the House, as if following a path only she could see. She paused before nearing the front door, let the tyre fall and bent down.

Esther had forgotten the bird.

Mother straightened and Esther was close enough to see the expression on her face, the frown and the way her eyes darted around to the top of the House and then directly to Esther's window. Esther didn't need to step back because the window was mirrored for privacy, but she did anyway. That frown was not sadness or disgust.

It was anger.

She disappeared out of view for a few minutes and came back with a shovel, which she used to jab a few times at the spring-soft earth, the grass shorter in front of the door. Esther wondered if the bird had died. A brown clod came away and Mother shook it onto the ground nearby but she didn't start digging again. Instead, she leant against the shovel, head bowed. Perhaps, Esther thought, she was briefly overcome with the fragility of life, the poignancy of the little dead carcass.

Perhaps she was praying.

'Dearly beloved, we are gathered here today for Bird …'

But Mother's next movements weren't mournful. She let the shovel drop and kicked at the earth she had uncovered, scattering some of it back into the small hole. Then she picked up the bird in her gloved hand and, with one powerful swing, she hurled it away from her.

Esther stared.

Maybe it had been the way the injured or dead bird had dangled from its wing, head lolling, or maybe it had been the viciousness of how the bird had been sent arcing into the sky, but there was something about what she had just seen her mother do that made Esther take another step backwards. The bird might still have been alive, but she had thrown the poor creature away from her as if it were a bit of rubbish.

Esther moved. Out of the room and down the stairs, hand on its chill rail, until she was back at the door once more, a blank of steel grey, huge and forbidding.

It opened.

Mother appeared, dusting her hands onto the back of her jeans, face calm.

'Was it alive?' Esther asked, too loud, too high.

Mother gave her a long look. 'The bird? No. Dead. They just can't cope in that rotten air, not even out here, away from the cities.'

It hadn't been dead, Esther thought, except she hadn't thought those words – she had said them.

Mother stopped dusting her hands. 'Sorry?'

All of the heat in Esther's body rushed to her face. 'It wasn't dead. I … I … saw it – from my window.' Mother tilted her head in an ironically bird-like gesture. 'You just threw it away. You could have … helped it.'

A blanket-lined box, seeds, water in a tiny bowl.

'The bird was dead, Pips.'

So you could have buried it, Esther thought. You could have folded its little wings neatly against its body and you could have laid it in the earth. With care. Instead you tossed it away. Esther made sure these thoughts stayed in her head this time. Her fingers traced the outline of pills in her pocket.

'Why are you back early?'

'Bloody flat tyre on the van!' Mother pushed past her, removing her mask as she headed into the tunnels.

'Wait!'

Mother paused and turned. She worked too hard, Esther thought, looking at the bruised hollows under her eyes, her sunken cheeks and reddened hands. Day by day: the constant checks and maintenance, the worry of being the only person in charge. Except that was where she was wrong, wasn't she? She was no longer the only person who could be in charge. It was time she let Esther share the load.

She pictured a man in a poorly chosen jacket, and she remembered the sound of those thuds echoing through the House.

'Mother, there was—'

'Esther, can't this wait?' Mother fluttered her free hand weakly.

'No! Just now—'

'Why are you wearing your overalls?'

Esther's heart lurched. She looked down at herself, at the overalls that normally hung on a peg by the front door, the ones she never wore because she never went anywhere. The ones she was quite clearly wearing right now.

'I …' She watched Mother's eyes flit about the porch, looking for other signs of disobedience. 'I was … I put them on in case you needed help with the tyre …'

She wasn't quite sure where that excuse had come from but it was good. She could tell by the way the frown between Mother's brows smoothed out a little. 'I don't need help.' She went over to where Esther's mask hung and stared at it for a second too long. Esther's heart would have lurched again but it seemed to have frozen in her chest. She would know, Esther thought, she would be able to tell that the mask had been used, that it had been worn. There would be something to give her away, a thumbprint or smudge of lip balm on that treacherous clear plastic.

Mother adjusted the strap on the mask. 'Take the overalls off, Esther,' she said and then walked into the darkness of the tunnel, returning a few minutes later rolling a new tyre in front of her.

There was no point telling her about the man who needed help because Mother wouldn't want to help him. No point in thinking that dead birds would be buried. Esther sighed and watched her mother readjust her own mask and roll the tyre out of the doorway into the bright daylight outside. But it was pollution and the air from which Esther had to be protected – not people.

'Can you help me?' the man had said.

A man, not a fairy-tale monster – possibly lost, bigger than a bird, harder to launch into the undergrowth, but no less vulnerable out here in Mother's kingdom. She could not let Mother get to him first.

* * *

43

Outside again, the world a dizzying swirl of colour.

Esther had waited an hour after Mother had left, just to be sure. Standing in the open doorway, masked and suited, she wondered if he would return, if he had even been real. But she did not have to stand there long. First as a small stick-like smudge under the trees and then growing larger and larger, he came towards the House. It was as if he had been waiting for her.

Esther's heart swelled in her chest, squeezing up against her demon who opened an eye and snuffled. She took a measured breath and gripped one hand in the other.

On he came, walking with long, purposeful strides and now he was a distinct figure in the scrubby grass and bracken that was the House's personal moat.

Heading straight for her.

Esther instinctively moved backwards, one hand stretched behind her, feeling for the reassuring solidity of the door frame at her back.

It was the intent with which he was moving. This time, there was no hesitant standing and staring. This time he was walking in a direct line to the door, as if he knew exactly what he was planning to do and wanted to get on with it. It didn't matter if previously he had asked for help, it didn't matter about his stupid unsuitable clothes or his brown curls. His moving forward made her want to scoot back, despite everything.

Of course, she was not expecting what happened next. How could she have expected that? She had not known about the danger lurking right there in front of the House. If she had known she would have warned him; she would have run out and yelled for him to stop.

But he did not stop. He kept on and Esther could only watch in horror as up from the long rough grass reared two huge snapping metal jaws. They caught the man's leg, mid shin, and brought him crashing to the ground.

Chapter 11

Hannah

Sixteen years ago

The afternoon it happened seared itself, barbecue-hot, onto the pink meat of Hannah's memory.

It started with sunshine and a back garden decorated with bunting and balloons and enough party food to give twice the number of children a sugar rush for days.

'I am five today!' Esther occasionally paused in her racing around to come and shout this at Hannah in case she had forgotten.

'I know, Pips.' Hannah smiled and smoothed her hot, flushed cheek. 'Now sit here by me and calm down a bit.'

'But I'm in the middle of a game!'

Hannah had seen the game, which was really a group of girls tearing around in a circle; girls she didn't know, just like she didn't know anyone in this new town.

'And now you're in the middle of a hug!' Hannah grabbed Esther and squeezed as the little girl giggled at first and then, as Hannah did not let go, wriggled, squirmed and twisted free.

'Great party! Grace is having a blast.' Another mother's face got in her way. Hannah couldn't remember her name. The woman took a swig from her glass, one she had filled from the wine bottle she had brought with her. 'Sunday afternoon treat, eh? Especially as Jonny's driving.' She smiled at Hannah and Hannah lifted the corners of her mouth in response, making a note to never let Esther go to a party at Grace's house. 'Want some?'

'Oh no – I have the party bags to sort out.'

'That sounds like the kind of thing wine was invented for …'

Ned played the monster and chased screaming children around their small back garden. As she cut the cake, Hannah watched him. People often referred to their spouse as their 'better half' and that's what Hannah had truly thought when she met him. He *was* better than her: kinder, more patient, more forgiving, slow to anger, quick to laugh. Hannah would zip through a day like a maddened wasp looking for someone to sting, whereas bumblebee Ned would linger over the pollen.

But she couldn't escape it – this was all his fault. A promotion he couldn't pass up. He had dragged them all out here to this dingy town with the massive, smoking steelworks on its edge. The dragon, it was called. A nickname for a monster. The huge structure and its outbuildings and the pipes coiling around it all cast a shadow on the houses and shops, the nurseries and the school that spread out around it. Before this they had lived in a leafy village, the kind of place you could imagine was almost in the countryside.

She forced a smile and busied herself, making the children eat their sandwiches before they went for the sweets. It was a happy day, she told herself.

Until the evening.

The guests were gone. There was nothing more to do but wipe up the icing smeared on the table, pick up the bits of wrapping paper and put the plates in the dishwasher. Esther toddled off to the lawn, happily pulling up handfuls of grass.

Until she wasn't.

Hannah could only have taken her eyes off her for a second whilst she emptied the bin. Then she turned and her little girl wasn't pulling up the grass but laid out on it, her lips turning blue. Hannah stumbled to her, out through the patio doors and only a few steps to her little body, Esther's chest heaving but with no breath for any wails or cries, panic making her eyes widen so she looked like one of those helpless baby seals Hannah saw on nature programmes. The ones that would soon be clubbed to death.

One of her fingers twitched.

She had never heard a wheeze like it, a death rattle. Hannah froze. She remembered reaching out a hand but not knowing where to put it, not knowing anything that she should do because she didn't know what was wrong. This was not a cut or a bruise or a temperature or a tooth coming through. This was nothing Hannah had ever seen before. She felt Ned push her away, moving through CPR steps that had been wiped clean from Hannah's brain, yelling at her to call an ambulance.

Then came a moment that was not a moment but a black void that nearly gulped Hannah whole. In the ambulance, balanced on a narrow seat, hands clasped as if in prayer but really just to stop them shaking, Hannah heard that terrible death-rattle wheezing stop.

Nothing gaped at her.

She moved but the paramedic moved faster, and she could only see his back as he did something she could not make out. Her hand fumbled for Ned's but Ned was in their car behind them, only room for one parent in the ambulance. There was no time to think. There was simply that aching silence where breath had once been before the paramedic performed some kind of magic spell, hands moving quickly and then there was a gasp and coughing and that dark mouth of black nothingness closed its rotten lips.

Help and hospital and calm, reassuring voices came next, and

Hannah sat in the waiting room chair with its back that dug into her shoulder blades, Ned's hand finally on hers.

A doctor told them about asthma and Hannah grabbed onto every word, listened so hard she could hear her heartbeat thud in her ears. Fine, fine, fine were the words she kept hearing; Esther would be fine. They would be able to take her home.

'What caused it? I mean, she's never had an asthma attack before.' Hannah twisted the tissue in her lap.

The doctor attached his pen to his clipboard. 'To be honest, medical science still hasn't worked out the cause of asthma. You have the leaflet about triggers, yes? But those triggers simply provoke an attack once a patient already has the condition. A trigger could be an allergen like dust or pollen, or it could have been exercise – she had been running around, you said? Smoke or pollution. But it can be certain foods, fragrances, additives …'

Smoke or pollution. Smoke or pollution. The air itself. All the poison she could not see, and if she couldn't see it, how could she protect Esther?

'But she's fine now, yes?' Ned touched her arm. 'We just have to keep a watch on her and use the pump like we were shown.'

Yes. From now on, she had to be vigilant; she had to keep watch, keep Esther in sight, keep her safe. Because that afternoon when she had frozen on a sun-drenched lawn in the middle of summer had shown her a truth she'd needed to see. Esther had to be kept safe, because if she got into trouble again the terrible truth was that Hannah couldn't trust herself to save her.

Chapter 12

Hannah hated the playground.

Not the fact that the paint was flaking and the safety flooring was cracked and uneven, nor that the turret at the end of the monkey bars always smelled of mould. No, though all of that was bad enough, it was not the actual playground that was at fault.

It was what loomed over it. The steelworks. Pipes coiled around its bulk as if the main building was a dying animal and those pipes were choking the life out of it. They slithered off into other outbuildings, connecting the whole thing together, a diseased, dirty town all of its own, with sheds and bridges and footpaths and towers. It was wreathed in smoke as it was almost every day of the year: 'carefully managed' reactions and 'a natural by-product' of the cooling system so the guidelines stated. The dying animal at the heart of it all was a dozing dragon. A light sleeper. It wouldn't take much to prod it into wakefulness when that smoke would belch and flame would spurt.

There was a beauty to Hell, however, Hannah had discovered. Often at sunset, the dying rays of light caught the smoke and made it glow, made the sky into a slab of gemstone that caused Hannah to sometimes stop and stare.

She did not look at it this morning. Three months had passed since Esther's first asthma attack. Whilst Esther played with a neighbour's child, a gentle boy a year or so older than her with messy hair and a ready laugh, Hannah read. Her local library had only a few reference books about asthma and Hannah currently had them all, as well as all the leaflets she had been able to find in her day job as a sales representative for a drug company, visiting GP surgeries trying to sell them new versions of antidepressants.

What Hannah did not now know about asthma was not worth knowing. She had learnt that, globally, it was more common in girls than boys after puberty and found more amongst city people than those who lived in rural areas. Doctors first thought it a neurological condition, the nervous system sending the wrong signals to the lungs, but now the popular idea was of it as an allergic reaction of some sort. In reality, from Hannah's reading, the true picture seemed to be more complicated than either theory.

Two things became ingrained on Hannah's retinas:

1) There was no cure.

2) The first few years of exposure were vital.

On her next trip to the library she was going to search out anything she could find about steelworks.

'Found it!' Ned appeared at her side, sat on the bench next to her and waggled the inhaler with a smile on his face that set Hannah's teeth tingling.

'I told you to check it was in the bag,' she said, not smiling in return.

'I know, I know, but no harm done, yeah? Our house is literally just over there' – he pointed off to where their road began – 'and it is stuffed full of the things. It would only take a sec to get one. We don't even need the bag.'

The bag. It sat between them and in it was everything Esther needed in order to leave the safety of the house. Every parent of a five-year-old had a similar thing, filled with wet wipes and a favourite toy, emergency snacks, a spare jumper and sun cream.

Hannah's bag had all of those things, of course, but more importantly it held the various inhalers that kept Esther from the massive black void that had waited for her in an ambulance months ago.

'Three.' Hannah put down her book.

'Hmm?'

'Three times this week so far.'

It was Saturday. Three asthma attacks: two mild, one less so. The shaking of the inhaler was a talisman, like a witch doctor waving a stick at the bad spirits. Be gone, foul demon! And it had, each time, but each time it returned and each time there were those terrifying gaps between Esther's wheezy, rattling breaths.

'I know.' Ned picked up her book, read the title, frowned and put it down again. 'But she's just a kid, yeah? I don't want to make a big deal about it. It'll scare her.'

'She should be scared!' Hannah lowered her voice. 'No, I don't mean that. I mean … *we* should be scared. We shouldn't have to go back to the house to get the inhaler; it should be ingrained on our brains that we bring it – we check the bag, we bring the bag. You weren't there in the ambulance with her.'

Perhaps that was the problem. He hadn't been there to feel the great aching void when Esther had stopped breathing, to feel the nothingness blow a freezing kiss at him. If he had, he would feel as she did. If he had, he would check the bloody inhaler was in the bloody bag.

She watched Ned run over to the swings and pick Esther up, whirling her around until she was red-faced and panting, the dragon steelworks waiting in the background.

Three asthma attacks this week.

Ned suddenly put Esther down and Hannah knew by the way Esther's shoulders hunched, by the way she crouched over, the way her hand went to her throat as if that could help.

Ned shouted and she gripped the inhaler, already on her feet.

Four.

Chapter 13

Hannah stuffed tissue into the cracks with a knife.

It was hardly going to make much of a difference, she realised, but she liked doing it. It was soothing, almost. Like meditation. The idea had come to her whilst she had sat at the reading of her aunt's will and it had taken all of her determination to stay in her seat and not dash out, past the open-mouthed faces in her haste to get home. Not that there had been many faces to rush past, just the solicitor and a distant cousin.

She was still wearing her smart black dress. The knife sank into the tissue as she wiggled it into the small spaces of the window frame, pushing and pushing until it wedged in tight.

Her house was a death trap. People said that, didn't they? About run-down places with dodgy floorboards and faulty wiring, with plaster hanging off the ceiling and sharp carpet tacks waiting to pierce a foot. But no one ever thought of the gaps, the cracks, the seams, the edges of things. Where the air got in.

Through the window she saw it.

The works.

It was a smoky God towering over the houses. She hated her street. The houses were squashed together with their dirty brick and shoddy windows, the little gaps between the roof tiles and the broken guttering hanging like a fractured finger pointing to the massive smoking chimneys beyond, too close, as if pasted onto the backdrop with a careless hand.

The pollution, however, was a grit on her eyeballs, scraping them with every blink. Ned told her she was imagining it. But it was everywhere. Because, and she hadn't realised this until now, there were places like this steelworks all over the country, all over the world. There were worse places even, and they all had their guidelines and regulations. They all had their lip service. Just because you couldn't see it, the air, didn't mean something hadn't gone badly wrong with it. Esther was proof of that.

Hannah stepped back, her hand aching. That was one window done. Sealed. With tissue, admittedly, and even that would probably not last long because Ned would come home and try to open the damn thing. But she could already feel the squeezing around her heart loosen slightly. The problem, now she was thinking of it, was that there were so many other places in the house she would have to sort. She could almost feel the draught.

Hannah had been thinking about Chernobyl a lot lately. She must have been around fifteen when she had seen the footage on the news. She thought not so much about the explosion of the Soviet reactor itself but afterwards, the invisible cloud of radioactive materials that had spread as far as Western Europe, nothing anyone could do to stop that poisoned air finding its way into millions of homes. And lungs. There had apparently been radioactive sheep in Wales.

But once you searched for Chernobyl on your desktop computer, well then it was only a few keyboard clicks to a whole raft of other stories. Take polycyclic aromatic hydrocarbons, the toxic component of traffic exhaust and cause of eye and lung irritation, blood and liver disease. Then there was tiny particulate matter which, when breathed deeply into the lungs, lodged fast, waiting, a patient assassin. The cause of cancer, heart disease, stroke. Some studies were beginning to link air pollution to dementia.

Asthma.

She had got a whole new set of books out of the library. Not about asthma or factories, but ones on architecture and planning laws.

Hannah began with a new tissue and a new window, stuffing the paper into the edges where she could feel the air chill her fingers.

'Why is she home?'

Hannah jumped. 'Jesus! You scared me!'

Ned came into the room. 'Why is Pips home?'

'School called. She had an attack.'

'Okay … but the school has her inhaler. They know how to use it. I thought we agreed she should always try to stay in school, even if she has an attack?'

'She was exhausted.'

Ned said nothing and then: 'What are you doing to Esther's window?'

Hannah didn't respond. He could see well enough, after all. Words weren't really working for them at the moment. She had tried them all, in all of their combinations: explaining, cajoling, pleading and reasoning.

There were other words in the inside pocket of the black handbag she had left in the hall. More useful words printed on a legal document that proclaimed her the only beneficiary of her distant aunt's considerable estate. She should tell him about that because that was the rule, wasn't it? No hiding things in a marriage. However, Hannah was beginning to believe that the exact opposite was true. Marriage only worked if you hid your true self. After all, look what happened when she showed her fear to Ned – he reasoned it away, shooed it off with a flick of his hand. She would tell him about the inheritance when the time was right.

She wasn't stupid – she knew that tissue paper was hardly the solution.

The solution would come from those legal words. Those words

would become numbers in a bank account, which would allow them to move away from the steelworks, find a corner surrounded by trees and hidden from the world, but even then, Hannah knew that the world would still find them. It would come and clamp its dirty mouth over theirs.

Nowhere was safe.

Unless she made it so. And she had a plan for that.

Chapter 14

Esther

The world stretched out around Esther, so much of it that she had to look down to the ground to anchor herself in case she floated off, away into the vastness. Her feet moved and then she was there, her own bedroom window above her on the first floor, its reflective glass glinting in the light.

The front of the House towered over her and she stared at it, mesmerised at being able to see it from the outside. The concrete looked rough like a lizard's skin.

In front of her a man was caught by the leg in a trap.

But Esther couldn't look at that yet.

Squinting, she turned her face to the sky. Rabbits froze in headlights, she'd read. She sympathised with them as she froze in this glaring new world, pinned by a spotlight sun, unsure of what to do next. If there had been a shadow somewhere, she would have crawled into it, happy to let the shade soothe her eyes.

She reasoned with herself. The damage was done. If the air was so toxic it could kill her through a mask, well, she was out in it now. The sky above her was the kind of blue that seemed lit up from within, a piece of curved stained glass into which a dead bird would no longer fly. The breeze tugged at her hood and the air moved against her forehead like breath.

The man swore.

Can you help me?

Yes, Mister Strange Man, I can, Esther thought. *I can and I will because that is the kind of person I am.*

When she started walking, she almost expected to bounce. Mother had taught her about the astronauts on the moon and how they had bobbed along in the dust, free of gravity. She was untethered from her space station, floating out into the void.

An explorer, an adventurer, someone brave.

Someone foolhardy.

There was a reason Mother kept them safe in the House. What was she doing? What made her think she could wander about with the demon in her chest and her heart banging hard like a frightened traveller pounding on a door.

What was she doing? *She was giving help.*

One foot moved in front of the other.

Beyond were the trees. Even after everything humans had thrown at them, trees had carried on photosynthesising and sheltering and filtering; they, miraculously, *continued* to help despite the pollution, the destruction, the strange diseases that ate away at them. And they hid, of course. The house was invisible from any main road though Esther didn't know how far the forest spread, or even if there *was* a road nearby.

Her feet kept moving.

Trees. They were just trees, she thought, forcing herself to look over to them, to concentrate on them because otherwise her breathing might begin to hitch and that would wake the chest demon. She wished she'd tucked Mr Wiffles into her overalls, if only to hear him grumble at the cold and tell her to 'Buck up, girl!'

That was another shock – the cold. Used to the ambient, controlled temperature of the House, the skin on her wrists prickled into goose bumps, though it was spring and the sun shone.

Then she stumbled to a halt. The bear trap. A bear trap had reared up from the grass – grass that she had stared at for sixteen years and that had never done anything interesting in all of that time. There were monsters waiting to take a bite out of her. How could she forget? One was already occupied, slowly chewing into the strange man's leg, but it might have friends. She studied the grass at her feet as she inched forward, this time at a much slower pace, watching out for a glimpse of rusted metal.

Sky, bird, tree.

The little fans in her mask whirred.

A man in a bear trap.

In a shuffling, careful way, she stopped as close to the man as she was willing to get. The trap was the kind of thing designed to bring down an animal twice the size of this man, a horrible, jagged-toothed monster of a thing that she'd had no clue was lurking so close to their front door.

The man gave a guttural cry. In the past few hours she had failed to save a bird and ventured into an outside so terrifying it could literally raise up jaws out of the ground.

Thoughts flashed across her mind but nothing coherent. Man. Mask. Teeth. Scream. Air.

Air, air, air. She'd breathed it in, great gulps of it, and it was as if she could feel it in her, something ragged in her lungs, scratching them with every new heave of her chest.

The man moaned.

The bear trap had clamped over his shin, a trap that might have easily bitten into her rather than him. How had Mother not noticed something like this when she was building the house—

Esther's brain stuttered to its realisation. She remembered her mother zigzagging across the grass as she had come towards the House, avoiding the dangers she already knew were there. Oh.

Mother knew all about the trap. At some point, probably early on, or maybe even as the House was being finished, she went out and found that monster, and maybe others lurking out there in the grass. She found them and then brought them here. Set them.

Mother did this.

The man carefully edged his leg straight out in front of him. How much damage did one of those traps do, she wondered? She couldn't believe Mother would set something that would break bone and she hoped a trap like that would be designed to catch and hold prey, not cut off a leg. It had probably been out there for years, the mechanisms weak.

He would be fine.

She wanted to run back to the porch and close the door behind her.

There wasn't any blood that she could see, and he hadn't fainted, but he didn't move, no longer staring up at the sky but at her. She couldn't meet his gaze, but focused instead on the mud on his trousers, his fingers red with the cold as they trembled near the trap's teeth.

What she should have done was obey her mother, even though she hid pills and threw injured birds away like litter. She should have stayed safe inside where she had always lived.

Instead, she cleared her throat and the words when they came were easy enough to say: 'I can help.'

Chapter 15

'Are you insane?' The man glared at Esther.

Esther opened her mouth and then closed it again.

'I mean, what kind of weirdos are you? Bear traps in your front yard?' He pushed himself up onto his elbows and grimaced at the pain, his face sheened with sweat.

Once again, Esther fish-gulped. He sat up straighter and brushed at his jacket, an oddly fussy gesture, to care about his clothes when his leg was stuck in a great big piece of metal.

If she had been expecting a Disney prince of some sort then that was what she got – except this was one of those early versions where the face was still a bit too bland, the skin too smooth and someone had gone a bit wild with the hair.

'Well, come on then? Help me!' He pointed to the trap as she stood unmoving. 'There are springs either side, you see? We need to push down on them and then I can ease my leg out. I tried to do it on my own but they're stiff, rusted I think. It'll need two of us—' His words were cut off by a grunt and he clutched his knee.

His voice was just a voice. Male. Impatient.

'How do you know my name?'

He paused. Esther gripped one of her hands in the other, thinking of nuns in convents standing peacefully in prayer poses. Calm. She needed to stay calm despite the fact she could hardly hear what he was saying over the sound of her own heart beating. He wore a flat bag across his chest and on its front flap was a big bright badge made up of red circles with a silver star in the middle.

'Why are you here?' Her voice was muffled by the mask, a robot question asked by a robot girl in a strange face shield. A weirdo. But feeling like a robot made her braver than she would otherwise have been, she needed to be robotic, to ask the questions that needed asking, to be cautious and careful – like Mother.

'I've been looking for you for days.' The man stared up at her, winced and went to rub his leg but stopped himself. 'Your mother needs to sign some paperwork, for the land she bought. This land. I got lumbered with hunting you out. Your lot—'

'My lot?'

'Doomsday preppers. Homesteaders …' Esther didn't know if he could see her expression but he faltered anyway, his face screwing up as he gingerly touched his leg. 'Fuck this hurts!'

Homesteader. The name made them sound like two characters in a western. People who stared at the intruder whilst standing on their wooden veranda, shading their eyes from the sun, chewing a stalk of straw, wearing gingham.

His expression softened. 'I'm Tom.' And he held out his hand to her as if they were business colleagues meeting up for the first time. She stared at his fingers whilst her heart tried to burst out from her throat. Eventually his hand dropped. 'So … if you could just …' He gestured towards the trap.

The man winced as rusting teeth from the trap dug slowly through the thick material of his trousers. She considered him. Tom. The only new person she had met in the last sixteen years. Someone who talked about the world so easily, a world she had only ever known neatly squared off in a television screen. Paperwork, land, preppers.

A potential threat.

A quick calculation. His leg was injured but even without that, he wasn't heavily built, didn't look muscular or all that strong. Not threatening – and Mother had taught her all about that.

He winced again and grasped at his leg.

Mother had taught her that people Out There looked ill, air-starved and grey of pallor, but this man didn't. His face could have been considered a bit pale but that was more likely to be caused by shock setting in.

Esther knelt next to him and looked at the trap. It was as he'd said: a thing with rusting teeth spread out wide enough to hold, but not seriously injure, an unwary leg. The springs on either side had also scabbed over in a rough rust but, she reasoned, if they'd moved to snap him, then they'd move back again, given a little push.

'I can help you open it, free your leg.'

'That'd be dandy. Thanks,' he muttered.

She could see in the way his jaw tensed that he was gritting his teeth. There was the red bump of a shaving nick on his chin.

'We have to work together,' she said.

They each placed a hand on one side. He had nice hands – slim fingers with nails that were clean and neat enough for even Mother to approve. Esther knew she should have been concentrating on freeing this man without severing his leg but for a moment all she could think about was how this couldn't possibly be her. This had to be a dream – her in the Out There, her hand only inches away from another person's, working together with a stranger to free him from a trap set by her own mother.

'Ready?' he asked.

She blinked and let her breath out slowly, like Mother had taught her when firing a gun. Steady the hand.

'On one, okay? Three ...'

His hair was an old velvet brown.

'Two ...'

62

The velvet brown was the colour of a much-loved teddy bear, a comfortable sofa, a well-worn pair of cords. Esther braced herself and stared at a spot just past his cheek. Not his eyes – she wasn't ready for those.

'One!'

Chapter 16

The trap fought them with an animal intensity, its springs creaking under the pressure in a squeal of pain.

As she pushed down, Esther wondered if this man might be stuck in it and what would she do then? Mother would stuff him and make him into a scarecrow to frighten away anyone else who stumbled onto their land.

The metal teeth widened a fraction.

'Keep pressing!' he said.

'I am!'

'You've got to press harder!'

'I am!'

The teeth widened a fraction more. They both watched the jaws stretch open in a ghastly yawn … more … a little more …

Knocking his hand away she kept up the pressure on both springs whilst he got ready to free his leg.

'Don't let go!' he said.

'Do you think I'm an idiot?'

No, a voice whispered in her head, *he thinks you're a weirdo who set the trap in the first place.*

With a grunt, she put all of her force behind her final shove at the springs and, with a gasp, he wriggled his leg out and scrambled away from the thing, breathing hard, holes in his trouser leg and his forehead sheened with sweat.

Esther allowed the teeth to gently close once more and then she kicked it from her.

They both lay on the grass for a moment appreciating legs that had not been chewed off and hinges that could still move.

Tom's chest heaved and he ran a hand over his face.

'You okay?' Esther sat up again.

Tom carefully prodded at his shin. His trouser leg was mangled but it didn't look as if the trap had bitten right through. Taking a few deep breaths each time he did so, he inched his trouser leg higher until they could both peer at his calf.

'Okay is probably stretching it a bit but I'll live.'

He'd been lucky – for a man who'd got caught in a bear trap. His shin was a mess of swollen red cuts and scrapes but within the swelling there was no wicked glint of bone.

He lay on the grass, staring at the sky.

'What's with the fancy dress?' he said, not looking at her but at the clouds.

'Huh?'

He waved dismissively in her direction. 'The get-up.'

She glanced down at her overalls, the tiny fans in her mask whirring away like polite bees. 'My asthma … the air …' was all she could manage of the eloquent explanation that formed in her brain but mangled itself in her mouth. 'I know in the cities it's worse but even out here I have to be careful.'

Tom frowned and turned his face to her. There was grass stuck in his hair. 'Careful of … the air?'

'Yes. I know you think it's safe here in the countryside and, well, it probably is for you but—' He looked at her strangely and she didn't know how to explain it. Possibly she needed diagrams and a flow chart.

She was cut off by his grunt of pain as he tried and failed to get to his feet.

'Can you stand?'

Stupid question, Esther, she berated herself. *He has just shown that he can't.*

But that wasn't the question she'd wanted to ask. What she'd wanted to say was: *'Can you leave now?'* Because she had a cold feeling in the pit of her stomach, her hands were shaking and she needed some time in the dim quiet to work out everything that had just happened.

He tried to haul himself up again, wobbled and sank back down onto the ground. 'Give me a minute.'

A minute wasn't going to solve it though. In a minute his leg would not marvellously heal itself so he could get up and hike down the hill for however long it would take him to get to his car, a car which he would then have to be able to drive using said leg. A lot could happen in a minute – but not that.

The problem was that there was another question Esther should be asking and that question was, *'Do you want me to help you inside?'* It clogged in her throat even though every heroine in every romantic film she had seen would have asked it by now, would have shouldered some of his weight and staggered across to the House, ready to tend to his leg (and this would probably have involved taking off his shirt, though the problem was with his shin, not his chest). Halfway through the film they would be nearly kissing but obviously interrupted because there was still half a film to go and—

The demon in her chest yawned and sucked all the air out of her lungs. She doubled over. Sinking to the ground, her world narrowed to the width of her windpipe.

A hand grabbed her arm. 'Esther?'

She was too busy fumbling in the pocket of her boiler suit for her inhaler to fully comprehend that there was a stranger's hand on her arm. If she hadn't already been having an asthma attack that would probably have caused one. But her head was too full as she told herself that there was nothing to worry about, she had had thousands of these kinds of attacks throughout her life, thousands, though it had been years since she had been outside whilst having one and, oh God, she had just realised that she would have to take her mask *off* to use the inhaler and everything in her screamed that that should not happen and all of those screaming voices were her mother's—

Her arms gave way.

At least she would be able to see the sky as she died, she thought, and not merely a tiny slice or circle of it but the whole glorious thing curving over her like a beautiful glass bowl in a blue she had never known was this vivid. In a film, this would be enough for the doomed heroine – the fact that she got to see the sky and she would die smiling … but Esther blinked and her chest rattled again. This wasn't enough; it wasn't enough at all. It wasn't a bloody film. She wanted more than one lousy glimpse of the sky.

The black spots in front of her eyes started to join up and she gave a little sob, which caused her lungs to tighten even more before hands tugged at her face and suddenly, coldly, shockingly – air rushed at her and her inhaler was shoved into her mouth.

Her mask was gone.

Chapter 17

Air. Real air. Raw.

Not purified, not sanitised, not safe and definitely not sound. She took a deep breath, almost expecting her throat to begin blistering and the demon to come roaring back to tear through her and leave her gasping on the ground.

That did not happen.

She felt flayed, half expecting her fingers to come away bloody if she touched her face. Her skin tingled, no not tingled – *stung*. Hands shoved her inhaler at her again and she sucked at it, but the attack had already begun to subside, the demon in her chest slinking away.

The sun, the air, the sound of the trees – everything was too bright, too loud, too cold, too much. Smells rushed at her, too many for her beleaguered senses to distinguish and that was perhaps most shocking of all. Filtered air smelled of nothing but here there was something earthy, something a bit smoky, something she couldn't identify at all.

There was grass and feet and air, so much air, pressing itself against her lips and teeth and there was Tom's voice though she didn't know what he was saying, and then she was pushing herself up from the ground and the world swirled with her but one point remained fixed.

The door.

She had to return to the House. Willing her feet to move, she stumbled back the way she had come: it had only seemed a few steps when she had first walked out to Tom but now they had turned to miles. She could hear him shouting something and she didn't care what he said, or that she was leaving him injured and possibly unable to follow her; she just needed to get back to the porch where she could close the door and breathe in filtered air.

The grass under her feet turned to a metal strip.

Darkness.

In the welcome gloom, Esther pressed her face against the cool concrete wall of the porch and focused on slow, calming breaths. The House. The place that had kept her safe all these years; the place that would continue to do so. Just as she was about to slam the button that would start the grinding sound as the door closed, a hand appeared on the door frame.

'Esther?'

With a gasp she scrambled backwards.

On his hands and knees, he held one hand out as if surrendering, dragging himself over the metal threshold. 'Hey, it's okay … you're okay. You're fine.'

In that outstretched hand he held her mask. She snatched at it. 'Get out!'

'You're fine,' he said again in that infuriating tone as if he was talking to an easily spooked horse.

She fumbled with the mask, her fingers numb and shaking because the door was still open and that air, the air her mother had spent every day warning her against, was curling in her lungs right at this very minute.

'You can't be in here!' she tried again but her voice was as broken as her fingers and the mask nearly dropped from them.

A quick calculation. Tom sat, blocking the door from being able to close. She couldn't shove him out of the door; he was bigger and stronger than her, even with an injured leg, but she needed that door shut before her chest demon woke up.

Awful, taut moments passed as she tried to decide what to do and, all the while, that outside air swirled around them. Tom dragged himself into the porch and she made her choice, her palm slapping the button as a clunking sound began.

Slumped against the wall, Tom stretched his injured leg out before him, chest heaving, but this time he reached across and put his hand on hers, the shock of his palm on her skin, his eyes concerned and warm as Esther slid her hand away.

She took another trembling breath but there was no rattle, no black spots swimming into her vision, no tightening band around her middle. She blinked.

'You're fine.'

And she was. She wasn't dead anyway, which was what she always half-believed would happen to her if she stepped into the Out There without any protection; she'd imagined herself plummeting to the ground like that injured bird she had seen.

She breathed again.

Fine.

No harm done. She had been lucky.

'I'm sorry—' Tom began.

'If I'm outside, I need the mask, my mother says. Asthma – I have asthma and this toxic air—'

'The air?'

'You probably think you're safe out here, but Mother says we're not. We're only safe here, in the House.'

Tom rubbed at his leg, his face angled downwards so she couldn't see his expression. Now her chest demon had slunk away, Esther remembered metal teeth rearing upwards. Closer to him, she could see that he had amber-flecked brown eyes and a face that seemed too young, too wrinkle-free, too tanned by a sun Esther's skin hadn't felt in years. She shifted away, scraping the hair from her face and twisting it behind her, hopefully neat, hopefully not too sweaty.

She tried to remember why she had gone out to this man in the first place. 'I guess we need to sort out your leg.'

Nuclear-strength heat rushed into Esther's cheeks. She didn't want to touch him; in fact she had only said those words because that was what she was meant to say. She was meant to want to help him, but really all she wanted was for him to leave – he took up too much space in this small porch.

Kneeling to him, she pushed the material of his trouser leg up a little further and made a mental note of the first-aid things she would need to get from the storeroom: tape and antiseptic lotion and bandages and—

He reached down to still her hand. 'You've been here a long time?' His voice and touch were soft but Esther gasped as if she had been burnt. 'I'm sorry, I didn't mean to—'

'No. I … umm …' She sat back on her heels, keeping her breath steady and holding the hand he had touched to her chest as if it had been hurt. The bruises on his skin were waiting to appear, sea creatures currently submerged, but they would come to the surface soon enough: big, dark shapes. She fixed her eyes on the hairs on his calf and it was a while before she could say, 'Sixteen years. I've been here for sixteen years.'

And she wanted to explain, to make him understand. Everything. About the demon in her chest and that this was to save her, that Mother had built a world for them both and that world had protected them … that he didn't have to look at her the way he was right then.

'Esther—'

Her name spoken by someone who wasn't Mother. The way he said it was gentler, and the "s" sound made her shiver.

'There,' she said, making as if to stand up. 'I need to get some first-aid stuff.'

He reached out again and caught her forearm this time. She

snatched it away as if he'd tried to bite it, but too late – once more the warmth of his fingers brushed hers. There was nothing but concern in his gold-flecked eyes and the shock of his touch on her skin.

'Esther, your mother is lying to you.'

Chapter 18

Tom talked and Esther watched his mouth move, knowing the words coming out of it should make sense but she couldn't make them fit together. She wasn't used to it, this new voice with its strange cadences and rhythm; she couldn't follow it fast enough.

Instead, she calculated how far he was to the door, how much it would take to force him to it and then out – out of the porch, out of her brain. Because he was wrong, she could see that. He was bad. The House did not want him.

'… but I mean … where do I start?' Esther said nothing. 'How do I even …?' Tom fumbled in his jacket pocket and brought out something that to Esther looked like a flat black piece of glossy plastic. Under his touch it sprang into colour, revealing itself to be a screen of some sort. 'It's probably best to just show you.'

'Is that a television?' Esther couldn't stop herself from asking.

'A television?' Tom smiled a little. 'Well, kind of, I guess, but mostly it's my phone, which connects to the internet so you can do pretty much everything on it.'

To Esther a phone was big, clunky and plastic and often attached to a wall with a long bouncing cord on the end of the receiver, which the people in the films she watched wound around their arm whilst they made plans and gossiped.

In order to see the screen, Esther had to move closer to Tom. He had his own smell too, she discovered: soap with a warm, spiced edge, though she didn't know what the spice was.

'We have no phone signal here,' she said, a headache beginning to pound her temples.

Tom tapped at the screen. 'Umm … I think you'll find you do.'

'What?'

'See?' He touched the plastic and it sprang into colour again. 'See those bars there – two are filled in. That means signal.'

'But … we have no need for a phone. It's an electric … net …' She faltered.

'Net?'

He didn't need to say it.

She had read about tinnitus, an insistent low-level humming or buzzing that suddenly happens for no apparent reason, that only the afflicted person can hear, and can continue for years. It felt like that, or as if she been left in the tumble dryer for too long, hot and full of static, liable to touch something metal and give herself a jolt.

She took a breath. Okay, Mother had lied about the phone. But there would be a reason, there would be an explanation.

Esther sank onto the bench next to him because her knees had suddenly disappeared. 'I do have asthma. You saw.'

'Yes.'

'Mother says that the air is wrong for me, too polluted. Everywhere.'

Tom tugged at his trouser leg. Esther tugged at the tattered remains of a life she'd thought she'd known.

'But you've been outside and you're fine,' he said.

It was coming, what Tom was trying to tell her. It was a volcano smoking away on the horizon, about to start pouring its lava down the hillside, killing all the tiny villagers in its path. She wanted to hold the lava back.

Remembering the name he had called her when she had first met him, Esther asked, 'What's a doomsday prepper?'

Tom turned back to his phone and she wondered if he was going to call someone and put them on the line, a calm voice to explain to her how Mother had been wrong, wrong, wrong all these years. So when he tapped at the screen again and swiped at it as if trying to remove a speck of dust, Esther couldn't help but crane her neck to get a better look.

'Here, this is from a newspaper. Doomsday prepper.'

He tilted the screen to her.

* * *

Saturday Feature: The Doom Boom

In search of people who close their door on the world

The end is nigh. The end is always nigh. War, nuclear weapons, pandemic, pollution, global warming. The fact that it hasn't ended so far, that's the miracle – but it's a miracle that some people aren't willing to take for granted.

And there is always someone around to cash in on fear. The Doom Boom is well and truly upon us. Out in the desert, in forests, farms, underground and in all the other forgotten spaces of the world, entrepreneurs have their eye on an apocalyptic future and are building for it.

Especially in America.

Oscar Stamp is ahead of them. Now in his fifties, he lives in a place I have vowed to not disclose where a small group of concrete fortresses jut out of the earth. He has a weather-beaten face that makes him look older than his years, a ready smile and a well-stocked armoury.

We drink coffee in a scene from an apocalyptic film.

'I don't want to go back,' he tells me, pouring us coffee the consistency of treacle. There is a level of luxury here that I am surprised to note. This place has a self-sufficient power supply, water from a nearby well, furnishings, cushions, even the odd decorative throw. This is no dark bunker; it has windows, even if the glass is bulletproof. The end of times looks pretty neat.

Twenty years ago, Oscar worked in a bank. I ask what made him give up a relatively secure job and life in a city. 'I was a Boy Scout – maybe that was the start of it all?' He laughs croakily, his voice unused to long conversations. 'Be prepared, hmm? People think I'm crazy, to have done this, but to me they're the crazy ones – I mean, with everything going on in the world, why wouldn't you get yourself a place like this? Somewhere safe, or, at least, safer, to wait out whatever catastrophe happens next. Disease, war, riot, wildfire, drought – you can't trust the government to look out for you no more.'

So, Oscar decided on the bunker life. 'I had the money and the know-how to build this little community, so I thought, heck, why not? The other plots are for my family, or my friends, whoever wants them. Though they don't want 'em just yet, unlike me!' He knows that he would be seen as an oddity, the doomsday prepper who didn't wait for doomsday. 'Me? I've had enough of people. I like the quiet.'

I tell him about my little apartment, my home comforts and a bit about my life. He listens patiently enough but then frowns. 'Frogs in a pot, hmm. Heard that saying? You're still a young'un. You're going to have it worse than me because odds, y'know? You're the frog in the pot – you just don't realise the water's boiling.'

I can't help but shiver. It feels like a story come to life, an ancient mariner predicting my doom. Oscar can live the rest of his life in this place and never have to come out if he doesn't want to. He has something called a deep larder with enough freeze-dried food to last for twenty-five years, a remote surveillance system, a panic room, and a nuclear-fallout shelter that doubles as a games room.

'Aren't you worried about falling ill? Or accidents?'

Oscar frowns again. 'Worrying about those things don't change 'em none, do they? If I get sick, I get sick. It's my choice how I deal with that ...' Rather chillingly, he nods towards the guns locked in a cupboard on the far wall.

A 2017 survey by the financial-tech company Finder suggested that roughly 20 per cent of Americans spent money on survival materials that year, and a further 35 per cent said they already had what they needed for an emergency. This year, those figures are bound to be higher. Meeting Oscar, who is friendly and thoughtful, has shown me that preparing for a less than rosy future needn't make you an oddity – it might actually be the only sane thing to do.

* * *

Esther handed back the phone, the glare from the screen making her temples throb even more. She pictured Oscar with his games room and deep larder and guns. When he died, however he died, perhaps no one would find him for months, maybe years ... if at all. He would be bone and mulch. She gripped the cold bench. 'People think Oscar is mad, to do what he's done?'

'Well. I mean, he's got a point, y'know. There are wars and diseases and fires and floods and pollution's pretty bad and when you look at it, it's a wonder more people aren't doing what your mum has done …' He caught the horror on Esther's face and added hurriedly, 'But there's all sorts of things being done to tackle pollution, to clean up the cities …'

'Mother isn't a doomsday prepper, though, and we're not in America. We know the world goes on outside. We don't think it's ended or anything …'

'No, but … you're still hiding from it, aren't you, like Oscar? Reading that feature, what I got from it – it's all about trust. Oscar doesn't trust anyone else to look out for him. Your mother doesn't trust anyone else to look out for you.'

Trust. Esther was having some problems with that word, mostly because of those hard little lumps in her jeans pocket. 'Mother has some pills. I mean, I found some pills of hers. She'd hidden them in a bear—'

'A bear?' Tom looked around as if a lumbering creature was about to swipe at him with one huge paw.

'A *wooden* bear. An ornament. Can your phone tell me what they are?'

'What do the pills look like?'

Esther held out her hand with the tablets nestled in her palm. Tom tapped and swiped at the screen once more, a whole universe of information at his fingertips. 'Can I?' he asked and she tipped the pills into his palm. People must be so clever, she thought, watching him. The knowledge they have, the ability to quickly get the answer to any question in moments. They were gods.

'*To what do we give thanks?*'

'*The House.*'

'*What protects the air we breathe?*'

'*The House.*'

'*What gives us plants and water and power and comfort?*'

'*The House.*'

The House. Mother. These were the things she knew. Enough. Tom, this stranger, this piece of grit in the eye of the House – he

78

couldn't stay. Once he gave her the answer, she would make him leave.

'Diazepam,' he said, just as Esther stood up. 'It's a sedative.'

Esther paused. Sedative. The kind of thing that settles to the bottom of rivers? Silt?

Tom continued to read aloud, 'This medication works by calming the brain and nerves and can treat anxiety, muscle spasms and seizures …' He glanced at her.

'I don't understand.'

'They … sedate. Make you calm – sleepy even – easy to manage …'

'Mother wouldn't take those …'

A silence and then Tom asked, 'So if they aren't for her … then who are they for?'

And just like that, the volcano belched and spewed. Had her quiet clockwork convent days been the result of little tablets dissolving into her bloodstream? Why would Mother have needed to do that? The weight of the last half an hour pushed at her and she felt like she needed to crouch under its pressure. This morning she had waved Mother off on the Yearly and everything had been like normal and now, as outside the light gave up against the darkness, here she was stood with a strange man who had ripped a hole in her life and wanted to keep on tearing.

Tom got up and shuffled a little towards her, limping on his injured leg, one arm slightly outstretched as if to stop her, as if to touch her again, and Esther flinched.

'Esther, I need to tell you—'

But he didn't get to finish his sentence. Instead, the outer door opened behind him and in the doorway stood Mother. Her face obscured by her mask, she pushed back her hood, saw the man in front of her and gripped what she held in her other hand.

'*What keeps us safe?*'

'*The House.*'

'*And the bloody gun.*'

Chapter 19

Hannah

Sixteen years ago

The door opened and Hannah was faced with her future self.

'Didn't you read the sign?' The woman frowned, gripping on to the collar of a dog that strained against her hold and lunged at Hannah. The sign had been hard to miss: it had been nailed to the gatepost and had used many red capital letters.

'I did but I—'

'No cold callers, no salespeople, no junk mail—' The door slowly began to close.

'I want to buy your land!'

The door stopped.

Hannah had found the listing whilst killing time before an appointment at an unfamiliar GP surgery. In the two months that had passed since the will reading she had been taking a lot of those appointments lately, the ones further afield where she could grab a coffee in the nearby town or village and stop by an estate agent's window.

'I want to buy your land for cash.'

'Good for you. I have an estate agent, so contact him.'

'I'm willing to pay a good price for it if we can keep this a private sale.'

The woman yanked on the dog's collar and gave Hannah a stare that could have kick-started a new ice age.

'You have five minutes.' She held the door open.

Future-Hannah was everything she would have wanted her to be. It wasn't just that this woman lived in a forbidding great fortress of a house in the middle of nowhere with antisocial signs and an even more antisocial dog. It was the stare. Her stare was one that pinned a person to the spot and kept them there, unable to remember what their limbs were for whilst she studied them.

The hallway that Hannah stepped into was a jumble of boxes piled high, bags, an upturned table and chairs stacked on top of each other. Just like Hannah had been sure there was actually a house under all that ivy as she'd walked up the drive, so she was sure there were walls and a floor somewhere underneath all of the stuff.

'Flood in the lower east wing. I've had to decamp.' The dog being held by Future-Hannah lunged again, its teeth almost grazing Hannah's coat. 'Sit, you stupid animal.'

Hannah nearly did.

'Your five minutes is fast disappearing.'

'Yes! Mrs ...' Hannah left an expectant pause.

'*Lady* Tregellen.'

'Lady Tregellen. I want to buy your land, for cash, for much more cash than you're asking, actually—'

'I said SIT!'

The dog gave one more rather half-hearted lunge and then did as it was told, almost as if it too was waiting for its mistress's reaction to Hannah's offer. A trail of slobber began to stretch from its chin.

Lady Tregellen raised her eyebrows. 'Go on – the catch ...'

'I will pay you much more money for the land if … you agree to keep my name out of it.'

'Out of it?'

'Out of all records. Land Registry, the contracts – everything. I will pay in cash, upfront, one lump sum.'

In the light from a nearby lamp Hannah took in how eccentrically Lady Tregellen was dressed: corduroy trousers tucked into knee socks and a padded gilet over a flowery shirt, bright green fingerless gloves topping off the outfit. Her hair was white and thin like strands of dried glue on paper.

'Drugs?'

'Sorry?' Was the woman asking for drugs? Is that what bored rich people did out here in the countryside all day? Actually, Hannah thought, that would explain a lot.

'Is this drug money?'

'Oh. No – an inheritance.'

The slobber from the dog's chin stretched out, longer and longer, and Hannah couldn't keep her eyes from it, until the animal shook its head, sending spray she could feel land on her neck. It gave a yawn.

'So why the cloak and dagger?'

Hannah sighed. She was prepared for this question, had been waiting for it since she'd walked up the drive. 'I just want … to be left alone.' She braced for the other questions she knew would be hot on its heels.

Lady Tregellen fondled the dog's ear. 'Sensible girl.' She plonked herself into an armchair squashed against what had once been a stuffed fox, though now it was mostly wire and skin. 'The ones who don't – they're the ones I don't understand.' It felt like Hannah had just played a really good move in a board game where no one had shown her the rules. She waited. The dog snarled but in a lazy way, its tail thumping a few times. 'It would take some … obscurification.'

'Yes.' A pause. 'How long have you lived here?'

'My whole life. When I was a girl we used to have weekend parties – hunting, shooting, fishing – then these big evening dinners. Awful, noisy things full of awful, noisy people. Papa died, and then Mama and my brother moved to Singapore and so there was just me. It's been glorious.' Lady Tregellen pulled some of the stuffing from the arm of the chair and placed it carefully on top of the fox's head as a little cloud-puff wig. 'There's that old bunker on that land I'm selling.'

'I know.'

'So you want to be alone in a bunker and you want to make sure no one finds you. Correct?'

'Yes.'

'Sounds like bliss. I have just the man for you.'

'A man?'

'For the obscuring. My solicitor. He'll work out the details. But no backsies, let me be clear.'

'Backsies?' Hannah was turning into one of those dim-witted people who repeated the final word of someone else's sentence because they could not keep up.

'Exactly. I don't want you clawing your way out of that place in a few years and banging on my door asking for sugar, got it? If you want the hole, then you have to stay in it, my unexpected little worm.'

Somehow, in this place with a smell of mildew catching in the back of her throat, amid beaten furniture and soggy cardboard boxes, decomposing foxes and dust shimmering in the light – she had found a kindred spirit.

Hannah smiled.

'Want to see the old place?' Lady Tregellen asked.

Chapter 20

'God, I love it out here!' Lady Tregellen stomped on ahead of her, wearing a headscarf and a man's wax jacket with loose seams and one pocket missing. Her dog raced around them in circles, swiping past them at speed and them dashing away again, tongue lolling.

Hannah waited for it. The feeling. It was the feeling that the countryside was meant to evoke: safer. Cleaner. Except – and Hannah knew this because in the months since Esther's demon had woken up, all she had done was read and watch programmes about this kind of thing – the rate of rot was too fast and had been going for too long. Everything posed a risk. The seas? Choked with plastic, its coral dying. The earth? Poisoned by chemicals. The animals? Their meat stuffed with drugs. And the sky? Well, the sky was worst of all.

You couldn't escape it. Not even here where birdsong and the rasp of branch against branch were the only sounds. You could buy your plot of land and build your house and sit in your garden with your home-grown fruit and filtered water and the rot would still get to you somehow. It would stroke your cheek as the soft wisp of a breeze. That air would bring the wheeze in your chest, the growth in your lung, the tightening band of heart muscle.

You had to be smarter.

Today was a Tuesday and it had already been three. Three asthma attacks. And she wasn't imagining it but every week, each time, one attack was always just a little bit worse, in a way that Ned could simply not see. Each week in one attack, the pauses between gasping breaths were wide enough for that black void of nothing to creep in. Hannah never wanted to sit in that ambulance again.

They marched on, Lady Tregellen setting a pace that Hannah struggled to maintain in a borrowed pair of wellies a size too big. Her feet slid about in them, making each step treacherous, her ankles wobbling, and there were so many of those steps. Hannah guessed it took them about an hour to reach the place where the trees thinned out.

She paused.

'Welcome to my little Cold War throwback.' Lady Tregellen swept an arm out towards the shape in the hill ahead of them. 'You can get rid of it if you need.'

Hannah wouldn't get rid of it. It was the reason she was here. The reason why she'd sent Esther to school that morning despite feeling sick and sweaty at the idea of her being out of sight all day. The reason why she'd used a day of annual leave and driven for hours and then walked until her toes throbbed.

It was their future.

The hill stretched up in front of them and in it like a tooth trying to break free of the gum was the bunker, only the front of it visible. Concrete. Hidden.

Home.

'Can I go in?'

'Do what you like. If you trip and fall in there though, I'll let my dog eat you up.'

The block of concrete in front of her was beautiful. A wall. Built to last and to protect. Hannah wasn't worried about the world ending. That missed the point. The world would probably end at some time – that was what worlds did eventually – but that was unlikely in her lifetime. What was more likely was the world limping on getting sicker and more diseased with every step, the bloated, parasitic people clinging to it.

This place would hide them from all of that. It was something to give to Esther. Not cuddly whales and pretty lace-topped socks, or flower hair grips and dolls with vacant smiles. All of that was useless. This would be a gift to last. Somewhere to stay, safe and secure, hers forever. She would never need to go into the world again. Hannah would make sure of it.

The door had been chained shut with a padlock but at some point someone or something had tried to force it open and there was a sliver of space through which Hannah could squeeze part of her shoulder and half of her face.

If the door hadn't let in a strip of light then she knew it would be the kind of dark where a person wouldn't know where *they* ended and *it* began. The kind of dark that got behind the eyeballs.

It was a dark that didn't say she was being ridiculous, stupid, that she was careering off with a half-baked plan that would never work, that she couldn't spend her inheritance on this.

Instead, it was a dark in which she could see the rest of her life – and the rest of Esther's too.

'It's amazing.'

It was hers.

Chapter 21

Three months on from buying the land, Hannah got out of her car, keys in hand, and froze. She recognised that laugh: joyful, delighted, high-pitched.

It sent her running in the opposite direction from her house, away from the car, across the road and straight into the park opposite with its patch of cracked safety matting and rusting play equipment.

'What are you doing?' She didn't like the shrill edge to her voice.

The four of them turned to her, frozen mid-frame in their fun family action shot that would have fitted perfectly into an advert for something wholesome. Ned paused his conversation with his younger brother, as Esther stood high on the stocky turret of the pirate's ship, which was really a few monkey bars, a grimy wheel and two slides on either end. The neighbour's child was at one lookout – that skinny boy a bit older than Esther whose name Hannah had forgotten. Esther was all she saw.

'Han—'

'We agreed! Not this park. Never this park!' Hannah barged past Ned and Adam, the smoking chimney stacks cutting chunks out of the skyline. She reached her arms out to her little girl with those big baby seal eyes. 'Esther, come down.'

She had not told Ned about the building site in the trees many, many miles away. Of course, she had tried, but there had never been the right moment and she knew he wouldn't understand. But once the place was finished, once she got the three of them there, once they had closed the door and were safe in the darkness then he would finally get it. He would see how she had saved them all.

And if he couldn't see that? Well, the fact that her name was hidden from the Land Registry was her safeguard because, if need be, she would take Esther anyway and no one would be able to find them. To the outside world Lady Tregellen owned the land and had the legal title but held it in trust for Hannah as a beneficiary, her name not registered. It was an unusual agreement, but not an illegal one.

'Can't you just leave her? She's having a bit of fun. No harm done,' Adam said. Hannah could hardly look at him, but that was okay, she didn't need to. She just had to keep her eyes on Esther. Ned was always more difficult when Adam was around, but that was fine because he wouldn't be around for much longer. *'No harm done.'*

Harm, Hannah thought, reaching again for Esther who hesitated on the turret, twisting the edge of her jacket in her chubby hand. What did Adam know about harm? He hadn't been there through all of those nights when Esther had woken, hot and afraid, struggling to breathe, taking great gulps that almost stopped Hannah's own heart, the pauses between them too long, too full of fear.

'Esther, come down. Now.'

Esther moved closer to her mother's waiting arms and then Adam was between them, trying to get in the way.

'Can't you just let her play? This once?'

Hannah turned on him. 'Can't you just stay out of it and mind your own damn business? This once?'

Though the daylight was fading, Hannah saw Adam's sneer. Light and dark, the two of them, their mother had once told her.

And it was Adam who was the darkness, despite his blond hair and handsome features, he was the one who was quick to snipe, quick to incite, too quick to get caught. Stood side by side like that, Hannah could see the similarities between the two brothers, but Ned's softer edges were chiselled to a sharpness in Adam's features – a sharpness that continued all the way to his tongue.

'Can't you just let her play?' Esther played, Hannah thought, she played all the time. Inside. With the windows shut.

Esther continued to scrunch up the edge of her jacket, her eyes moving between them, caught on the pirate ship sailing a sea of indecision. The boy with his curly hair and snub nose stuck his head further out from the lookout, 'It's been fun,' he said, rubbing his sleeve over the handrail in an awkward way. Giving up on getting her to move, Hannah stood on tiptoe and reached up, half-pulling, half-dragging the little girl closer.

She felt Ned's hand on her sleeve. 'Enough, Hannah. She's been enjoying herself.'

Hannah turned to him. 'You know! You know the reasons why. Look at it. It's right there. Do you think it's a bloody coincidence that we move to this hell town and Pips' asthma starts? You're not bloody stupid. We said, we agreed not to let her play anywhere near here.'

'It's just this once. While Adam's here. It's his last visit for so long.'

And Hannah couldn't have been happier about it. Soon he would be on the other side of the world for a job opportunity he couldn't pass up in whatever he did, something slimy in banking mostly involving the attempt to hide rich clients' money from the taxman.

'Stop it, you're making a scene. Listen to me.' Ned's voice was low but there was nothing light about it this time. He kept his grip on her arm; she kept her grip on Esther.

The little boy rubbed some more at an imaginary spot on the handrail.

Most of Hannah's problems had come from listening to Ned. 'We'll get a better place, further out from the works,' he'd told her when he showed her his job application. 'We won't live right by it,' he'd said and, fool that she was, she'd believed him. And now he said, 'We'll move as soon as we can, to the edge of town.'

She wouldn't be a fool any longer.

It didn't matter where they went. The demon was in her baby girl's chest. It would never sleep properly until they were under that hill, behind a thick door with an air-conditioning system that would filter out the poison.

Hannah shrugged Ned off and lifted Esther down. 'It's getting late.' She aimed this at the boy. 'You should go home.'

'It's only five,' he sniffed and ran his sleeve over his nose before rubbing it back on the handrail.

In her arms, Esther did not complain but her body went floppy, a dead weight drooping onto Hannah's shoulder. She thought she heard Adam mutter, 'For fuck's sake,' as she walked past but she didn't care.

And then the wheezing began, as Hannah knew it would.

'Bag,' she said, not looking at Ned but holding out her hand.

'We haven't got it.'

'Oh my God – how many times do I have to tell you?' She shifted Esther's weight, the little girl's head on her shoulder, and felt her hot, laboured breath in her ear as she hurried off towards the house.

'We can literally see our front door, Hannah! We don't need the bloody bag!'

Wrong. There were too many what-ifs in the world for that kind of thinking. What if they forgot their keys and were locked out? What if they couldn't get Esther back to the house in time? What if something happened to the house while they were gone – fire, flood, burglary – and they couldn't get to the inhalers?

Crouched on the hall floor, Hannah grabbed the bag from under the bench where they sat to put on their outdoor shoes.

She shook the plastic tube and Esther sucked in deep, refreshing breaths; Hannah breathing along with her as she watched Ned and Adam saunter closer through the open front door. That was the problem with Ned, she realised, that saunter. Too slow. Whilst she waited for him to catch up, that aching black void of nothingness that had nearly swallowed her in the ambulance when Esther's breaths had stopped – that was still waiting for them, around every corner, in every playground, garden, street and schoolyard. He would be too slow to save Esther from it.

She couldn't trust him to do it.

Later that evening, when the two of them thought she was busy putting Esther to bed, Hannah crept down the stairs to hear their hushed conversation.

'She needs help, mate,' Adam's voice floated to her.

Hannah couldn't disagree with him. She did need help. But it wouldn't come from a therapy session, or mindfulness, or the kind of antidepressants she sold every day to beleaguered doctors. No, her help was sealed thick concrete and narrow windows as far away from smoke and traffic fumes as she could get. Her safe house.

Chapter 22

Esther

All eyes were fixed on the gun.

Mother had never looked that way before: the set of her jaw, the narrowing of her eyes and the way her body tensed, as if she could leap and attack at any moment. That soft shabbiness of her cardigan was merely fur on a wild animal and beneath it were claws.

'Mother?'

'Mrs Allbright—?'

But Mother did something Esther had never heard her do before: she roared, with a brutal vehemence, 'GET OUT!'

Tom's words stuttered to a halt. Esther could not stop staring at the gun in her mother's steady hand: it was not the familiar shotgun because that had been left in the House. No, this was a slim handgun, something that could be hidden easily – something that must have been, for years, because Esther had never seen it before.

'GET OUT OF MY HOUSE!'

'Mother!' Esther stood and instinctively put an arm out in front of Tom as if he needed shielding, as if this scene was hazardous material and he should keep back.

Esther pushed Tom behind her as he tried and failed to get to his feet. She had been mistaken, when she had first tried to identify that scent on him; it wasn't spiced but something else, something other people probably instantly recognised but which baffled her, though she liked it. However, it was instantly wrong to be facing Mother, to not be on her side. She could rectify that with a few steps, but there was too much new information swirling in her brain, too much doubt.

'Mother?' she said softly, her hands raised in surrender. 'You can't do this.'

Mother's hands shook, and there was a harsh edge to her voice. 'Get out of the way, Esther.'

Esther, fetch this; Esther, read that; Esther, stand here – Esther, Esther, Esther. Sixteen years of it.

Esther stood firm.

'I don't care who you are.' Mother pointed the gun at Tom but looked at her daughter. 'Get out of my house.' Her voice broke. 'And you, Esther, what are you thinking? You let him in, this … this … man, and now—'

'I had to – he was hurt by one of your traps!'

Her words dropped like tombstones. Quiet settled.

'You went outside?' Mother's voice was strangely toneless and her question was followed by a sigh that made her shoulders sag.

'It was—'

'Without your mask?'

Esther had never seen her mother look like that, the way her eyes widened and the colour drained from her face.

She opened her mouth to speak but Mother cut her off, keeping her gun trained on Tom but her eyes on Esther. 'Are you okay? How's your breathing? Do you need your inhaler? Where is it? Should I get the nebuliser? Get your inhaler now—'

'I'm fine, I promise!'

'You wore your mask the whole time?'

The lie, when it came, was so easy: 'Yes.' And a little voice only she could hear added, *'When I took it off, the fresh air helped me stop my asthma attack. And the air did seem like that – fresh. Not dirty, not polluted.'*

Mother sighed again. 'Well, I guess you've been lucky. The mask saved you. And it *is* cleaner here, but it's not just the air, Pips, it's never just been about that. It's dangerous out there. What has he told you?'

Esther thought, *The only danger at the moment is that bear trap – and that gun …*

'He hasn't said anything.'

'Good.' She waved the gun at Tom. 'You don't speak to my daughter, is that clear? You keep your mouth shut. Why are you here?'

'Trust me, I—'

'No! I don't trust you! Do you think I'm stupid? Esther and I, we only ever trust each other … and the House.'

Esther flinched and took a step away from Tom. She should have been standing with Mother, not defending a man she barely knew. Esther looked down, away from Mother's stare. How could she? It was Mother who had kept her safe all these years. She had given up her own life for her daughter's, had hidden them away so she could grow up being able to breathe easy, sheltered from the world. And Esther had loved her life: her daydreaming, rosary hours, the minutes slipping from her like someone running prayer beads through their hands. She had loved it. Hadn't she?

'Esther. Come here.'

'We only ever trust each other …' Except, Mother was hiding pills and bear traps and a working phone signal. But there would be a reason for that, a logical, rational explanation. There always was.

Instinctively, Esther moved to her.

She could only have taken a few steps, but that was all Mother needed. Esther saw the gleam in her eye as she raised the muzzle of the gun.

Chapter 23

'Please! Wait! Don't shoot me – Jesus!' Tom raised his arm as if that would stop a bullet, his other hand clutching the strap of his bag. 'I'll leave, I promise – but I was sent to tell you … Lady Tregellen is dead!'

Esther saw her mother's hand tremble, before she steadied it. She stared at Tom with a gaze of stone. 'Dead?'

'Yes. Her solicitor, Snipes and Son, I work in the office and there's some paperwork you have to sign, y'know, as the beneficiary of the trust? They sent me to search you out.' He kept his palm outstretched whilst he fumbled in his bag with the strange bright circle on it, drawing out a crumpled envelope. 'You see?'

'Beneficiary of what trust?' Esther frowned.

'Ssh, Esther.' Mother lowered the gun a fraction. 'How did she die?'

'Heart failure. Brought on by liver disease. Umm … she was a bit of a drinker, it seemed. She got pretty sick at the end but wouldn't leave the house. Said she wanted to …' He eyed the gun. 'Die there and let the dogs eat her.'

The muzzle lowered another fraction.

'Sounds like her,' Mother muttered.

'So then there was all this paperwork, the estate and

everything and, of course, old Mr Snipes was dead by then too and it took us a while to work it all out ... y'know – the agreement with you.'

'So if Lady Tregellen is dead, that means I now own the legal title to the land? My name will be shown on the Land Registry?'

'Umm ... yes ...'

'What agreement does he mean?' Esther asked.

'Shush, Esther – I'm trying to think!'

'No!' The word was out before Esther could stop it and then the others tumbled free as well. 'I won't shush and will you put that gun down? Are you really going to shoot this man here in our own porch? For doing his job? You've already nearly killed him with a bloody great big bear trap!' In her bedroom she could almost hear Mr Wiffles flapping his fins together in applause.

Esther took a breath. Mother flicked her a glance. 'It wouldn't have killed him. I made sure of that when I set them.'

Them. More than one. Deliberately set.

'But ... I don't get it.' Esther touched her mother's arm. 'It's the air we're hiding from, right? Not the people?' Mother's shoulders sagged. 'All we have to do is bandage his leg and sign his papers and off he goes. No harm done.'

She couldn't let him disappear so soon. The gloom of the House, the darkness of their mole lives under the hill, was waiting to claim her and snuff out the questions she had – questions to which Tom might have the answers. What Mother said next, and how Esther reacted, would never be more important.

Mother frowned, but then Mother frowned all the time – that was no indicator. But she was thinking of what had just been said, Esther could tell, and then she seemed to come to some sort of decision and motioned with the gun.

'You stay here – understood?' she said and Esther stopped herself from smiling. She had persuaded her mother; she had actually offered a different point of view and Mother had accepted it. Tom nodded. 'You don't move and we'll fix your leg and sign the paperwork and then you go and you don't come back. Understood?'

Another nod. Tom cleared his throat. 'Excellent. Happy to leave with all my limbs so I'll do whatever you say … but could I have a glass of water? I don't feel too good …' He tugged at one arm of his jacket, trying to get it off.

'Mother, you can't leave him in the porch. He needs a hot drink and it's cold here. We could let him sit in the gym. He won't be able to climb the stairs anyway.'

Then an alarm went off somewhere and, confused, Esther wondered if the House had some sort of warning system the minute they considered allowing anybody else in. But she realised that the alarm was musical, though a bit tinny, and that Tom had once again brought out that slim bit of plastic that contained the whole world as well as a telephone. A telephone that, she realised now, was ringing.

Esther marvelled at how cool and innocent her voice sounded. 'But how is that phone working, Mother? We don't have a signal out here, do we?'

But Mother didn't seem to hear her.

'Give me that.' Mother gestured for the phone.

'It's the office, I should really—' He began to tap on the screen.

'Now!' Mother stomped across as he tapped faster before she swiped the thing out of his hands. 'You can have it back when you leave. Which, believe me, won't be long.'

'You didn't answer my question?' Esther could only see the back of her mother's head, the tangle of short curls and the fraying collar of her shirt, but she noted the way her shoulders squared. 'You've always said we have no phone signal.'

The words were placed deliberately before her mother like tumblers in a magic trick. Would Mother be able to spirit away the ball hidden beneath them?

Mother turned to Esther, her expression guarded. 'We don't. Maybe a new mast has gone up somewhere – how would I know?'

Her tone was light but forced, whipped as stiff as meringue and liable to crack as easily.

Esther said nothing in return.

There would be a time for this conversation, she thought. But it would have to take a ticket and get in line with all the other conversations they needed to have about hidden pills and paperwork designed to keep them secret for reasons about which Esther knew nothing. But the time now was for helping Tom – because if she had lots of questions jostling for position in her brain then it looked as if he had some of the answers. The truthful ones anyway.

Mother had lied.

That was too sharp a thought. It didn't matter if she could explain it all, logically, rationally – Esther was twenty-one now and there was no need to hide anything from her. No need at all.

But Esther was the one doing the hiding as she nodded and said, 'Yes, a new mast. That's probably it.'

Satisfied, Mother lowered the gun and gave yet another sigh. 'Let's get this over with then. But he stays in the porch – hear that, you? You stay in the porch.'

Tom would have answered if he could but instead, whilst the two of them had been distracted, he had slumped over against the wall with his eyes closed, pale and unmoving.

Chapter 24

Moving a body was hard.

'Watch his head.'

'I am watching his head! He's lucky I am, getting himself stuck in my trap and then fainting in my porch—'

'He was only doing his job! Traipsing around trying to find us in the middle of nowhere— Mind his head!'

'I am!' Mother dropped his shoulders onto the floor of the gym but Esther placed his ankles gently down, as if that would be the thing to wake him, not the way his skull had just been thumped onto concrete.

The two of them stared at him. Esther thought he looked younger with his eyes closed, the eyelashes dark and long, his breathing even and shallow.

'He's not even dressed properly,' Mother muttered. 'I mean, look at his boots ... no grip to those cheap soles. No, don't take them off!'

But Esther already had the offending shoe in her hand. 'I thought that's what you do?'

'No, his bloody foot will swell now and we won't be able to get the thing back on. Do not touch the other boot. He can damn well hop home for all I care.'

His socks were bright blue, nowhere near thick enough, and were printed with a cartoon character of a strange yellow person with a spiky head and bulging eyes. This alien had a speech bubble coming from his mouth that said, 'Don't have a cow, man.' Esther wasn't sure why the alien could not have the cow he wanted but that was the least of the mysteries she needed solved.

'He might have blood poisoning or something. From the trap,' Esther muttered.

This time Mother bent and inspected his leg, the trouser still rolled up from earlier. 'Poppycock. The teeth didn't even break the skin. Those traps are so old now, I'm surprised they are still working.'

'Why?'

'Rust, I guess. I mean, I haven't been—'

'No – I don't mean that. Why did you set traps outside the house?'

Mother concentrated on getting a closer look at Tom's injury, jerking her head to make her glasses fall from their perch and land on her nose. 'We'll need an ice pack and some alcohol wipes but I'm not wasting a bandage on him.'

'Mother!'

Standing up from her crouch, Mother's knees clicked like little pistons, as if she were a robot woman, malfunctioning quietly here in this bunker. 'We're two women alone in the middle of nowhere. Why wouldn't you set a few traps?'

'Two women alone *in a bunker*! An actual bunker! How much more protection do we need?'

'You don't understand. You don't know – what it's like Out There.'

'No, that's right, I don't – how could I? You won't even let me go on the Yearly with you.'

'Oh, this again? Not now, Esther.' She rummaged in his inside jacket pocket and brought out the envelope he had shown them earlier. 'You know what, after this – you can do what you want,

okay? Walk all the way to the nearest city if it makes you happy …
stand in the traffic without your mask, breathing in as much of
that *fresh air* as you want. You're not a prisoner and I'm not your
bloody gaoler. I'm only trying to keep you safe.'

She ripped the envelope open with such force it tore along
the front before she crushed it into a ball and scanned the pages
within. Esther rolled Tom onto his side and opened his mouth
a little, remembering the first-aid DVD Mother made her watch
every month, aware of her cold fingers on his warm jaw. She
couldn't be sure, but she thought she saw his eyelids flutter.

When she looked up, Mother was staring down at him. It
was familiar, that stare, one she had seen many times before on
her face, her eyes blank and cold while her brain worked out
the solution to the problem in front of her. The flickering of a
motherboard behind her eyes.

'Esther, can you fetch the first-aid kit from the storeroom?'

And she nearly did. Her legs moved instinctively, pushing
herself up from where she knelt, and she was about to dutifully
trot off amongst the shelves and leave her mother alone …

… in the dark …

… with Tom.

But those eyes. If her mother was a malfunctioning robot with
her circuitry fritzing as she trundled through the grooves of her
day, then the thing obstructing those very grooves was laid out
on the floor at their feet.

Tom.

Mother's eyes had the gleam of calculation. And it wasn't as if
Esther did not trust her mother; no, that was completely wrong
– she had no reason to mistrust her, no reason at all.

Except …

… pills hidden in the belly of a bear, the rusted teeth of a trap
and the shrill ring of a phone that should not work …

To Esther it felt urgent that she should not leave Tom alone
with Mother – and that, if she did, she would return to find that

something convenient had happened to him. He would have woken and rushed off and that would be it: the darkness would close over her once more and she would never get a chance like this again.

'I don't know where the kit is. You rearranged yesterday.' If Mother could make her gaze inscrutable, then so could Esther. She had learnt from the best.

Mother huffed. 'Fine.'

Later, when she had a chance to think about the day, she realised that she should have been more suspicious of what happened next. Because it was almost as if Tom had been awake the whole time, only pretending unconsciousness so that when Mother left the room he could open his eyes all of a sudden and they were eyes that didn't seem confused at all.

'I have to tell you something else,' he whispered. 'It's important.'

'The pills, I know – you don't think they were meant for her. You think—'

'No, Esther, your mother is lying to you about more than just sedatives. She's—'

But she was on her way back, a dark shadow at first but then that shadow took form, a form that should have been as familiar to Esther as the House around her: baggy cardigan, broken shoes, a nest of hair, a woman she had known her entire life – who had *been* her entire life.

Tom let his head flop and closed his eyes once more.

Chapter 25

Something somewhere dripped.

It was a noise that was beginning to make Esther itch. In fact, she had already scratched a small red welt onto the soft skin between finger and thumb.

'He'll need to use the toilet.'

Mother stirred a pot on the stove before sliding a newly sliced carrot from the chopping board into the stew. She didn't even turn her head. 'I put a bucket in there. He'll make do.'

Darkness had laid an inky finger over Mother's plans. By the time she had sorted out Tom's leg and given him a drink and a painkiller, the sky outside had softened and smudged into a deep grey that threatened black. Then she had had to read the paperwork that needed signing, frowning over each page until finally she had clicked the pen and made a scribbled flourish. With her jaw set, Mother had considered what was unmistakably a night sky but hoisted Tom up anyway and barrelled them both through the front door despite Esther's protestations.

'You can't be thinking of walking him back to his car in the dark!'

'I can.'

'He's hurt his leg!'

'Needs must when the devil drives.'

It had only taken them minutes to return.

'I could break a bloody ankle out there!' Mother had fumed as she let go of Tom rather more abruptly than was strictly necessary. He had wobbled before leaning against the wall. 'You'll have to stay the night. In the gym. You don't move from there, you don't speak to us and first light – we're walking to your car.'

'What if I can't drive it?'

'I'll drive you.'

Another drip. Esther scratched at her hand. It wasn't a drip but the House tutting slightly under its breath, disappointed that there was a stranger inside its walls. Disappointed in them. She watched Mother sprinkle some herbs into the pot and give it another stir.

Esther touched the outline of the pills in her jeans pocket.

'So if they aren't for her … who are they for?'

Tom's words hung about in her brain like a mob of teenagers, scaring the locals and throwing cans at her neurons.

'Mother, do you ever have trouble sleeping?' Esther asked.

The hand paused in its stirring. 'Trouble sleeping?' She left the stove, wiped her fingers on a tea towel and came closer to Esther, fixing her with a look. 'Esther, people who have trouble sleeping have simply not worked hard enough in the day. I'm so bloody exhausted I'm out like a light as soon as my head hits the pillow.'

'Thought so.'

'So if they aren't for her … who are they for?'

'Are you okay, Pips? Have you been struggling to sleep? Because that can cause stress and we've discussed it, haven't we, how stress is a major player in an asthma attack?' Mother's voice took on that hectic edge that was so familiar to Esther.

'I'm fine.'

And she was. Never a problem sleeping. Every evening candle-light and reading, dinner finished early so they could fit in a cup of tea and chocolate before bed. Half the time her eyelids were heavy before she even made it to her bedroom, brushing her teeth whilst her brain packed up for the day. She didn't even wake on those occasions when her body decided to sleepwalk to the front door.

'So if they aren't for her … who are they for?'

But tonight a cold hand held her eyelids wide open. Because she knew the logical conclusion to what Tom had told her. If the sedatives weren't for Mother then she was either stockpiling them for no reason in a hidden place she thought no one would find or …

… they were for Esther.

But it made no sense. Why would Mother sedate her? She didn't need to. It was hardly as if Esther was bouncing off the walls, wrecking the furniture or trying to claw her way out through the skylight. She had been happy with those calm, ordered days of hers.

But cold fingers stretched her eyelids a little more. Perhaps, though, her tranquil days had not been down to her own quiet temperament, the way she carefully sliced up time to make a manageable bite of day. Perhaps, instead, it had been caused by chemicals dissolving in her bloodstream, a neurological blanket laid over her frayed nerves.

The House tutted again.

No.

Her mother would not do that. How did she know this man was telling the truth? Her fingernails scraped at the raw skin on her hand. She didn't; she knew nothing about him. He could be mistaken about what the pills were used for, the flat black bit of plastic that he claimed was a world and a phone all in one could be faulty.

The only solution was to talk to him. And he wanted to talk to her, didn't he? *'I have to tell you something else.'*

'I'll take his meal down; you sit.' Esther took a bowl from the shelf and held it out for her mother to ladle the stew into it. She

106

was disappointed. Vegetable. It was always vegetable. Meat was tricky to store but there was some salted stuff: hard and thick and possibly more useful as a weapon. However, this was the golden time after the Yearly when Mother usually brought back some fresh produce. Perhaps she didn't want to share it with Tom.

'No, you're not going near him.' Mother tried to take the bowl from her, but Esther gripped on and the result was a tiny, ridiculous tug of war. Esther let go. 'He could be dangerous.'

'He doesn't seem dangerous. And he can hardly walk.'

But Mother had already slopped some of the stew into the bowl and walked away, leaving Esther with the steaming pan. She looked in.

She trusted her mother.

But she did not eat the stew that night, claiming a lack of appetite, and when Mother made the nettle tea – dank and sour-smelling and cloudy – Esther let hers go cold and then tipped it into her bathroom sink before bed. Watching the nettles swirl and then clog the plughole, she decided that tonight was not a night for sleeping.

It was a night for answers.

Chapter 26

Esther had to wait.

Her mother had to fall asleep first. She had left her bedroom door wide open to see the stairs in case Tom dragged himself up them with an injured leg and tried to kill them both with the axe he had successfully hidden until this point. It took a while for her to drift off, but Esther knew it was a waiting game: after all, as her mother had said, insomnia was a problem for the lazy.

Tiptoe. Darkness. The round moon of their skylight and then the stairs to the gym door where she opened it and—

Something large swung across her face, just missing her nose.

'Jesus! I thought you were your mother come to kill me!' Tom steadied himself against the wall, eyes blurry from sleep.

Esther considered for a beat. 'So you were going to defend yourself with a … yoga mat?'

Tom hugged the rolled-up plastic. 'Didn't have much choice.'

'Well, there's a barbell in the corner …'

'There is?'

An attempt had been made at comfort, Esther noted. The sleeping bag and a blow-up mattress underneath, a glass of water and the infamous bucket, which Esther avoided.

Tom limped over to prop the yoga mat against the wall, sat

down and ran a hand through his hair, which immediately flopped back into messy curls. When she had first seen him, she had thought him a disappointing Disney prince and that held true here in this room: he was too lanky, lacking the required square in his jaw and muscle in his shoulder – the cartoon illustrator had a lot of work left to do.

Esther had been preparing for small talk her entire life with the help of the films she had seen. The weather. There was always a general agreement that that was a good place to start and though she really did have other more important things to talk about, she couldn't help but give it a go. 'There have been lovely cloud formations today,' she began, pleased with herself.

Tom looked a bit puzzled, which wasn't the expected response, but she really didn't have time to dazzle him with more of her thoughts on the trees, the temperature, or the sudden rainfall. 'You have something to tell me?'

He sighed and his shoulders slumped. 'I do.'

In her pyjama pocket were a few hard, round little shapes. Her T-shirt had a picture of a cartoon whale on it but one eye was now drooping, its print flaking away. 'Oh, and how does your leg feel? Are you okay?' She blushed at this because she remembered that that bit should perhaps have come before the small talk – after all, the man had been stuck in a bear trap.

Tom tried to sit up some more and winced. 'Fabulous.'

Esther could recognise sarcasm, though Mother never really used it. So she knew how he probably meant that word but she decided to take it at face value and be pleased at his positivity. He was clearly a man who liked to look on the bright side of things, which was exactly what was needed in this situation: the bright side.

'And I've been thinking, y'know – about the pills. Maybe they are for emergencies. Mother may never have used them.'

Another long hard look. 'Maybe.'

In the spaces between her words though, that was where the

shadows lurked and those shadows were twisting themselves into shapes, into pictures: her mother sprinkling something in a drink, a tea that already tasted so foul no one would suspect it had anything else in it. To keep her daughter calm, to keep her docile. To keep her sane.

In the corner of the room was his bag, the one with a badge of red circles and the silver star in the middle. 'Is that your solicitor's logo?' she asked, pointing.

Tom smiled and then laughed. 'Captain America.' Esther must have looked blank because he added, 'The films? Or, well, the comics first, I guess. He's a superhero – it's his shield … Oh God, you have no idea what I'm talking about, do you? Marvel?'

To marvel: to become filled with surprise or wonder at something. Esther often flicked through their battered dictionary when she was bored. Did he want her to marvel at his bag? She guessed it was nice enough, but it wasn't anything to make a fuss over …

'I mean – fuck! Where do I start?' He sighed. 'Look, Esther, I haven't done this right at all and things like this, they're meant to be handled delicately, which is exactly what I'm not doing, but I need to tell you more – if you'll listen. Are you listening?'

Esther had always thought herself nun-like, her days little rosary beads of peaceful routine. But had that been down to chemicals? And, if so, then she had no idea who she was *without* the pills.

'… you know that, right?'

'Huh?'

Tom repeated himself, slower, 'The air here is fine.'

Esther blinked. 'Yes. Of course. It's cleaner here, which is why Mother chose this spot. But cleaner doesn't mean clean. I still need a mask, to be safe.' But those were Mother's words. Again, what would Esther have said? Not Esther on pills or Esther influenced by Mother, the Other Esther – the one she didn't know yet.

'What do you think the outside world is like? Not here but say, a city?' Tom asked.

'The cities are polluted and the air is toxic but, well, not everyone Out There understands this because … people can be stupid and blinkered, but the air is dangerous. People get sick from it. It can cause cancers and diseases, dementia and breathing problems. Too dangerous for me, with my asthma.' Again, these were not her words.

Tom patted the floor next to him. 'Sit.'

She did. Her legs felt too bendy anyway, like she was an over-heated Barbie.

'You're kind of right, y'know. This is why this is so hard, and I'm completely not cut out to explain all of this to you. Cities *are* polluted. But there are plenty of people just like you, with asthma, with pretty bad asthma, who don't hide themselves away in bunkers in the middle of nowhere. They live and work in those cities. Without masks.'

Esther studied the concrete floor. 'I'm different. Out There is not for me … for us.'

'So your mother says …'

More shadows formed in the spaces between those words. *She also said we had no phone signal, and she keeps a hidden stash of sedatives and pulled a gun on a man who had been injured by her own trap.*

'There's something else.'

Esther wasn't sure how much more she could take in.

'Something I should have told you straight away, but I just didn't know how …'

Out There was a place she could walk without a mask? On city streets, crossing roads clogged with traffic, roads that could take her to other places, other cities – a whole world she could experience, bigger than she could imagine. He had plonked that in her lap: the world. Anything else he said could not affect her.

'Your father is still alive.'

111

Suddenly the concrete underneath her melted and she braced her hands against the wall, a thousand questions on her tongue, but before she could say any of them there was a yell from upstairs, someone calling her name.

Mother.

Chapter 27

Hannah

Sixteen years ago

Hannah's beloved dark had been ruined.

She knew she shouldn't have trusted his opinion. City. Expensively educated with a sense of entitlement sewn into his pocket square. Even in his hard hat and hi-vis jacket you could have plonked him in a London wine bar and he would have fit right in. She imagined a factory line of similar men, teeth-gleaming grins, each one toppling off the end to scamper away in Italian leather shoes.

'You agreed. We went over the plans,' he said.

Yes, she had, Hannah had to admit. She'd needed the best, to get the job done quickly and well. The "well" bit was important. They were going to live in this place for the rest of their lives and there was no room for slapdash, or that'll do. She'd needed precision and that had cost money – it had cost *him*. The best in the bunker business. Project Manager for the End Times: Edward Monten.

'It's got to go.' She stared upwards.

He took off his glasses and rubbed one eye, 'But I really don't see—'

'It's got to go.'

They both gazed at the ceiling. She didn't expect him to understand. The darkness. People always wanted to fix it, didn't they? Human beings spent so much of their time pushing it back – street lamps and security sensors and silly little fairy lights in twee gardens – as if that light could protect them somehow. Light doesn't protect. It attracts. It makes you visible, marks you out as a glowing little morsel amongst the great hulking monsters stalking the edges.

Hannah wanted the dark. Currently there was a bloody great round hole in it.

'A skylight. We talked about it, something to lift the gloom.'

She gazed at the round white moon in her dark bunker sky, remembering the discussion. At the time it had seemed sensible to have an extra light source and Edward had been insistent, that the place would be 'untenable without it' and, at that moment, probably dazzled by the glint from his unfeasibly large watch, she had agreed with him.

After all, she did not know what she was doing.

But the thing was, as the House had begun to take shape around her in the month since that afternoon at the playground with Ned and Adam, as it grew its capital H in her mind, she began to realise that she *did* know what she was doing. It was her doing it, after all. Her who would live in it afterwards. This was all hers. And if she wanted darkness, she would have it.

A boy scuttled in a corner. Hannah guessed he was around mid-twenties, but he looked as if he had only started shaving a day or so ago. Badly. Edward had introduced him as the air filtration expert. This was the other thing she was determined to have, because this was the whole point of well … everything she was doing. Air. Breath. She wanted to give her daughter the gift

114

of security, thick walls, small windows, safety, toughened glass and concrete but most importantly she wanted to gift her the very air she would breathe until her lungs gave out at hopefully a ripe old age.

Safe air.

The filtration system would be cutting-edge. More importantly, it would be foolproof – easy to maintain and fix, forever, or at least, for an average lifetime. This boy had already won awards for his designs.

'It will take money.' Edward put his glasses back on.

Their fake moon shone down upon them. She should have trusted her gut, Hannah thought. She should never have agreed to it. After all, she had bought the place because of its darkness, not despite it.

She pressed her lips together. Cash wasn't an issue; she had more than enough of her aunt's money left in that bank account that Ned knew nothing about. It still surprised her, what you could achieve so quickly and easily if you had those extra zeros in your balance statement, though it shouldn't have really. That was how the world worked.

'Diane?' Edward turned to her.

Lying wasn't an issue now either, not for Hannah – or rather, Diane, as Edward knew her. And she would have liked to have said that that had been a surprise too, the ease with which she lied, but those false words seemed to trip too freely from her tongue for that to be the case. Lies had given her so much. She and Esther would be safely hidden.

Not that they needed to hide from anyone. Ned would be coming with them.

But it never hurt to plan ahead.

'Spend the money, get rid of the skylight.'

They already had enough light from the two narrow front windows in each main bedroom, light that could, thankfully, be closed off with a simple shut door. And those weren't lying in the field above, waiting to be stepped upon by intruders, to be peered through, vulnerable and easily stumbled over.

'It will add more time.' Edward unrolled a design and switched on the torch attached to his helmet so he could peer at it.

Hannah crossed her arms. 'No.'

'I'm afraid there's no way round it.'

She pressed her lips together again, this time so hard that she could feel them numb a little. Time. It was the only thing she could not manipulate and she could not wait any longer for this place than was absolutely necessary – her little girl depended on her.

Edward showed her the plans. 'The skylight would be fully reinforced and have a high-tech kind of security glass that means we could blend it in to its surroundings but if you insist ...' He deliberately let his words hang there in the dim air.

Hannah sighed. Damn him.

'Fine. Keep the skylight but I have a few additions I want put in and these ones aren't going to take any extra time at all ...'

Chapter 28

Hannah knew as soon as she got in and saw him sitting in the living-room chair.

The plans were spread out before him.

Things had been going so well. Her double life. Three months of a particular routine. She had given up her real job without telling Ned and instead, after walking Esther to school, travelled to her other 'job' at the bunker, watching it transform into a home, or better, a fortress. It nearly made her want to scratch off her own skin, how much time she spent away from Esther, but she knew that she had to think long-term: the bunker and the forever years of safety that it would give.

'What are these?' Ned said, gesturing to the plans laid out on their coffee table.

Hannah gave Esther a cuddle and sent her upstairs with a biscuit. Ned didn't normally snoop, in fact the opposite – he barely knew where anything was kept in the house apart from maybe his own clothes. His working hours were long and when he got home all he often managed to do was eat a meal with her before dragging himself into the shower and then bed. She knew that she had hidden those plans and hidden them well. He would have had to search hard to find them.

Ned raised his head, his eyes bleary like he was about to cry.

He could bloody cry. Hannah felt like wailing from the rooftops. This was not part of the plan. Not yet.

'Where have you been when you've said you've been in work?' he asked her. She frowned and he held up a hand as if to shush her. 'I saw Tricia, bumped into her in town. She asked about you, which I thought was odd as you'd seen each other yesterday at work. She asked what you were doing … since you'd left your job *in November.*' Hannah opened her mouth but Ned stood up. 'In November, Hannah! That's over three months! What have you been doing for three months?'

'*Building Esther's future,*' Hannah wanted to say.

He walked over to the living-room door, closed it and rested his forehead against the painted wood. Usually Hannah had the words. They came hot and fierce from her and those words were always just the right thing to say. Usually they were fast and clever and convincing. Usually Ned listened and agreed.

Now there was silence.

He swivelled his head so it still touched the door, but she could see his eyes, red-rimmed, bloodshot. 'You actually want to build something like this?'

Hannah almost laughed as the realisation hit: he thought those plans were just that, plans. Not concrete under earth in a faraway hill.

Ned turned so the back of his head was now pressed against the door and rubbed his hand over his face. 'This is … you can't … you need help …'

'Look, I—'

'You want to bury us in a fucking bunker?' He lurched from the door straight to Hannah as if he was going to grab her, hit her, choke her, shake her. But he pulled up short, breathing heavily. 'You are fucking insane!'

That was the word that was always thrown. Insane. Crazy. Paranoid. So easy to dismiss her with the swipe of that word, not listen to her, not even bother. At one time she had thought that she would try to explain it to him, with those words of hers that tripped off the tongue. But now she found she hadn't the energy.

His next sentence was a smash to her temple, spoken in a cold tone she had never heard him use before. 'Esther is going nowhere.' Heat rushed to her face as he continued speaking. 'You don't get to involve our daughter in all of this.'

He pushed past her and went to the dining table, which had Esther's unicorn bag on it with its huge eyes and pointed horn – a bag stuffed with socks and pyjamas and Esther's spare asthma kit.

'What are you doing?' A stupid question, Hannah thought. She knew exactly what he was doing.

'We're going to my mum's for a few days. Me and Pips.'

'No.'

She wanted the word to puff up like a venomous snake, its head swaying, something that would hypnotise Ned into staying still. He zipped up the unicorn and pulled a larger rucksack towards him. 'We need some time … away from you.'

Almost dizzy at the thought that he would leave with Esther, Hannah knew she had to be smarter. She softened, smoothed off the hard edge to her stare and let her shoulders slump as if someone had undone a knot in her middle.

'I'm … I'm … so sorry,' she whispered, taking a step back.

Ned paused. What she did next was vital, because, after all, he was packed – what could stop him from leaving now? She couldn't let that happen. Hannah let her head dip, so that at least some of her hair hung over her face. Behind her back, the fingers of one hand dug into her palm, the pain a point on which to focus.

Ned twitched, almost as if her snake word – 'No' – had sunk its fangs into his leg. 'Han, I'm …' but the sentence hung there, limp.

Hannah knew him. Ned. Who liked *Star Trek* and tatty books bought from second-hand shops that stank of mildew, who preferred a cup of tea to a glass of beer, who genuinely found tax laws interesting and liked to make cute little claymation films for Pips. Patient, kind, level-headed Ned. Who loved her.

'I'm sorry, Ned.' She made her voice crack just the right amount. 'It's just, I'm …'

She didn't know what else to say but then, she didn't have to as that was when the sky outside exploded into flaming colours and a deep booming sound shook the floor where they stood.

The steelworks had erupted into flames.

Chapter 29

Esther

Esther lay in the darkness by the front door, heart pounding, eyes closed.

Mother's voice: 'Esther? I told you not to come down here tonight.'

For a second, as Esther peeped from one half-opened eye, it didn't look like her mother, hunched over itself as it was – just a shape in the gloom. It looked like the kind of vague monster children scared themselves with each night, the kind that lived under the bed.

The kind that kept their daughter hidden from their father.

Who was alive.

Esther closed her eyes again. She didn't know what to think of that just yet so she did the easiest thing: not think of it at all. Just get through this bit. It was the best plan she could come up with in the few seconds she had had after hearing her mother's voice and dashing out of the gym, leaving Tom inside.

There was something in her hand, she realised in a dazed way, an envelope that Tom must have given to her though she couldn't remember that happening. She tucked it into the waistband of her pyjamas. There definitely wasn't time to read mysterious letters.

The figure at the top of the stairs muttered to itself.

'Esther?'

Time for her performance. She moved in what she hoped was a just-waking-up kind of way and pushed herself into a seated position, making her voice sound weak and sleepy. 'Mother?'

To her side was the rough arch into the tunnels with its packed earth floor, a dry, grave-like smell, those alcoves filled with machinery and tools and appliances and dried food in mouse-proof boxes. The sound of her mother's slippers against the floor was a kind of shuffling, a kind of scraping, a sigh.

Shuffle, scrape, sigh. The combination of sounds was suddenly a cold finger between Esther's eyes pushing hard and for a moment she felt as if the House around her could tilt and tip into something else … a memory … a dream … the dream she had had only a few days before, the last time she had found herself lying here by the front door, instead of in her bed.

Her mother took her by the arm. 'Have you been sleepwalking again?'

'Is everything okay? Mrs Allbright?' Tom's voice came from behind the closed gym door.

'Yes, yes! Stay where you are!' Mother shouted and then turned back to Esther who was now doing what she hoped was a passable impression of someone just awake and rather confused. 'Pips?'

'I'm sorry, I don't know how … I must have …'

Mother gripped her tightly under one arm, leading her back to the stairs. 'We can't have you wandering around the place. You'll hurt yourself.'

'Maybe I need something to help me sleep better?' *Like the pills you might already be slipping into my food?*

Mother did not look at her and did not respond to that. 'I thought you'd gone to talk to him.'

'Tom? Really?' Esther was proud of her innocent tone and a

little bit shocked as to how quickly lying to her mother came to her. 'Why would I? You told me not to.'

'I did. You're a good girl.' Mother patted her hand as they got to the top step but this time the phrase did not sound quite as loving as it normally did. The softness had gone and in its place was a sharper scratch, something that wanted to scrape a little more.

This time, when she looked at Esther, it wasn't simply out of panic and concern, a searching for a flushed cheek or a wheezy breath; no, this time, there was something else mixed in with all of that – something that made her eyes flick from Esther's hands to her feet, to the print on her pyjama top, trying to catch her out.

Esther yawned. 'Gosh, I need to go back to bed. I'm shattered.'

'Yes. Though … you didn't speak to him, did you, Esther?'

Esther put a hand to the waistband of her pyjama bottoms, feeling the square shape of the piece of paper stuffed there. 'No,' she said and the word was strong. She was pleased with it and the extra shades of indignation she laid upon it.

There was silence as Mother didn't move, didn't take her eyes off Esther, didn't say anything in return. It would have been easy at that point, to lay it all out in front of her and explain everything Tom had told her, every last detail. She was a tree trunk and running through her were the age circles representing the years of always obeying and trusting Mother.

Mother pulled her cardigan tighter around her, knotting the belt. 'You see we have to be careful. We don't know him.'

Stood in front of her was the person Esther was supposed to know.

'Well, I'm off to bed. See you in the morning,' Esther said. There was no reply. Mother remained at the top of the stairs, looking down.

'Do you believe that's what he came for? Paper signing?' Mother asked.

'Yes.' Like her 'no' before it, this word was also firm and steady.

Mother sighed. 'Well, it's only a couple of hours until morning and then he can go. I'm awake now. I'll make a cup of tea, get a jump-start on the day.'

'Okay then.'

Closing her bedroom door, Esther made it to her bed before the shaking began.

'*Hello, girlie,*' Mr Wiffles greeted her from the bedspread. '*We've got ourselves into a bit of a pickle, haven't we?*'

Outside her door she could hear the soft soles of Mother's slippers shuffling around, making her tea, so she had told Esther, but Esther knew the truth. She was patrolling, keeping watch – making sure Esther did not leave her room again that night. As she flopped back onto her pillow, the edge of the letter tucked in her pyjama waistband dug into her stomach.

It was a plain white envelope with nothing written on it, the ghost of someone's handwriting just about visible through the thin paper.

There would be no sleep for her tonight either.

Chapter 30

The envelope wasn't even stuck down properly. Inside was a letter and two photographs.

Dear Pips (or do you prefer Esther now?)

What did she tell you about me? I'm guessing she told you I died that night in the explosion at the steelworks and, if I'm honest, there were times that evening when I wondered if I would survive. And, in those times, I thought of you.

When it was over, when I'd done all I could to help, which wasn't near enough, all I could focus on was getting back to our home. To you.

Except, when I got there – you both had gone.

I should have known she would do something like that. It was my mistake. And it's a mistake I have had to live with for the rest of my life. But I didn't have time. I found those plans of hers, of the house, the one you're probably in right now, and we argued and I knew then that I would have to take you away. That your mother was a lot sicker than I had realised. But that was when the sky exploded. It felt like a giant had slapped his hand down hard on the town. My steelworks.

My area staff on their shifts. Of course I had to go – I didn't even stop to think about it.

Chaos. Smoke and fire and people and a lot to do, so much, and too much that I wasn't able to do ... I got home dirty, saddened and exhausted and found an empty house. I was left with nothing. No clue, no note ...

No you.

Your sweet little face, with your big serious eyes and your hair in plaits with the bobbles in the shape of shells because you loved the sea. The way you adored that toy I got you, Mr Wiffles, which was always clutched in your hand.

God, the planning that went into something like that – the sheer scale of this whole other life your mother had going on! Hidden bank accounts, I mean, I still don't know where she got the money to build that thing, or renovate it, or whatever she did. Before she left, she took all of the information with her.

I couldn't believe it at first. I gave myself reasons, as I stood there in our house, the smoke in my hair, my clothes, the pores of my skin. She had run to a neighbour, I thought, frightened by the roar of the flames and a night sky turned red. But none of the neighbours knew anything. It was Mr Wiffles that convinced me. He was missing from your bed. I knew he lived on your duvet – it was his sea and whales can't live out of the water, can they? I remember tearing through the rooms, seeing that some of your clothes were missing, a suitcase, your shoes, coats. I remember the sound that came from me, from deep in my stomach, a wailing I'd never heard myself make.

I want you to know that I tried.

I had the memory of those architect's plans. The house. A black blot on a hill where she could seal you up. But it could have been anywhere.

I reported it, obviously. But there isn't much the police can do when a person has left no paper trail, no e-trail, someone who has disappeared like a smoke ring. Uncle Adam came back to help. Anything I earned, after food and bills, I put aside into a fund to find you. I got cleverer and did my own research, narrowing down the places in the world with the cleanest air. I did my homework.

If I make it sound business-like, that is not how it was. I was ... broken, I guess. There are piggy banks you have to smash to get at the coins inside and this had smashed me open like that. There were only bits of me left to deal with everything, but I remembered what it was like to be whole and I yearned for it. I would wake up from a dream where I'd been watching you sleep and the pain of it, of knowing that I was forgetting how your hair smelled, that pain was almost too much.

But I've found you. A piece of luck. And I was due that luck after all this time, lately on my own, my whole world narrowed to one focus: finding you. People have been kind, but they have their own lives and commitments: Adam had to go back overseas for work; the police could not keep searching indefinitely.

Esther, your mother is ill. She has been ill for a very long time and, when she was with me, I should have done more to help. When she looks at the world, she sees only its dangers and her solution has been to hide away from it all, telling herself that she is keeping you safe. And she is, I suppose, though at every doctor's appointment I went to with you, they all said your asthma was only moderate and would never have to affect your life, as long as you had your inhaler.

I can't tell you the world is safe, because it is not. But we live in it, Esther. We do the best we can. There are regulations being brought in to try to curb the air pollution in the cities and I won't say governments are doing their best because that is not what governments do, in my experience. But the alternative is hiding in a hill and, as your father, I would advise you not to waste your life doing that.

So here I am. I've written it all in this letter more for me than for you, to try to explain it all to myself, this crazy life I've been forced to live without you. I don't know if I'll even give it to you.

One thing I do know though: now it is up to you. You have a father who loves you. I'm here alone, no police, nothing to scare your mother because I really don't know how she's going to react to me turning up like this. I want you to leave this place.

I love you, have always loved you, always will,
Your father

Esther spent a while smoothing over the handwritten sentences, imagining her father writing them, noticing the wobble on the loops of his letter "y" and the way his capital "I" looked more like a "Z". Real words written by a real person, a tangible, very much not-dead father.

It therefore took her a while to see that, tucked in the envelope, were two pictures. One was familiar because they had its twin in their own possession. It was of them all on the grass, her mother holding her up and her father sat behind. In theirs her mother was caught mid-gesture, her arm stretched to someone out of shot; in this one Esther had caught her finger and there was the start of a smile. Her father was their bulky, strong backdrop, his blond hair blown across his forehead, big smile, kind eyes, sweatshirt and jeans.

That photo did not prove anything. It only proved what had been. Past, history, done and dusted.

The second photo fast-forwarded sixteen years. Before and after. There was only one person in the picture, a man in his fifties, in walking boots with his trousers tucked into his thick socks, a backpack on his shoulder and a T-shirt with an embroidered badge Esther could not read. The blond hair now more white than grey, the bulky frame somewhat deflated, the sharper smile a pale ghost of the one in the first photo. The kind eyes now wrinkled and shadowed. Haunted.

Unmistakably her father.

Chapter 31

Breakfast the next morning was served with a side order of suspicion and a garnish of exhaustion.

Esther drank tea that she made herself and declined her mother's home-made flapjack all the while admiring how her body did those things so calmly whilst her brain churned through the same thoughts and questions that had kept her up all night, clutching the letter and those two photographs.

Her father was alive – if she believed Tom and the paper now stuffed under her mattress.

Her father was dead – if she believed her mother.

'You can't possibly be thinking of going out there in this weather?' she said, as her mother stood and reached for her waterproofs.

'He's not staying a minute longer.'

Overnight the rain and wind had wound itself into a frenzy and Esther had got out of bed to see the view from her bedroom window distorted by a blur of water.

'He can't walk in this weather.'

'He'll manage. I can get my wellies on over his leg despite the swelling. He's got small feet for a man.'

'Umm … they're average-sized …' Tom put his coat on as

slowly as he could, casting Esther a glance. She was supposed to know what that look meant, but it skimmed over her, merely a movement of eyebrows.

Esther stood too, only knowing that she didn't want Tom to go. She had no clue what was true or not, who to trust or what to believe but she knew if Mother walked him out of the House there was little chance of her ever seeing him again.

Or finding out more about her father.

Her father was, simultaneously, dead and alive. Undead. A ghost who would haunt her for the rest of her days if she didn't at least try to find out if Tom was telling the truth.

And that meant he couldn't leave.

But things moved too quickly for her. Her mother had the waterproof coat on and had found the spare wellies and still Esther was stuck at the table, trying to think what to do. The letter. She had to show her the letter, she had to ask her why she had lied, *if* she had lied.

The letter.

Esther dashed to her room to get it but, as she had hidden it under the mattress, by the time she came out again, her mother had gone. She ran down the stairs, but she knew before she'd even opened the door that the gym would be empty. Her mother had left without her.

Again.

Something hot welled up in her chest and Esther gave a half-scream, half-wail as she thumped the front door.

Except.

This time she wasn't going to be left in this place, a moth under glass. Barely registering if she had put on a coat and boots, she fastened her mask and opened the door with shaking hands.

Rain stung her face, a weird, prickling sensation that she hadn't experienced in years. Screwing up her eyes, she tried to see if she could spot them but it didn't matter if she couldn't. Moving was the thing, and so she did, and it was nowhere near as hard as last time. In mere seconds she was beyond the door with the wind yelling and tugging her, her eyes on the ground to watch out for traps lurking like alligators in the grass.

She would stop them and bring Tom back and then they would all sit down and work out what the hell was going on and it would be weird and probably hard, but it would be the right thing to do – even Mother would see that. Esther would make her see.

Her foot slipped in the mud slurry that had become the dirt track leading between the trees, and she teetered to a stop, wrenching her ankle. Ahead of her was the treeline though the rain lashed at her face so hard she could only take quick glimpses from under her hood, water already seeping coldly onto her neck.

There they were.

Esther slithered closer, the mud underfoot sucking at her feet one moment and then letting her slide the next. She tried to shout but all she got in her first attempt was a mouthful of rain and a slap from the wind. Because her mask did not seal to her face, the rain got in and she could hear the fans within labouring.

They both had their backs to her and now she understood why they had stopped. The path that should have led down to the trees was no longer there – in its way was a floodwater river.

Slick as seals, Tom and her mother stood side by side, gazing at the water as it gushed past them, the rain flattening their hoods to their heads, their cuffs dripping, and as Esther looked at them, clambering closer down the mud slide, it was almost as if they were a team, working together.

If it hadn't been for the rock in Mother's fist.

Esther could only watch in horror as her mother took a step back from Tom and raised her fist and there was still a part of her that couldn't believe she would use that rock as a weapon. It was unthinkable that she would even consider hurting Tom on purpose – or even try to kill him. But then she remembered pills and guns and letters from undead fathers.

Water, rock, her mother's face. She could only see her profile, her hood pushed back so that strands of her hair were plastered to her face by the rain.

Rock.

When she had been a child, Esther had loved her history lessons with Mother most of all. They had done a whole month's worth of work on the Georgians who thought it fashionable to create silhouette portraits, those pictures of people taken side-on, a dark outline against a white background. They nicknamed them shades and, as Esther stared at her mother in that long stretched-out moment, she knew that was what her mother had become to her. A shade. A dark version of her former self.

She didn't know what her mother was capable of and she would never be able to stumble her way to them in time so she did the only thing left for her to do. She wrenched the mask from her face and screamed, 'Stop!'

Chapter 32

The sound of Esther's voice stilled her mother's hand.

'Stop! You have to stop, please—' Esther slipped and slid towards them, wiping the water from her face with wet hands, the cold rain that had begun to seep down her neck now trailing a finger along her spine.

When she got nearer, she saw Mother's aghast face. 'Esther? Your … your …'

Mask. Esther held it by its strap, the thing rendered useless by the rain anyway. Tom turned to them both, his gaze flitting to the rock in Mother's hand.

'Put it back on!' Mother rushed to her and fumbled with it, trying to take it from her.

'Stop! The air's fine here.'

'Put it on!'

Mother tried to rip it from her hands and Esther gripped on, each pulling against the other, until Esther yanked her hand away with such force she brought the mask with her and nearly tipped her mother off balance.

'Will you just STOP!' she cried, her chest heaving, not because her demon was awake but because (and she'd never really experienced it before) she was angry. She had been tired and frustrated

134

and bored and excited and sad, but this heat that made her throat prickle and fizzed in her brain, she had never experienced *this*. It made her feel as if she could … she didn't know, pick up a car like a weightlifter, muscles bulging. The rain came down hard between them and her mother's face was a pale little circle with her mouth open in shock. 'You have to stop – all of this,' Esther found herself shouting. 'It's too much. It's all too much. I'm safe. I mean, what were you even going to do?' Her voice broke.

Tom picked up the rock and frowned at it.

Mother's eyes shifted from ground to flood to daughter.

'You were probably about to check the depth of the water, weren't you, Mrs Allbright? We were wondering if we could wade through …' Tom dropped the rock and wiped his hands on his trousers, pushing his hood back so he could see.

'Yes …' Her mother took an eager step forward. 'That was it – checking …'

The rain was loud in Esther's ears, a roar of noise that suited the static in her brain. One thing was certain: her mother had not been checking anything unless it was how hard a rock would have to be smashed against a young man's skull in order to break it. And after his brain had seeped out like yolk? Would she have pushed him in the floodwater and cried accident?

'We are done here. You are both coming back inside – *now*.' The steel in Esther's voice was new and she liked it.

'Esther, I—'

'I don't want to hear it! The path is blocked. No one can leave and there's no point us standing here getting soaked in the rain. Move!'

Mother opened her mouth again, probably to fuss about the mask, or ask if she felt okay, or if she needed her inhaler. The streaks on Esther's face weren't all down to the rain and she wanted to walk fast, away from the both of them and what could have happened out there in the trees.

But there was a limping Tom to help, so she forced herself

to take his side and work together with her mother once more, one on either side of him, supporting his steps all the way back to the House.

Shelter.

Home.

In the rain, its dark, crying face waited for them.

* * *

The suspicion and exhaustion that had been served with breakfast continued as a garnish sprinkled upon the tea break the three of them had back at the House as their clothes dried.

Tom wore a pair of Mother's corduroy trousers, the hems high on his ankles, making him look like a child who had suddenly had a growth spurt. He limped quietly from one bit of the kitchen to the other. This time there had been no discussion about him staying in the gym; this time Esther had simply continued to propel him up the stairs where they then collapsed in a muddy wet heap.

'I'll make tea,' Esther had said, giving her hair a final pat with her towel.

'Nah, least I can do.' Tom had flicked the switch on the kettle.

Mother was silent as she drank her tea. Esther wasn't sure if that was an improvement. Silent meant thinking and thinking meant plotting. More lies. More explanations. The figure slumped on the sofa was not the mother Esther had grown up with and this new woman, the one who drew a gun and picked up a rock so easily, who could hide a father for a whole lifetime – she wasn't sure how to talk to this woman.

So she didn't.

She fetched a wooden bear instead and plonked it on the low coffee table in front of her mother.

'Do you want to tell me the truth about this?' she demanded.

Her mother had spent the entire time since they had got back

136

staring at her hands, which were clasped in her lap. But the bear drew her gaze, if not any words.

'Nothing? Well, I guess I don't need to say much either.' Esther grasped the wooden figure and gave it a twist so it split in half, tablets spilling from its stomach like undigested food. 'They're sedatives.'

The wooden bear looked at all of them at once with his cross-eyed stare. Her mother concentrated on her empty mug and then spoke in barely a whisper, 'They're mine.'

'I don't believe you.'

'For when I have trouble sleeping.' Mother slumped back on the sofa.

'You don't have trouble sleeping.'

'Well, sometimes I do.'

But Esther reminded herself of the letter under her mattress and the woman described in it, one who lied about nearly everything to the man she was supposed to love the most. The words nearly said themselves, '*I know my father is alive*,' but she knew that wasn't the way to go about it. It had to be worked up to, something as big as that, lie by lie, small to large, creeping up to it like you would if you were trying to catch a bug with a net.

Esther let the silence sit with her mother for a while.

'Want to know what I think?' Finally Esther spoke but when she reached to put her mug on the coffee table, she noticed her hands were shaking and she saw Mother register that too. 'I think you've been using them on me.'

Mother darted her gaze back to her lap.

'I think you've been using them to keep me … docile. Like a pet who can't cause too much bother. Calm. Quiet. Too dumb to notice the lies – because you lied about us not having a phone signal and you've been hiding these pills, and setting traps around the House and pulling a gun on strangers and that's not the end of it, is it? Because actually there's something much bigger that you're trying to keep from me …'

'Esther?' Tom leant forward in his chair.

Her mother's head drooped but Esther continued as she stood and turned away.

'… and it's much worse than all the rest of it because it means you've been lying to me for nearly my entire life …'

'Esther!'

There was a crash of china as the mug tilted and slid from her mother's grasp.

'What?'

'Your mother is asleep.'

'Huh? How can she have fallen—'

'I put the sedatives in her tea.'

Chapter 33

The demon in her chest wriggled.

Esther heard her voice wheeze, 'What the hell?' She dashed over to her mother who had keeled over on the sofa at a drunken angle. 'What do you think you're doing?'

She did not expect Tom to laugh, but that is what he did – a weird kind of choking snort. 'I don't know! I have no clue what I'm doing – this wasn't how it was meant to go ... I mean, Jesus! She nearly brained me with a rock!'

'But how did—?'

'I kept a couple from the ones you gave me to look up on my phone. Guessed a dose from Dr Google that would knock her out and put it in the tea when I made it. They work quick.'

Esther dragged her mother clumsily from the sofa and let her body flop onto the floor where, for the second time, her first-aid skills came in handy and she put her into the recovery position. 'You don't know what you're doing! You could have hurt her!'

Suddenly it all welled up in her. Here she was in a bunker with literally no one around to hear her scream. She had to make a decision – who to trust? The man she didn't know who had just drugged her mother and given her a long-lost father, or the woman she had thought she'd known, who had told her

139

lies about life Out There and who was behaving more strangely hour by hour …

'Esther?' Tom moved to her, dressed in her mother's old trousers and sweatshirt.

'Stay away from me!'

What she wanted was to rewind, go back to the moment Tom had been caught in the bear trap's jaws, knowing everything she knew now, so she could watch and take notice, of every gesture and inflection, every hidden meaning behind innocent words. So that, when she got to this bit – she would know what to do.

'Here.' Tom put one hand up as if in surrender and with the other he carefully reached into his trouser pocket. 'Your mother gave my phone back to me, before we left. Look – I've unlocked it so it will stay unlocked and … there … I've put 999 in so all you have to do, if you feel scared, is press the green phone symbol and you can ask for the police. Battery's a bit low but it will last while we talk. Signal's okay for now, though these thick walls don't do it any good.' He placed the phone on the coffee table and slid it over to her. 'All I want is for you to let me explain it properly and then … well, you can kick me out if you want.'

Esther picked up the phone by its edges and cradled it in her palm, careful not to touch the screen. With her other hand she held on to Mother's ankle.

Tom sat. 'I knew you as a child.'

Of course he had, Esther thought dully – and the moon is made of cheese and the earth is also flat and a giant beetle drags the sun out into the sky each morning.

'Only briefly. You probably don't remember me. You'd only have been about four or five. I was seven. You lived next door and when your mother was out, your father used to take you to the park and we would play together.'

Esther might have remembered a play frame with a turret on one side, the grit of flaking paint under her palms. But memories were just like everything else – sneaky and not to be trusted.

'I remember you disappearing. The whole town buzzed with it. Your father, the hero who helped save three men in the steel-works explosion, who then came back to find his wife had left him. Rumours she wasn't right in the head and far too protective of her little girl – of you. I remember you – you were a serious little thing with big eyes and that toy whale you used to drag around with you.'

From the bedroom, Esther heard the faint voice of Mr Wiffles: *'The cheek! I'm not a toy, I'm a massive bloody leviathan of the massive bloody seas!'*

'You gave me my career, kind of – you know that?'

Esther straightened her mother's sock, pulling it up to cover the bare skin of her ankle.

'I'm a journalist, local newspaper, y'know: births, deaths, summer fetes, all that sort of stuff. It was you disappearing, my playmate, that stuck with me though. For years afterwards I'd often go and hang around our playground, just in case you ever came back there, even though that's such a stupid idea, isn't it? That you'd just be sitting there on a swing, waiting to be found … Whenever I could, I tried to follow up any leads that sounded a bit like you or your mum. And then your dad came back to our town, still looking for you, and my mum gave him my details. Meeting him gave me some of the final bits of the puzzle, as well as Lady Tregellen dying. I came here on a whim before telling your dad and I know I should have told him first, but I wanted to check it out myself – thank God I managed to get a message to him before your mother took my phone.'

The wooden bear wouldn't let go of Esther's gaze, his wonky stare irritating her, with those white pills surrounding him in a chemical snow. She put the phone down on the table and scooped the tablets into her hand.

'But … you had paperwork …' She gazed at the pills.

'Ah … yeah. Well, I downloaded something that looked a bit official, guessed your mother wouldn't be able to tell what those documents looked like now after all this time. And I know what you're thinking – you need some kind of proof right? Something more than just a photo and a letter that could be faked from a stranger who has turned up out of the blue. So your dad gave me a bit of info to tell you, something only you three would know. Something about that toy he gave you, Mr Wiffles?'

There came a faint, grumpy voice once again: '*Not a toy, lad – NOT A TOY!*'

Esther walked over to the kitchen and opened a bottom cupboard, taking out a pestle and mortar into which she tipped the contents of her hand. She needed something to do and this was exactly the right thing. She never wanted to see these pills again. The rhythmic moving of hand and wrist was soothing, obliterating the things and grinding them into dust.

'So,' Tom followed her to the kitchen with wary steps. 'Your father told me to say that Mr Wiffles has one black eye and one blue eye made out of a button because you pulled off the original when you were very small. And the button is cracked where you dropped him off a balcony when you were four.'

From the bedroom: '*Bloody hell! I still get flashbacks about that balcony. PTSD it is. And my eyesight has never been the same …*'

Finally, Esther looked up and her hand stilled. The only people who could know about Mr Wiffles and his button eye were either sleeping peacefully on the floor or … Out There, waiting for her. Alive. Her father.

She moved with the bowl, past Tom as if she couldn't see him, towards her bathroom where she watched the powder flush away.

'Thing is – are you listening, Esther?' Tom followed her into the doorway of the bathroom and then back out again as she once more sat at her mother's feet. She nodded. 'Right, well, thing is, if I stay much longer there is a very good chance that your mother will actually succeed in killing me.'

One powerful slam to the back of the head, a few more against his temple until the rain watered down the blood and hurried it away into the soil, the floodwater, into the roots of the trees themselves.

'Esther?' Tom had moved to crouch near her. 'You understand, don't you?' he said softly, one knee bent as if this was a proposal, except there was no diamond ring in his pocket, just secrets. All the secrets that had held her together through the years. All the secrets he'd now unpicked so she would unravel and slither to the floor.

She nodded again.

'She's ill, Esther. Like I said. Your mother – she needs help.'

Esther was wrong, she realised, she did not have a thousand questions, but only one: 'Why?'

Three letters, one small word. She put her chin onto her knees as Tom sat next to her. They both stayed silent for a while. 'I don't know, Esther. I've never met anyone who's done something like this before. To protect you? And you have every right to be angry.' But Esther was too numb for a hot feeling like anger; she was an ice sculpture newly wheeled out of the fridge.

When someone's love grasped on to the other person so hard that it choked them, was that love then? Was that protection? It wasn't love that lied to a person, that took them away from their father, that made them believe that that father was dead. Not love – something else.

Esther's head pounded.

'But you have to work out what you want to do next.'

'Next?'

There was a next after all of this? Esther couldn't imagine hauling herself up off the floor, let alone anything to come after that.

Tom was too close with his curly hair and eyes that sent glances she did not understand. Mother had taught her how to change a plug a few years back and she had learnt about live wires. Tom was one of those; if she touched him, the shocking zing of electric would fizz straight through her.

'I want you to come with me.'

He may as well have scraped a fork across her teeth.

'What?'

'I mean, it's your decision and I totally get if you want to stay here with your mother. At least you know now – about the lies, the way she's kept you a prisoner when you could have gone outside and lived a normal life with a father.'

Esther tried to imagine the Out There version of herself, a young woman who wore bright dresses and rode a bicycle with a basket on the front, hopping on it to get fresh croissants from the local bakery every morning. That woman lived in a flat with two others and was part way through her university degree, turning up to lectures with a pretty notebook and a ring binder of revision in her best handwriting. At Christmas and other holidays she went home to the cottage where she grew up, to a mother who cooked her favourite meal and a father who oiled her bicycle pedals.

Lost in her own thoughts, she almost missed what Tom said next.

'Esther? Did you hear me? I've had a message back from your father. He's waiting – he wants to meet you.'

Chapter 34

'Slow down!'

The world attacked her in a jumble of images that flashed at her and then away again, so quickly she couldn't take it all in. She gripped on to the car seat. 'Please! Slow down!'

Tom gave her a quick glance. 'Esther, if I slow down any more, we will stop. I'm only doing fifteen miles per hour.'

Look before you leap. But she had leapt with abandon, jumped straight into this rushing, flashing world with no other thought than him – her father.

They had had to wait a while for the rain to ease and even then, as they set out, they hadn't been sure that the flash flood would have subsided enough for them to cross. But it had. There should have been more ceremony about it, the leaving. In the end though, there had just been the late afternoon sun in her eyes and the sucking sound of mud under her trainers as she had walked to the car, Tom limping next to her. It seemed as if the very earth itself was trying to cling on to her feet, to hold her back.

Before she had left, she had stuffed Mr Wiffles into the ruck-sack, her face burning as she hid him under a spare jumper (she did not know how cold it was going to be), some snack bars (she did not know how long she would be gone) and a spare inhaler (you *never* knew). He grumbled at being squished.

Her one last look at her mother had nearly undone her. Esther had repeated *pills, bear trap, father* in her mind and then left her sleeping after a final adjustment of her note so it would definitely be the first thing her mother saw when she woke up. Leaving her had felt like ripping a plaster away from her eyeball.

And then: Out There.

This had been the first time she had deliberately stepped outside without her mask. Of course, she had it in her rucksack, ready for the more polluted towns and cities she might come across, but here, where it was so green and peaceful, she had felt it wasn't needed.

Not needing it was a delicious feeling.

They'd taken the dirt track through the trees, Tom stepping carefully on his injured leg, dressed once more in his own soggy trousers. For Esther it would have almost been pleasant if her heart hadn't been hammering away at her ribcage. She had liked the way the branches made a latticework above her because, if she hadn't looked too hard, it had felt like a ceiling. The smell of them was fresh and green, clean, as if the very air itself could clear a stuffy head, or soothe a dizzied mind.

But the trees had thinned out and the dirt track had eventually ended at a road.

'Is this the main road?' she had asked, thinking she could cope with this, this tarmac tongue barely wide enough to fit one car, the trees keeping back from it as if it was a red carpet laid out for a celebrity.

Tom had smiled. 'No, Esther. The main road is about an hour away.'

In her imagination the main road was made up of lanes of cars gliding in the same direction, gracefully moving around each other as onboard computers calculated the best route and drove the vehicles for their owners, a Sixties film view of the future.

146

'Here we are,' Tom had said when they eventually reached his car.

The cars in her imaginary motorway hadn't looked anything like what was in front of her at that moment. She had been expecting something small for a start, a sleek beetle curve of shiny metal.

Tom had followed her gaze. 'I didn't know exactly how hard it was going to be getting to you, or whether I'd have access to charging points so I needed something ... sturdy. We had to go old-school.'

Esther did not understand why schools were involved in the making of cars, and why those schools had to be old.

Big wheels, big bumper, big globs of mud on the paintwork. 'Not mine. I don't own a car, back home. I live in the city so the buses are good and I bike everywhere else.'

Buses. Esther was almost sure she actually remembered them, from before they left for the House. Steamed-up windows and the smell of damp upholstery. "Stop" buttons grimy around the edges that had made a pleasing ping when she had pressed them.

'Lucky it's an automatic or, with this leg, I don't think I'd be able to drive.'

Esther looked around her now as they hurtled along the road. There was a comfortable leather seat and a dashboard that was lit up in a way that suggested the car knew what it was doing. Here the fresh green smell of the trees gave way to a whiff of new plastic and another chemical tang, something perhaps used to clean the inside, which made her eyes sting and her brain ache.

Everything was fine, she told herself, completely and utterly fine. The car was moving but she was not, she was strapped into it, which was okay because the thing was going slowly even though the road disappeared beneath the bonnet in a way that made her head spin ...

They may only have been going at fifteen miles per hour, like Tom said, but that was fifteen miles per hour faster than she had ever travelled in the past sixteen years. She was one of the bugs splatted onto the windscreen, terrified in its dying moments at a world that had suddenly shifted gear.

Tom, however, did not need to shift gear. The car did that for him.

Teeth gritted and hands clutched, she endured the lifetime it took to drive to the village.

Trees.

Trees.

A signpost flashed past and with a jolt she realised that, without Tom, there was no way she would be able to find her way back to the House. She dug her fingernails into her palm in punishment at finding herself once again reliant on someone else. It was time to stop all of that. The first chance she got, she would buy a map so she would always know how to get home. And she would need money and some kind of transport and … all sorts of things she didn't even know she needed yet.

Trees.

Trees.

Wall.

Then house.

Her first view of a house that was not the House. A fleeting glimpse of light brown stone, a grey door with a happy splodge of yellow plant next to it. She tried to turn her head to keep it in sight through the rear window but that made the sickness that broiled in her stomach overspill into her throat so she turned back.

Buildings loomed in from every side, crowding close to the car like curious natives: the same light brown stone, tiled roofs and, in the shops (for she saw then that this was a shopping street) big glass windows with mysterious and interesting things in them.

Suddenly she was grateful for the firmly shut windows of the car.

Because it wasn't just houses Out There, it wasn't just happy yellow plants and flag bunting in shop windows and pavement signs in doorways that had messages on them she wasn't close enough to read. It wasn't just that.

There were people too.

Chapter 35

Esther had prepared for one. A person. Him.

She was not prepared for many. Plural. People.

But there they were.

She took a deep breath, glancing over at Tom who still gripped the steering wheel as if the car was in motion. A man walked past them, so close she could have rolled down the window and flicked the sleeve of his coat. It looked like a normal coat – blue, waterproof. He looked like a normal man.

But she didn't know what was normal.

'We've arranged to—' Tom began, grasping the door handle. 'Just give me a sec.'

Someone had flicked on a boiler inside her and her heart, which had been hammering before, now began to thump in a way that made her feel each meaty thud. This rhythm carried to her head, which seemed to be growing at an alarming rate, so fast that her skin was stretched tight over it. Her fingers tingled.

She heard a seatbelt unclick and something warm covered her hands. 'Esther, you are safe.' (That's probably what Tom said – she didn't know for sure as she was busy trying to keep her skull from splitting through her flesh.)

She had been a fool. Of course she was safe in the air outside the House because Mother had chosen that place carefully for that very purpose. But she wasn't there any longer. She was somewhere she didn't know, with air that was at that moment seeping through cracks in the windows and vents in the dashboard.

The demon in her chest flickered an eyelid.

'This isn't a city, Esther.' Tom's voice came to her through a tunnel, one where a howling wind raged down it and evil imps banged on its metal sides. 'This is just a small village, still in the countryside. The air is as unpolluted as you're going to get.'

Green for countryside. Green for go, like a traffic light.

Minutes passed. Esther's head returned to its usual size, her fingers stopped sparking and her heart started to remember its normal rhythm. Her demon closed its eyes again.

'Okay?'

'Okay.'

She took her mask with her and her rucksack with Mr Wiffles in it even though she knew he was only some stuffing wrapped in velvet with plastic eyes.

'Some stuffing with plastic eyes? I'm a wonder of the bloody oceans, my girl!' he grouched at her through a hole in the canvas.

They had parked outside a small row of shops: a butcher's, a baker's, a candlestick maker's … except she didn't know if people even used candles much Out There.

Sunlight, breeze – and smell. So much scent. Dogs navigated the world by their nose, she remembered reading, with many more scent receptors than humans. Right now she felt very dog, the smells creating a whole new world on top of the one she could see. There was a bitter scent of coffee she recognised, mixed with something sugary but then she moved nearer a bin and the sweet rush of rot made her take a step back. Steadying herself, she rested her hip against the truck but there was no respite there, the lingering of acrid exhaust fumes was worse than the bin.

Another headache formed like a fist pushing down on her eyes.

Birdsong. She peered upwards in amazement at the shapes wheeling in the sky. 'I've never seen so many,' she whispered.

Tom came to stand next to her, shoulder to shoulder, following her gaze. 'The birds? Yeah, it was weird how few I saw around your house. I think your mother was using some kind of deterrent to keep them away.'

The shapes swooped and soared, flitting this way and that as if they were being scored on their choreography. Esther would have given them top marks. She could have watched them for hours.

'Your father's waiting for you in the café.'

It was a few steps away but the space between her and the doorway could have been miles. Sweat prickled under her arms. She could almost hear her mother's voice: *'Esther – how can you trust him more than me?'*

Tom took her hand and she dragged her gaze away from the sky. 'It's so busy.' She kept her voice low as if she was a presenter on a nature documentary who didn't want to frighten away the native wildlife.

Tom couldn't help but smile. 'It's a Sunday afternoon in a tiny village, Esther. This is quiet.'

A woman in wellies marched past her, loudly talking to herself, or to someone invisible. Like an invisible friend … some children had them, maybe here adults did too.

'She's on her phone, except you can't see it because she's using headphones.'

Esther nodded as if she understood and ducked her head out of the path of the woman's perfume, a strong swipe of heady flowers.

The nearby bin was a painted black metal thing with a mouth that drooled some kind of whitish ooze. She blinked, almost sure she could see the germs squirming in the air around her, tiny spores ready to cling to her skin and rush up her nose, waiting to fell her like a doomed Martian.

'I need my mask.' She fumbled in her rucksack.

There was too much movement. The freewheeling birds in the

sky, the people walking past, signs swinging, doors opening, even the wind itself blowing a paper wrapper across the street, tugging at her jacket, her hair whipping across her face.

She jerked away as a man's elbow jogged her arm.

'Is she all right, mate?' the man stopped and asked Tom, frowning in concern, his round face chubby-cheeked and red-nosed.

The man's little dog snuffled at her feet whilst she completed a tricky yoga pose in her attempt to get away from it. She might have squealed. The dog continued to snuffle, unperturbed.

What could Tom have said? *'Nah, it's okay, mate – she's just never stepped foot outside her own house before because her mother told her that her father was dead and that the air was so polluted she might die and this is the first time she's been out because she's going to meet her not-dead father in that café behind you …'*

Instead he went with: 'Oh yes, she's fine.'

The dog snuffled some more but the man tugged on its lead and it trotted away.

Esther was ready to be inside again. The café door was open and it was warm when they stepped through the door.

At a side table a man in a jumper the colour of dried blood stood up.

Chapter 36

Hannah

Present

Hannah woke up, and in those sleep-blurred moments of peace as she let the world settle into focus around her, she did not remember.

Then she sat up and threw the covers from her.

Why was she on the sofa? The last thing she remembered was sitting with that wooden bear on the coffee table next to her empty mug and the pile of ...

... sedatives.

Realisation dawned fiery-bright. They had used her own pills against her, or rather that wretched young man had, because it had been him who had made the tea. And now she had been asleep for who knows how long, completely useless whilst who knew what had happened.

There was a piece of paper propped up on the coffee table, resting against the bear's stomach, the stupid creature holding it out like a gift. It was Esther's handwriting but the words wouldn't focus until Hannah shook her head and sniffed.

Mother,
Please don't worry. I am safe and with Tom. I will come back.
Pips

So few words.

The living room was empty and Hannah knew it even as she checked in the other bedroom and the bathroom. She knew it as she ran down the stairs to the laundry room and flung the door open on the store and the gym.

Esther was gone.

A few halting steps and she crumpled onto the bottom step of the stairs, one hand clutching the handrail as if she was on a storm-tossed ship and had to keep her balance.

Esther was gone.

The realisation was not a punch to her gut; it was a hand scooping out that gut and everything else inside her until she was a hollow woman, one that, if flicked too hard, would simply crack and fall to shards.

Out There right now, her Esther, her wheezy, fragile, vulnerable Esther could literally be fighting for her breath in air even more polluted than it was when Hannah had originally fled.

In an instant she was back in the ambulance sixteen years or so ago, helpless and mute as a paramedic worked that magic spell over the still body of her only child. She remembered all too well that great gaping black void waiting to swirl Esther away into its nothingness. Who would keep that at bay, if Hannah wasn't there?

Not Tom.

No one could say she hadn't had ample chance. She should have shot him, or caved in his skull with that rock. She would have, if Esther hadn't stopped her, because she had known the whole time, hadn't she? A warning itch. Something about him had not been right, not from the start. Hearing that Lady Tregellen was dead had been a shock and the urgency of signing that paperwork and getting rid of him had blinded her to the way he had barged into their lives in the first place. The papers she had signed had probably been fake.

It had been no coincidence that he had got himself caught in that trap on the only day of the year Esther was left on her own.

He must have watched.

And waited.

Why?

What had he told Esther?

It was only the tingling in her arm that made her realise she was still gripping the handrail. Flexing her fingers, she massaged life back into her palm and stood up, smoothing out the note that had become a crushed ball in her other fist; that word, Pips, at the end of the message her lifeline and her torture. Her daughter hadn't been angry enough at whatever she had been told to sign off formally but the very nickname itself reminded Hannah of a chubby, snub-nosed face and hair in curled pigtails like speech marks around it.

Her Pips.

The sedatives had been a mistake. No, that was wrong – her hiding place for them had been a mistake, not the sedatives themselves. She knew about medicines; there was no way, in her hands, that she would have let anything awful happen. It hadn't – for years. She had only ever been thinking of Esther. Life in a glorified bunker had edges, the kind of nasty rusting blades that sliced the brain and made it bleed, but a little chemical airbag every now and then worked a treat. She should know; she used them herself … had to, otherwise sometimes the glorious aloneness of the whole place dazzled her so much it hurt.

Which wasn't a weakness in the place – it was a weakness in her.

She knew what she had to do. It was what she had built her life around – keep Esther safe. And that meant sleep rubbed from the corner of her eyes, coat on, door open and …

… Out There. Esther's name for it.

Massive sky, hillside, treeline.

She had been out in the world every year for sixteen years. This would be no different.

Except …

Masked, she stepped over the threshold like she had done every year for sixteen years. This would be no different.

Except …

She walked that path to the van like she had done every year, the vehicle hidden in an old shed disguised from the road by as many branches as she had been able to pile around it, kicking and hammering the corrugated metal shed walls to make it look even more abandoned than it was.

No different.

Except …

Each time she had known exactly where she was going and what she was going for, a little toy train on its short track. The out-of-town shopping centre where the DIY store was and the garden centre, a discount food shop and a coffee place. She knew almost exactly how long she would be gone.

The van door creaked as she opened it. Like her, her knee bones, her neck; age creeping its fingers into the whites of her eyes, the grey in her hair, the twinge in her back. Right. So she only really knew now how to get to the DIY store. Then that is where she would go. It would be a start. From there she would get directions to the nearest town or village, she would top up with petrol and buy a map. The next step would come to her – it had to. Esther's life depended on it.

The engine thrummed to life, its power not dimmed by the years. Hannah drove away.

Chapter 37

Esther

The reunion should have played out under the strains of a sweeping classical soundtrack. Her father should have rushed towards her and taken her in his arms and they both wouldn't have been able to choose between laughing and crying as they tried to fit a lifetime into one hug.

Instead, the three of them stood motionless.

Cutlery chinked. Bustling around them was the café, a cutely decorated place with a half-net in the window, potted plants in the corners and little sprigs of flowers on each table. Gold lettering on the window spelled "Tea and Sympathy" in reverse. Here the smell was a hug, something buttery and warm. It promised hot drinks and food and friendly chat.

Her father was only a few feet away.

'What are you standing around for, girl? Get moving!' Being squished was not putting Mr Wiffles off voicing his opinion.

After seeing her father's photo, she'd expected hiking boots, trousers tucked into socks and the ruddy cheeks of a man who had been out in the elements all day.

The man in front of her kept his arms firmly at his sides. The hair was ice-grey and smoothly combed, not wind-blown. The trousers were smartly creased down the front and met shoes at just the perfect length, not tucked into socks. Polished shoes too, the fancy kind with punched decoration and shiny leather.

Finally she let herself look at his face. She had thought that this moment would trigger something deep within, some dormant cells in her recognising those exact same dormant cells in him. Family. Instead the face was merely a collection of parts, all put together in the regular way. The man in the photo had been whittled down to a sharpness: more wrinkles, no smile – wary eyes. A stranger.

'I—' She began but then stopped.

Tom gave her a nudge and then said, oddly formal, 'This is your father.'

The man hesitated at that but quickly opened his arms to her and she couldn't remember crossing the last few steps to his side of the table but suddenly she was in his embrace and his jumper was soft and smelled like something she had long forgotten she desperately needed to smell once more.

'I've waited so long for this,' he whispered into her hair.

Esther wanted to speak, to cry, scream, laugh – something, but she couldn't manage a single word. Her lozenge heart cracked and the syrup that oozed out clogged her throat.

How long they stood like that, or what kind of spectacle they presented to the other customers in the café, Esther did not know. Tom cleared his throat. Her father pushed her back a little. 'Let's get a better look at you.'

It seemed immeasurably colder out of his arms.

'You look so like—' But he stopped himself.

Maybe it was Mother. Maybe that resemblance was a knife to him. A small frown appeared between his brows as he searched for … Esther did not know what.

'I'll leave you guys to it,' Tom said, already backing away, nodding at Esther, and she wanted to run after him, make him sit with them, press his hand down onto the table and keep it there.

Instead she put down her mask with an unintentional thunk. Ned's eyes widened at the sight of it, a chunky, alien object. A man at the table next to them nudged his partner.

'We could maybe put that on the floor, hmm?' Ned said, smiling gently.

Esther stuffed the mask under the table along with her rucksack, hearing Mr Wiffles grumble something about him being a wild creature who shouldn't be confined to a bag.

There was a television in the corner, sound muted, and she couldn't stop her eyes from sliding over to it. It was nothing like the television at the House, but more like a bigger version of what Tom had shown her in his palm: images appearing on a slim flat screen. On it, a cartoon piece of toast was lathering itself with some kind of spread, which she guessed was an advert but who knew? Sentient bread could be a thing in the Out There.

Ned stared at her. 'I'm sorry, I just—'

'I know.'

And she did. Here he was with the daughter he thought he might not ever see again, her with a father raised from the dead. They shared another smile but then he fiddled with a knife, the frown reappearing.

'I kept looking for you,' he said.

'I know.' At some point Esther was aware she was going to have to try some different words.

'I would never have given up.' He put the knife down and began twisting a ring on his finger. It was gold with a flat, blank front.

A silence settled between them, like grave dirt. Under her T-shirt and jacket, Esther could feel herself sweating. The temperature in the House was always the same, always ambient, not too hot or too cold, but here in this tearoom the air was a fug that wrapped her too tightly. Ned sank back in his chair, teeth gnawing on his bottom lip once more as he dabbed at his eyes with a tissue. 'Sorry, sorry, it's just – I never dreamed that I would … and it's all a bit …'

Yes. Yes, it was "all a bit". Definitely. Esther placed her hands on the table, palms flat, to try to stop them shaking. Maybe it was time to break out the small talk again. Her brain tried its best and came up with: 'Do you want something to eat?'

She could almost hear Mr Wiffles sigh from the depths of her rucksack. Good job she probably had her foot on his head and was muffling his mouth. But she was hungry all of a sudden, for food that could not possibly be laced with any type of sedative. Around her people sliced toast and spooned beans; they buttered croissants and scooped eggs whilst they talked, grasping the handles of their coffee mugs and smiling with greasy lips.

Ned sniffed and snapped back to a tarnished brightness. 'Of course. Fuel. We have so much to talk about.' His face fell again. 'And I have something I need to explain …'

Chapter 38

Esther stared at the waitress's nails, each one a perfect rainbow of colours. How long had it taken her to do them, she wondered, and did you have to buy tiny, pointed nail paintbrushes to get each clean stripe of colour?

On the television in the corner, the toast had disappeared and now there was a female presenter with Barbie-blonde hair and a band of writing underneath the picture that Esther wasn't quick enough to catch. The presenter then cut away and there was a windswept reporter standing outside a very glossy black door. Esther knew that door – she had seen it many times in films. Downing Street. The Prime Minister.

'Should I give you a minute?' the waitress asked. Her dark hair was tied up but the ends were all different colours like her nails. Esther stared at her more than the menu.

Ned glanced at her and then smiled apologetically. 'I'll have a latte and a croissant and, Esther, do you like coffee? Would you want the same?'

The choices on the menu made her sight swim. All the foods they could not have in the House danced before her vision like a street parade. 'I'll have, yes, a coffee – but also … eggs. Scrambled eggs on toast, or – wait, no … eggs benedict, that sounds nice.

With extra bacon. And the croissant ...' the waitress tapped something on a small screen in her hand '... and a glass of milk ...' the waitress was about to turn away '... and a peach. Please.'

Ned unsuccessfully hid his smile and cleared his throat. 'That's going to be quite a lot of ... never mind. Look, I need to explain something to you ...'

Her mother would not be eating so well, Esther thought. She would be awake by now, alone in the gloom with her Checklist and chores and no one to make her even a cup of tea. Esther nearly slid into sympathy for her, but the footholds that stopped her slide were those words repeated in her mind once again: *pills, bear trap, father.* Ned dug his fork into the tablecloth.

Unexpectedly, a ragged sob burst from her, excruciatingly loud in the muffled hum of the café. She shoved her hand against her mouth, pressing hard, fearful of what would come out next. But it was too late.

Keeping her hand stuffed against her mouth only lent her sobs a distressingly distorted quality. The man at the table next to them paused mid slurp of soup to raise his eyebrows.

Esther found an arm around her shoulder and heard a whispered, 'Let's take some air, shall we?'

The irony of that phrase wasn't lost on either of them.

For the first time in sixteen years, Esther sat outside. She did not walk anywhere, or run from anyone. She wasn't in a mad panic – she simply sat on a low stone wall a little way out of the passing foot traffic and adopted the brace position because it did feel, in some way, as if she was about to crash. Ned came back with cardboard cups of coffee and their pastries wrapped in napkins.

'Here.' He nudged her. 'Eat something. It will make you feel better.'

Esther straightened up and picked at the buttery layers of the croissant, peeling them away before eating them.

'Don't worry – they're keeping your eggs warm for you.'

'I bet they all think I'm crazy.'

'Well, who cares what they think?' Ned said. 'And, hate to break it to you, but you've been hidden away from the world for sixteen years so, well – you might be.'

The bite of croissant suddenly became concrete in her throat. Her mother would never have agreed. Her mother would have defended why Esther had behaved the way she had. She would have patted her arm and … She realised that Ned was smiling.

Esther's sniff turned into a laugh and she swallowed. Ah, this was banter. Ned gave her a sideways glance with a glint in his eye as she tore strips from the pastry. He was funny – another point to add to her list of things she knew about him. It was a short list.

Nearby a fat-breasted pigeon waddled over to peck at the pavement, its little bulging eye scoping the ground for breadcrumbs. In her mind, Esther saw another bird, smaller, one that did not get a burial.

'It seems okay. Healthy,' she said.

'The pigeon? Umm … yes? Why wouldn't it be?'

'Mother said …' But she didn't finish her sentence. There was no point. Mother had lied again. On the way to this village she had lost count of the birds she had seen perched on telephone wires, in the sky and now here on the ground. She would have to get Tom to look up how a person could deter birds from their property; there was probably some way. His phone would tell her.

She also realised she should get herself one of those phones. Esther continued to torture the croissant and Ned clenched his fists in his lap. 'I can't, Esther. I can't talk about her yet. It's too hard …'

Little burning sips of coffee, the hard wall beneath them and sticky flakes of croissant on her lips. People walked past but she was getting used to them. They didn't seem so much of a horde now – more of a … zoo. The women in particular were fascinating, dressed in puffy jackets and bright leggings that looked uncomfortably tight. Her best pair of jeans and least washed T-shirt seemed shapeless and dull compared to them and she tucked her feet under her, not wanting to look at her scuffed trainers, brushing errant pastry flakes from her knees.

'Stroll?' Ned stood up and offered his hand. Esther put her own into it, expecting rough skin but his were softer than her mother's. Ned laughed again, a quick snort. 'Your rubbish! Give it here and I'll put it in the bin.'

There were only a few shops on the street and they puzzled Esther. People in this village didn't seem to need meat or vegetables but seemingly lived for hiking gear, trinkets, garden ornaments, woollen shawls and afternoon tea.

There was one shop window on the small street that made Esther pause. Miss B's Boutique. In it was a frankly terrifying faceless mannequin with a wash of smooth plastic where eyes, nose and mouth should have been. But this faceless woman was wearing the type of jeans she had spotted on many of those other women, the women with actual faces who had walked past her.

'It's a clothes shop.' Ned glanced away, down the street. 'I'm not sure—'

'I know what a clothes shop is,' Esther laughed. Did he think she was some kind of cavewoman dragging her club on the floor behind her, stopping to "ook" at all the strange things?

'Sorry. Of course.' He reached for the door handle. 'Do you want to go in?'

Esther didn't think she had ever wanted anything more, apart from a mother who hadn't lied to her and maybe the past sixteen years back. 'Hold on, you said you had something to explain?'

'It can wait.' He opened the door and glanced inside. 'I don't think it's a really up-to-the-minute kind of shop …'

That was not going to be a problem. Esther smiled. Up-to-the-century would do.

Chapter 39

Esther knew exactly how this scene played out.

Because she was in a film now, wasn't she? That was the only logical explanation to the strange turn her little mole life had taken. And she knew how this scene went – she had seen it a hundred times in the many films she had watched.

Transformation.

She couldn't stop herself from touching the material. No threadbare cotton to be seen: her hands smoothed thick tweed that caught her nails and a velvet so soft it felt alive.

A shop assistant wearing green eyeshadow and a massive enamelled bracelet with the word "smile" on it came over. Perhaps it was even Miss B herself. Her glasses dominated her face with thick, bright red frames. 'Can I help?'

Esther opened her mouth. What she wanted to say was, *'Yes! You can help! I've been waiting sixteen years to step into a shop like this and I have only ever touched one lovely dress my whole life and that was my mother's and probably well over twenty years old. You can help me by making me as bright as you – I want all the colour and I'd also quite like your eyeshadow too please …'*

Nothing came out.

The shop assistant smiled. 'This your father? Would he like to take a seat?'

The shop doorbell tinkled again and Tom appeared, limping in. 'Ah, here you are! Thought you'd skipped town without me.'

Ned's phone rang. 'Sorry, got to take this. Here.' Placing what Esther recognised as a credit card into her hand he retreated outside, the bell above the door tinkling again as he stepped through. Esther could see him pacing outside the shop window.

'Well, I am going to be of absolutely no use at all with this.' Tom gestured to the women's clothes around him.

'I often find the partners prefer to sit this bit out ...' the shop assistant began.

'Oh no – we're not—'

'No, no – we're just—'

Esther wondered why the shop was so hot whilst Tom became very interested in the floor tiling. Luckily the assistant whisked her through the rails, holding up clothes and then swiping them away again as she asked question after question that Esther struggled to keep up with. Short, midi, maxi? Tight, relaxed, loose? Cotton, acrylic, silk?

Then there was a tiny dressing room where Esther kept bashing her elbows and, on one occasion, even her forehead when she got stuck in a polo neck. Esther had never owned a skirt: they were impractical, Mother said, cold in winter, and it was easier to cut the legs off old trousers and make shorts when it got warm. But in the House, seasons really didn't mean much, just a change of colours in the scene outside their bedroom windows. Esther tried on a skirt that fell to mid-calf in a soft, pleated material but the strange, unfettered feeling when she wore it was so off-putting, she quickly stepped out of it again.

The tops were a revelation too. If the skirt made her feel unfettered, then the tops did the exact opposite – slim-fitting things that clung to her arms and chest, making sweat prickle on her skin and embarrassment prickle on her cheeks. They were as far from her usual baggy cotton T-shirts as she could get.

She finally stepped out in front of the mirror.

Transformation? In the films this bit of the scene was always accompanied by a volumising bounce to the heroine's hair, a blush to her cheeks and a bold shade of lipstick she hadn't been wearing before. Esther's shoulders sagged – that was still her pale face on top of the different clothes; no change at all.

'Here, do you mind? You have such lovely hair. Thick. It's a shame to keep it tied back all the time.' The woman stood behind her and gently loosened her hair from its ponytail, smoothed it over her shoulders and tucked one side behind her ear. Esther had never really spent much time thinking about it. It had always been just another chore to her, something to wash and condition and dry, something that fell in her face, got stuck on lip balm and tangled itself into knots that snagged on her brush.

Maybe the bounce would come later.

Tom cleared his throat. 'You look great,' he said and there was a new look on his face, something surprised, something twinkly. Esther had never understood that before when she'd read the phrase: *his eyes twinkled*. Eyes were not fairy lights. But now she got it – the twinkle was not a light, it was … an intention …

Standing in front of the mirror, it was easier to imagine the woman she could have been Out There. Her jeans fitted snugly, the denim not thin from too many washes and her purple velvet sloppy jumper slopped fashionably, not because it had been in the tumble dryer too many times. Her trainers with their cracked soles had been replaced by boots with a block heel that she'd expected to wobble in, but which actually gave her a pleasing stomp instead. Their post-box red was a brighter shade of her father's jumper.

The doorbell tinkled again. 'Pips. You look …'

Then Ned stood by her side and finally she saw it. The resemblance. Something in the set of the mouth, the curve of jawline, the straight nose. He had the same colour eyes as her – brown but with swirls of green that intensified after crying. Today the green glimmered.

Something broke in Ned's expression. Esther expected tears and then a hug and they would stand there in the middle of the shop floor with the assistant watching on, bemused. It would be an important emotional moment, a breakthrough, something desperately needed.

Instead, Ned simply tilted his head into hers as they stood side by side. It was only a small gesture but then she felt the weight of his arm across her shoulders and suddenly she didn't need the tears and the big moment anymore because her life was now going to be made up of these small moments, and all of those put together would eclipse a few seconds standing in this shop.

She smiled and so did he. Their smiles were almost exactly the same.

Chapter 40

A strange dinner ended their day.

Esther had never had any alcohol except in medicines or mouthwash. Mother hadn't classed it as an essential or a luxury.

It had been Ned's idea. 'Just one glass, a spritzer – celebration?' So she did. She could do anything in the Out There and that was such a hulking thought that she needed a sip or two of alcohol to even think it. She had expected it to taste better but it was surprising how quickly she got used to the tart tingle that fizzed all the way to her brain. A spritzer. It sounded glamorous.

The pub in which they sat had old beams and mismatched chairs. There was a lot of inexplicable brass hanging from the walls and hundreds of framed prints and paintings, mostly of animals and farms and weirdly proportioned pigs. They sat away from the big fire in its dusty grate in case Esther's demon did not like fire smoke. But that ashy feel got into her mouth anyway and she could imagine the fine grit settling onto her – her hair, her eyelashes, sinking into her pores. That night before she got into bed, she reassured herself, taking careful breaths, she would get into the shower and scrub at every last inch of her to get the dirt off.

Whether they held a normal conversation was beyond Esther's

judgement. They talked about Ned's journey here and the traffic jams and Tom, inspired by the burger in front of him, explained how to make burgers that had no meat in them at all, a recipe that Esther tried to remember for Mother. It was skating-pond chat. They zipped about on the surface and ignored the dark shapes flitting underneath the ice. Esther had a thousand questions glued up in her mind that never made it onto her tongue and though she spoke a little, she watched more.

She watched the way her father ate his food, leaving his roast potatoes until last, perhaps his favourite bit of the meal. That nugget of knowledge she stored away. She watched him place his knife and fork neatly at an angle when he had finished, and she watched as he rubbed at his chin sometimes when he was thinking of the right words to say. For her the right words didn't come; her answers to questions were short and halting, her face on fire, but she tried to listen to what he said about his job as manager of a factory, not the steelworks anymore, about his life in his flat, no new wife, no more children.

Brothers or sisters – Esther hadn't thought of them until now. They appeared as shadowy figures in her mind and puffed away to dust just as quickly, a dust that stung her eyes.

After a while, Ned yawned and pushed his glass away. 'I think it's bedtime for the old fogey, yes? Good night's sleep, clear head for tomorrow.' He reached out as if to smooth Esther's loose hair but his hand froze over her head, an awkward papal blessing. 'Lots of things to work out.'

Esther tightened her grip on her knife. What if he left, walked out of this pub restaurant and never reappeared again? What if he fell on the stairs up to his room, his ankle twisting, a tumble to the bottom, skull meeting floor?

Ned let his hand fall away, leaning over her so she could see the red etchings in the whites of his eyes and the darker shadow of stubble. 'We'll see each other in the morning, Esther. I've booked two more rooms here at the pub, for you and Tom.'

For a second, the world tilted. Esther had been expecting another car journey in the darkness and then House and Mother ... and whatever lay beyond that. It had never crossed her mind that she would spend a night away. A whole night.

'What?' she asked, continuing to grip the knife.

Tom, who had been about to take a sip of his drink, put his glass down. 'I thought we'd go back tonight – check on Esther's mum and then take it from there. We probably need to involve the police pretty soon ...'

'No!' Ned said rather too vehemently. 'No police, not yet – I don't know what that woman will do if we send over a police car. We can wait, do that tomorrow – it's late, we could all do with some sleep.'

That woman. Her mother. Esther didn't like the way the two of them were talking over her. 'You should have asked me,' she said to no one because the two men weren't listening.

Ned continued, 'It's more sensible to stay here for the night—'

'Yeah, but you can't just assume that's what Esther would want to do—'

Esther let her knife clatter onto her empty plate. 'Hello? Are you going to let me speak?' She heard her mother's tone in her voice. Tom and Ned looked at her. 'Thank you.'

Deciding to go back was tempting if only to show her father that he didn't need to make decisions for her because she was done with people doing that but ... she had spent so little time in the Out There and there was so much of it to experience. She wasn't ready to leave it yet.

'Exactly,' Ned said once she had haltingly explained that. He kissed her on the cheek, his lips warm. 'I'm off to bed but you two stay up, enjoy yourselves. Goodnight, Pips.'

And he was gone, leaving an empty chair between her and Tom.

Suddenly the effects of the small glass of white wine hit her all at once. Her cheeks flamed and the pub became spongy in a way that was actually rather nice, suggesting that, if she fell over, the floor would just gently bounce her back up again – no harm done.

'I can drive you back to your mum, if you need,' Tom said, his hand loose on a half-full glass of beer, his injured leg propped up on a chair.

She swirled the part-wine-mostly-lemonade and thought. Back at the House there was just chilly concrete and a mother she didn't know anymore … and maybe didn't even want to know. The pub on the other hand was warm and had those soft, bouncy walls that would keep her safe. It had her father, tucked up in a small bed in its roof somewhere, like a bird in its high nest, but not a bird who would be tossed away like rubbish.

'No,' she said, her words sounding as rubbery as the walls. 'I don't want to go back.' Tom opened his mouth but she interrupted him, 'And I don't want to talk about Mother, or the House, or how I'm feeling either.'

He took a sip of beer. The pub was too dimly lit for Esther to catch his expression but there was a definite smile. 'So, what *do* you want to talk about then?'

'First I'd like another drink. Another spritzer but without the spritz bit please.'

'So, just the alcohol then?'

'Yep. That's it.' She could understand why people drank – it loosened the connection between brain and mouth so mouth could do what it liked while brain fumbled to catch up. 'And then … then you're going to catch me up on what I've missed.'

'Huh?'

'The last sixteen years.'

'The last … umm – rightio …'

Tom gave it his best shot. He talked about technology and television, illnesses and inventions, climate and capital cities, work, workouts and what to dance to.

The pub was just scenery and the people in it merely extras who would never get a speaking part. Halfway through explaining,

Tom moved his chair closer to hers and though their legs didn't touch, merely the thought of his knee so near hers did strange things to her stomach.

'... you know, we're trying to learn. Mostly. But it's an uphill struggle – we have a lot of things about pollution and the environment that we have to try to tackle. But I like to think we will, y'know – we'll work it out because we have to. We have no choice. And certainly no one is hiding away in bunkers like your mother.'

And just like that, the mention of Mother flashed an image of her into Esther's head: alone, unable to haul herself out of bed, in a dark room without even a glass of water.

She must have staggered when she stood because Tom was suddenly at her side. 'Whoa there, buddy. Take your time. Are we leaving?'

She wanted to say: *I am not your buddy.* She wanted to make the point that the word "buddy" suggested hand-shaking, high fives and beers after work and that was not them. It was not them at all. But her lips had become as spongy as the walls and she couldn't trust them to say anything that would make sense.

'I should have cut you off earlier,' he said, breath warm on her ear.

Esther had no idea what that meant. Hadn't she already been cut off, for so many years? Why would he want to do it again? There was too much that she did not understand, for example why women wore boots with little heels that helped you stomp but also made you wobble.

'I think I need to go to bed,' she managed to blurt out.

Tom smiled indulgently. 'It can hit you all of a sudden sometimes.'

The woman behind the bar had big jangly plastic earrings and, rather alarmingly, two sets of eyebrows. Esther briefly thought this was some kind of worrying mutation until she realised that the top ones had been pencilled in just a little too high above the originals.

'Be there now in a minute, loves,' she called over to them whilst pulling a pint.

'What are you doing?' Tom said as Esther bent down.

It wasn't obvious to him because he wasn't wearing them but those boots with their stompy wibbly-wobbly heels – they needed to come off. Now. She pulled at one and threatened to send both of them toppling backwards.

'Your rooms, is it?' The woman appeared before them. Esther showed her the boot; she looked surprised but that might just have been the eyebrows.

'Yes please,' said Tom.

'Lucky we had a cancellation, you are – we were fully booked until yesterday. It's that music festival that's set up in the field over that way.' She waved vaguely. 'It's been a goldmine this weekend. You here for that?'

'No.' Tom caught Esther's expression. 'No?'

'No ...' Esther thought she said quietly but by the way those nearest to them turned their heads, she may have misjudged that.

'No – I don't think you're quite ready for that.'

There he went again, telling her what to do.

'Probably not,' she agreed, but that wasn't going to stop her.

Chapter 41

Stars. Esther knew they were formed by the gravitational collapse of large clouds of cold gas and that they did not actually twinkle, it was just the way human eyes processed the light.

'As clouds of gas,' she said to Tom, 'they don't really care what humans do. But that doesn't seem to matter to us because, y'know – wish upon a star and all that ...'

She had not spent enough time gazing at them wistfully, like many of the heroines did in some of the films she had seen.

'You okay, Esther?'

The stars were dizzying.

Currently she was sprawled over an outdoor pub bench, her feet on the seat with her back on the table. Tom was laid out in the same way at her side. She was glad to be lying down, because the sky reeled over her in a way that made her stomach lurch. There was just a bit too much of it, now she was lying underneath it and it wasn't safely squared off by thick windows. She had the feeling that actually, the sky was blinding white and those stars were just pinpricks in the material thrown across to protect everyone below, material that was slowly weakening and tearing ...

'Esther?' Tom said.

She made a sound.

'Are you okay?'

She made another sound that was meant to approximate the word, 'Fine'.

'Because you're gripping the table quite hard?'

Esther looked down at her white knuckles, loosened her grasp and edged up onto her elbows.

'Do you need to go back inside? Because y'know, if the stars are too much for you then ...'

Deliberate pause. Tom stared at her rather too intently, though the gloom prevented her from seeing the amber flecks in his eyes. The flimsy jacket he wore couldn't have kept him warm, Esther thought. Next time he went searching for two people who had hidden themselves away from the world, he would perhaps dress more appropriately.

This was acclimatising, so he told her. If she wanted to see the nearby music festival – which she very much did because it was just the Out There kind of thing she should see – then she had to get used to wide open sky above her.

'You're missing the best bit – look.' He shifted around to face the opposite way, Esther following his lead.

'Oh ...'

Esther had not seen the moon for such a long time. Due to their positioning, the windows in the House had shown two narrow slices of the world and that world had been both sun and moonless. Sunrise and sunset had been merely a soft glow starting on one side and ending on the other, the edges of marvellous oranges and pinks lit up from within hinting at the glorious colour that lay out of view. Once she had left the House, Esther knew not to stare at the sun because that would have burnt out her retinas.

But she could stare at the moon. It was much bigger than she remembered and brighter too, its white pockmarked by shadow, not an eye, not a torch beam, not any of those comparisons because there was nothing even remotely like it in terms of sheer luminous beauty. Esther could understand why people worshipped it. After all, it was a whole, huge, shining world hung above their heads.

'Know the names of any star constellations?' Tom asked.

'No.'

They gazed.

'Luckily, I'm an expert.' Tom grinned and then squinted, waving his finger at the sky. 'Well, I think you'll find over there is the … the … saucepan …'

'The saucepan?' Esther smiled and turned her head to watch him, not the stars.

'Yep, well-known constellation, I'll have you know. And there, just there, is the zigzag, only seen on certain nights so we're very lucky to glimpse that one …'

Esther laughed.

'And then finally, the jewel in the night sky is the … wizard's hat, just there.' He pointed again, and she saw more random stars refusing to get into any formation. 'It's lucky you have me with you, otherwise you'd have missed out on all of those.'

He squirmed around to lie on his side and face her as she was facing him, both of them smiling. But then, of course, they were only staring at each other, not the sky, and that became a very different situation altogether. Heat rose in Esther's face.

'I can't believe I found you,' he said. 'You don't remember, do you, us playing together when we were little?'

'Oh … umm … I mean, I'm sure I do—'

'It's all right. Obviously I'm mortally wounded by the way I left completely no impression on you but it's fine … fine …' He laughed. 'You liked the turret the best. I was a few years older than you, so I was bit taller and could do the monkey bars better, which really annoyed you. I remember you hanging there from them, desperately trying to move. In the end your dad would hold your feet to help swing you to the next rung.'

Esther could see what he was describing in her mind: a small girl in plaits clinging on to the brightly painted bars, her tongue

178

poking out in determination, a curly haired boy encouraging her from below, but she knew she was just seeing what Tom had described – it wasn't her memory.

'My father is alive. And my mother tried to keep me from him.'

Tom shifted up into a sitting position, winced a little and rubbed at his leg before passing her a piece of the chocolate bar they had been sharing.

'I think your mum is ill. Her mind. But she just wanted to protect you, like most mums.'

'But most mums don't lie to their daughters about the world outside.'

'Well, no – but I haven't really met anyone like you two. You've been on your own for so long. She probably believed what she was saying. And I haven't met anyone who's grown up in …'

'Captivity?'

It was meant to be a joke. Esther had been aiming for light and witty and entertaining and not some strange person to be pitied and spoken to in soft tones. Tom's face fell.

'It's not – I didn't mean—'

'No, I know!'

Esther had seen zoos, places where cities kept animals, some-times to keep them safe, but mostly so people who'd never seen those kinds of creatures before could spend a day gawping at them in between slurping ice-cream. A lot of dates took place in them.

'What is your life like?' Esther asked.

Tom fiddled with a loose thread on the zip of his jacket.

'Me? I'm pretty standard. It may surprise you that I very rarely get my leg stuck in bear traps. Got my job. Got a flat, and parents who nag me to eat my vegetables. You know, the usual.'

Then he paused awkwardly. The usual, Esther thought. He could have told her he talked to aliens on a Saturday and walked his pet fish every evening, going back to his igloo for a meal of dried feet and tree sap.

'Tired?'

She shook her head. She had never been more alert. Maybe it was Mother's low-level sedatives finally leaving her system, but it felt as if the edges of the sky had sharpened and that she could peel them back, see what was underneath.

She sat up. 'Well, that's enough sitting in the dark talking. I've done plenty of that already. Come on – I've acclimatised.' She hadn't. 'I don't want to sleep and I might still be a bit drunk … no, wait – I am definitely still a bit drunk … but I'm done sitting on this bench. Festival please.'

'You're sure?'

Stupid question, Tom, she thought. Sure wasn't something she could ever be again because all of her knowledge and beliefs were built on a white powder of sedatives and lies. So no, she wasn't sure. It wasn't about being sure. It was about need.

Chapter 42

Streetlights flashed past her like fish, fat and golden.

There was a headache lurking tight at the sides of Esther's eyes and, worryingly, her tongue was beginning to take on the texture of dried meat. Tom glanced at his watch. 'Well, it's pretty late. Sure you don't just want to have a rest?'

At rest. Laid to rest. Stillness. Death.

It hadn't taken them long to get back into the car, Tom reassuring her that he had only had a half-pint and was fine to drive, though she hadn't thought to worry about that. There was a lot she was going to have to start thinking about.

'Not in a creepy way, either,' Tom had been at pains to explain. 'Y'know, me not drinking. I'm on painkillers for the leg and I just didn't know how you'd react to the alcohol and being somewhere strange so I decided I wanted to have a clear head in case ...'

In case she went full crazy. He made her drink a cup of coffee and as much water as she could stand before they left.

Being in the car was better at night. The darkness blacked out a lot of the things that were rushing past and she had the goldfish lights to keep her company as they swam alongside the car.

They parked in a field, which was apparently normal, and paid a man whose face was lost amongst his beard and hair. He stood next to a bucket of change and a folding table and had been in the process of packing up as it was late but took pity on them, took their money and handed them a wristband each.

Beyond the hedge and some hulking trees there was a blue glow and the throb of music. Down a wooded path they went, and for a second the gloom reminded her of the House but then she saw the lights strung amongst the branches, big warm bulbs like glowing fruits that if she reached up and ate, would make her shine too.

Then the path ended.

Esther had thought that her heart would race and her fists would clench, like they had when she had stepped out of the car at the village café. But this time, she looked around her and took a breath and it was as if the scene opened up like a beautiful clockwork music box. And, if it was a music box then she was the tiny plastic ballerina in the middle of it all, waiting to dance but worried her spindly legs would snap.

There were more people in one place than she had ever seen in her entire life, swaying to the music, talking, laughing, singing and drinking from bottles. Too many different outfits to take in, too many different faces and hairstyles and accents and perfumes. And if, occasionally, she saw amongst those faces another face, one tired and worn, with eyes that reproached her, then she kept that to herself.

On a stage ahead of them a band played, the music more of a thump than a melody, something that punched at her from the ground. She couldn't believe the power of it, the strength of the sound way beyond the highest volume setting on Mother's record player back at the House. This music thundered at her; it filled her ears and then passed through them into her brain.

The smells thundered at her too, a rush of alcohol and after-shaves, greasy food and something earthier that Esther couldn't define. Stopping at a candy floss stall was a relief as Esther let the hot sugar scent push all the others to one side.

She paused. She should have felt afraid, the mass of bodies, the noise, the bright lights swinging over everyone so it was hard to tell if the smiles were in fact snarls. But the sky above was her balance with its aching emptiness apart from those needlepoints of stars. The music filling her left no room for fear and it was too loud to hear Mother's voice in her mind.

The place was the sea, and she was about to dive.

'Wait!' Tom pulled at her. 'Are you okay to do this? Like, have you had all your jabs and everything?'

Esther raised her eyebrows. 'Mother put me in a bunker to stop me from getting sick – what do you think?'

She couldn't waste time explaining it to him though, how the beat of the music pulled her by the heart. Before she plunged, Tom managed to grab her, but she dragged him along with her, hand in hand, feeling the rough skin of his knuckles and the way her fingers curled snugly over his.

She was a deep-sea explorer once more. The people were blue-lit, a mass of faces and arms and shoulders and all the time moving, swaying like coral, the thump of the music echoing in her chest, hollowing out her body.

This should have been the exact kind of thing that would have sent her running back to the thick, cold walls of the House. Instead, she swam, holding Tom's hand and steering their course until they were as close to the middle as she could get.

The music was loud enough to justify the way Tom leant in to her to speak, his breath on her neck; it justified the way she moved closer, though, in the end, they didn't need words. The crowd pushed them together.

Tom pulled out a blanket from his Captain America bag and draped it around her shoulders. 'Brought it from the car – thought you'd get cold!' he shouted, not moving away after he had wrapped her up.

It was only her imagination, but she could feel the heat of his hands through the blanket and the velvet of her jumper. The music thudded in her stomach. She had to look away every so often because it was all so intense, the darkness, the light sliding over her, him standing there, his hands on her arms – broad-shouldered, looking at her properly for the first time, not seeing the girl in the weird mask who'd helped him out of the bear trap, but someone else altogether. Because of his leg they didn't so much dance as sway in a gentle languid rhythm.

The crowd moved them and they, caught in its current, moved together, something more serious in the way they stared at each other, more electric in the brushing of her fingers against his arm.

He anchored her to the ground so those dizzying stars above them couldn't sweep her away into the dark.

And though she wanted to, though the static between them made her blood fizz and his amber-flecked eyes gazed at her in a way that made her heart fizz too, they didn't kiss that night, didn't do anything other than move together in time – not to the music but to something else entirely.

That was enough.

Chapter 43

In her dream that night, tucked into a strange bed after a night in a field full of people, Esther is young.

She knows it because her nose is nearly touching the door handle as she faces it in the darkness. Standing there is important, Mother told her. No, not told – shouted, an angry voice out of the black. Esther's heart is still thumping from it.

Her feet are cold. Barefoot. Where are her fluffy slippers with the pom-poms? Back in her bedroom most likely. She doesn't know why she is here in the dark, facing the door; she only knows that this is what she has to do.

Behind her there are sounds in the darkness. Esther does not know what those sounds are. A kind of shuffling, a kind of scraping, a kind of sigh. Perhaps, if Mother let her, Esther could turn and help – hold a lantern for her perhaps, because it is very hard to see and the metal of the door is a cold kiss against her nose.

Esther is not afraid of the dark. She is proud of this. In the films she watches with Mother, children often are, they cower on their beds and imagine monsters under them. But the gloom is where she lives. It is her home – and in the deep seas where Mr Wiffles would swim.

Maybe it is not quite this dark though. She wishes she had Mr Wiffles with her as she clenches her hands.

Something has changed about the shuffling sounds.

They are coming nearer.

'Mother?' she calls, a weak little voice from a weak little figure.

But Mother does not answer.

The sound gets nearer still.

It is hard to keep her back turned to it; the shuffling sound is a beckoning finger and she wants to move her head and find out where it wants her to go.

She is a good girl though – she will not disobey Mother.

Shuffle, shuffle.

And then she knows with a total certainty that there is someone behind her and that someone is not Mother. It is a prickle along her hairline, a needle in her chest where her demon sleeps and, for once, she wishes it would wake up because maybe it could help her fight whatever is closing in upon her.

'Mother?'

This time, when she tries to move, she finds that she cannot. There is now a strange warmth upon her feet, which she realises with a gasp is like hands holding down her toes. That cannot be, she tells herself. She squirms but now she cannot move her arms or her torso either and the shuffling is getting nearer and nearer and—

There is silence.

Esther breathes out and her demon does nothing but open one eye.

Darkness.

Stillness.

And then with a scream a hand slams down onto her shoulder, the weight of it pressing at her, almost forcing her to kneel, and she cannot make a sound as she uses all of her strength to turn her head and even though it should be too dark to see she can see this, this hand made of earth clamped upon her shoulder, with small things wriggling in it.

She knows the hand will continue to press her down until the concrete cracks beneath her and then she will be forced under the earth, soil filling her nostrils, her ears, her eyes, her mouth as it clogs her screams. Those hands at her feet will help and under she will go.

The hand upon her shoulder breaks apart, the earth loosening and sliding away, leaving the small white grubs to writhe alone.

Esther wakes with force, sweat-drenched.

Chapter 44

The next morning, after a fitful, nightmare-disturbed night in her room above the pub, Esther knew she couldn't be dying – but it certainly felt like that.

'Sleep okay?' Tom asked when she had got herself washed and dressed and out of the door despite the fact her head suddenly weighed a lot more than it had last night. He stood at the bottom of the stairs, using the newel post as support to take the pressure off his injured leg.

'Yes.'

A lie. A nightmare she had never had before, one of darkness and shuffling sounds and a clutching hand of earth. Of course, she had had nightmares in the past but afterwards, in the morning, she had only been able to remember fragments of them. This was still whole in her mind.

'How do you feel?' Tom grinned at her.

'Fine.'

Also, a lie. Overnight, her tongue had turned to compost in her mouth and the daylight was dangerously bright. Something heavy sat on her brain and squashed it against her skull, making her temples throb.

'Some breakfast will make you feel better,' Tom said but the easy grin faded as Esther got nearer, replaced by something more awkward, a memory of the two of them underwater and alone in a crowd of people. Esther dug one nail into her palm and swallowed.

Of the journey back to the pub last night, Esther had little memory. She might have been asleep for most of it. There had been the ghost of music ringing in her ears and blisters beginning to sting on her heels from her new boots. Then darkness, followed by morning.

Films had lied about hangovers. In them, after a big night out, the hero or heroine had woken up pleasingly dishevelled and had moped for maybe a few minutes tops before getting on with the rest of the story. Esther tried to wet her lips with her Sahara tongue and wished the day would go away for a bit.

When she had first woken, she had made herself coffee using the world's smallest kettle, which people Out There confusingly kept in the wardrobe for whatever reason Esther could not fathom.

The trend for tiny continued at the pub's breakfast buffet sideboard with dinky packets of cereals and even dinkier pots of jam and marmalade. Perhaps, Out There portion control was very strict, some kind of government scheme to keep people healthy. But it was the fresh fruit that mesmerised her the most, so much of it. Back at the House, they had had fruit, of course, after one of Mother's shopping trips or in tins, but never so much or so colourful. She marvelled at each new lovely thing until the man next to her cleared his throat and made her jump.

'So ... who's Mr Wiffles, then?' Tom appeared at her elbow.

Esther fumbled the apple she had been considering and it slammed down onto the sideboard. 'What?'

Had he been rummaging through her rucksack? That was near impossible as she had practically slept on it last night and even now it hung as a weight on her shoulder. A wave of heat spread from the small of her back to her temples.

'You mentioned him last night?' Tom's words grew slower as

he noticed her horrified expression. 'You said … he … liked … the sea …?'

'Oh God.' Esther put the apple back in the bowl, the spot where she had dropped it already a brown soft bruise. 'Oh God.'

'I thought he might've been an old neighbour or something, but I didn't remember anyone with that name …'

'Oh God.' Her face felt so hot it might explode, spraying little bits of embarrassment around the room. Sprinkles of shame would land on people's morning toast.

There was no way around it. She glanced behind her and swung her bag between them, opening it a little so Tom could see inside, their bodies blocking the view for anyone else.

'Mr Wiffles.' Esther stared down at the cuddly whale's mismatched eyes.

'*Wotcha*,' Mr Wiffles said, though Tom could not hear him.

Tom could not seem to help the little smile that edged up the corner of his mouth. 'Ah. You made it sound like a person, not a toy.'

'*Not a bloody toy!*' Mr Wiffles grumbled.

Esther closed the bag, not sure why it was so important that Tom understand. 'He is a person.' Tom raised his eyebrows. 'No! Not like that, I mean – I don't actually think … It's okay, I know he's a toy.'

'*Not a bloody toy, girlie …*'

'It's just, he's *like* a person. I talk to him sometimes.' The eyebrows went higher. 'No! I know he can't answer back or anything—'

'*Yes I can—*'

'It's just a way for me to … Umm … I guess it was …'

A friend, a confidant, a lifeline.

'Some company?' Tom offered.

Quiet: 'Yes.' She picked up the apple again; she couldn't leave it there, bruised in the bowl for someone else to take.

'I get it. I had Socksy.'

'Socksy?'

'He was a knitted monkey. Took him everywhere with me when I was little. My parents still have him in their attic.'

'Don't even think about shoving me in an attic, girlie. I don't like heights. I like depths.'

Tom smiled at her in a way that was supposed to show he understood. But he didn't, Esther thought, swinging the rucksack over her shoulder. She was the weird girl once more, not the woman he had swayed with in an underwater, blue-hued music festival.

Ned sat at a table across the room. *Father,* she corrected herself. She had to start calling him Father. But that word reminded her of the opposite: Mother. After breakfast, perhaps she would take herself somewhere quiet, sit and think through the events of the previous day.

The woman behind the bar from last night wore a fresh pair of plastic earrings but had stuck to her two sets of eyebrows; she held out a machine to Ned and Esther expected him to use a credit card but he waved his phone over it, a baffling magic money trick.

'So – what do we do now?' Ned asked as Esther sat down, her precariously piled fruit plate wobbling. Tom took his place with a coffee and what looked like a slab of sponge with chocolate swirled through it.

'Are you having cake for breakfast?' Esther's fruit suddenly didn't look so appealing anymore.

'It's a continental breakfast, apparently.'

'Which continent?'

'Don't know. But they've clearly nailed breakfast wherever they are.'

Ned clattered his spoon against his cereal bowl. 'So what do we do now?'

Tom broke a piece from his cake. 'Eat breakfast. And then Esther gets to decide what we do.'

'Of course, of course. That's what I meant.'

Silence fell. Esther paused mid-bite of banana and looked up to find the two of them staring at her. She chewed slowly.

'You probably want to talk it all through a bit more ...' Ned said.

Oh no – she'd done enough of that.

'Decide what we do regarding your mother ...'

No.

'Perhaps you would want me to talk to her ...'

Hell no.

She cleared her throat, a lump of banana lodged in it. 'I know what I want to do today.'

Tom leant forward. 'Good! That's great – we'll take your lead, yeah, Ned?'

He nodded, rotating his coffee cup in its saucer so the china screeched.

Esther smiled. 'I want to see a whale.'

Chapter 45

A whale was difficult to rustle up on demand, she soon discovered.

It wasn't even for her, not really. It was for Mr Wiffles: a whale for a whale, a gift from her to him, a marker in the sand where reality could meet imagination and then maybe she could … let him swim free.

She was grateful she didn't have to explain that to Tom and Ned.

Her father, she should start calling him that.

Rain dripped from the aquarium awning. The building had seemed to be red brick and boring until they had rounded a corner to find a glass curve bulging from the side like a shining soap bubble stretched tight. A massive octopus painted on the glass gazed down at them in an interested fashion, its tentacles reaching out as if to snag passing people.

'No whales, sorry. But lots of fish.' Tom held the door open for her. Mr Wiffles grumbled something in her bag.

Beyond the awning the rain had become a shimmering curtain that Esther felt she could lift, peek through and see the audience beyond, waiting for the next act of the play.

Inside, walking next to the curved aquarium glass, it was

almost as if she was back in that festival from last night. A blue-green light slipped and slid over the three of them as on either side, bright coral swayed and fish darted in and out of sight. Mother had got it wrong choosing a bunker in which to live, Esther decided. They should have dug their home out of an old submarine at the bottom of the sea and, instead of a skylight, there could have been a sealight where she could have popped her head up and said hello to a manta ray each morning.

Ned stuck to her side, pointing out fish and enthusiastically reading the information panels.

That had been taken from them too, she realised. Days like this, day trips where she would have trailed around family-friendly attractions as a little girl, her hand in his, ice-cream for tea and an overpriced souvenir from an overheated gift shop. How would she have behaved? Would she have silently gazed and obediently eaten her packed lunch or would she have thrown a temper tantrum halfway through and demanded to sit on his shoulders for the rest of the trip?

'You'll love this.' Tom took her arm and she knew there was a lot of material between his skin and hers – a velvet jumper and her coat – but it felt as if all of that had melted away at his touch.

He was right. She did love it, even though it was a tunnel and tunnels to her meant gloom and dry earth and shelves stuffed with supplies. This tunnel was light and movement, fish swimming over her head or lazily sucking, open-mouthed on the glass as if desperate to give her a French kiss. Bright shapes zipped in and out of view as quick as panicked thoughts and the soft glow made Esther's throat ache. She was being hugged by the sea. Day-trippers walked slowly underneath, heads upturned, the paler, smooth skin of some of their throats the same as the bellies of the creatures swimming above them.

Esther wanted to stay in there forever. It was warm and blue and she liked the shuffling people around her who didn't give her any notice. She even liked it when a teenager gave a deep booming yell, which the tunnel broke up and gave back to him, the girl with him pulling his jacket and rolling her eyes.

'Sorry about the lack of whales.' Tom closed the leaflet he'd been reading.

He had nothing to be sorry for, Esther thought, watching a plant shaped like a green elephant's ear float hypnotically. He had brought her to the best place, an underwater world that she could walk in, and that right now, from the opening at the top of her bag, Mr Wiffles could see. He was very quiet. She took that as a sign of his awe.

'This is perfect.'

Tom sidestepped a small child who was using the tunnel for their own personal sprint practice, zooming around in trainers that lit up with each step. Next to his head was a smudged handprint on the glass and someone had left a takeaway cup on the floor, lipstick smeared on its lid. And then they were through into a wider open space where Ned already stood, a living wall of underwater movement behind him, held back by floor-to-ceiling glass.

'Reminds me of your old toy fish, Mr Wiffles,' Ned said. Esther waited for Mr Wiffles to say, *'I'm not a bloody fish – I'm a leviathan of the oceans!'* It didn't come. 'You carried that toy around with you all the time back when you were little.'

Esther adjusted her rucksack. It would have been easy enough to open it up and show him, like she'd done with Tom, but she didn't reach inside the bag, not here with all the people around her, people of her age who were not accompanied everywhere by a grumpy velvet whale.

Ned's phone rang – a lilting melody, soft at first then insistently loud. He glanced at it. 'Sorry, I have to take this. Excuse me. Work. Won't be a minute.'

That was what people did, Esther thought, watching him walk away, the device already clamped to his ear. People Out

There had jobs that demanded things of them. The House had been a kind of job for her, she supposed, but it was unlikely to ring her up right now.

A picture in her head: her mother alone in the gloom, quiet and still on the sofa, one hand lolling towards the floor.

The light from the underwater wall lit up that picture until it overexposed in her brain, brighter and brighter, her mother's face fading to an imprint, a tracing paper outline seen through thick paper.

'Are you okay?' Tom came to stand beside her. A fat fish with a large droopy mouth swam up to nibble at his shoulder. Esther's eyes stung as she watched fish flit and fronds wave, the blue light slipping over her hand on the glass making it seem almost a part of the scene. She was a deep sea fish gazing up at the shimmering light beyond the water, wondering how she could ever swim so far. 'It's understandable to feel a bit overwhelmed, y'know. Totally natural.' The fat fish moved to nibble his ear. He swivelled to her, stooping a bit so his body made a curve that blocked her from view, protected her – made her safe. She could stay that way forever, the sea at her back and him her whole view of the future.

Because she knew what came next. The fish whispered it to her, each child's yell was an instruction, the underwater plants waved it as semaphore. This blue place was the festival from the night before, and she and Tom were dancing once again, the thud of the music her heartbeat and his, joined together, everything else a blur, the only focus on the two of them.

It hardly took any movement, so close was he: she just had to tilt her face and lean forward.

So she did … just as he pulled back.

'I mean, I—'

'Oh, I'm—'

Now the fish were shouting at her, the children were jeering and the underwater plants were turning their fronds away from her in shame. The sea at her back became a crushing weight and she had to get away from it before it broke the glass and crashed over her, sending her sliding across the floor in a melee of flapping fish, rocks and seaweed.

Her only thought was to get away.

Chapter 46

Water stopped her.

Out of the aquarium, Esther rushed onto a street and from there her steps took her to a small marina where boats bobbed. To her right a square stretched away from her, its cobbles furred with grass, the broken smile of a curved building at its end. Inexplicably the trees planted at intervals behind her were each surrounded by their own hedge as brambly chastity belts.

Esther held on to the railing that separated the harbour from the walkway and tried to breathe. Her chest demon clawed its way up her throat and, for a second, she left her inhaler in its pocket. She deserved the rasp of its fingers on her lungs, the tightening as it squeezed her chest and then upwards onto her throat. But her hands acted on their own and the rattle of the inhaler brought relief too quickly.

She was an idiot.

Why had she done it? Because he had been nice to her. Because he had told her the truth and given her a father and a world and all of that was so dazzling she needed something to hold on to, to make her way through it. Not something – some*one*.

But she was a weirdo from a bunker, a mole, a child who still carried around her favourite toy. What had she thought she was doing?

'Esther?'

She considered throwing herself off this walkway and onto one of the waiting boats where she could escape out into the open sea, a sea she must have seen as a child but could not remember. Knowing her luck though, the stolen boat would probably leap out of her control and she would end up crashing it into one of those skirted trees on the pavement behind her, a beached sea creature for people to come and gawk at.

Ned appeared at her side. 'Esther? You left pretty quickly.'

What was worse, Esther thought – having this conversation with the man you'd tried to snog, or having it with a father you'd just met?

'Did you—?'

'I just saw you leave. Tom looked a bit confused.'

Esther couldn't work out if he was lying or not. She couldn't work out if anyone was lying because she had had no practice at it and their expressions were just movements of muscle and tendon beneath flesh, nothing more.

'I needed some air.'

Ned gazed out at the boats with their furled sails and mini curtains at their windows. The rain had stopped but left pools of water on the walkways.

'I'm not so good at all of this, y'know.' He gestured like he meant the marina and its walkways. 'Look, Tom didn't say what happened just then but … well, it's okay. We're all floundering a bit here.'

Flounder. In real life an ugly flat fish, in a Disney cartoon a chubby, big-eyed cute side-kick. Real life was turning out to be a continual disappointment. Ned's grey hair lifted and flattened in the breeze, the silver of a newly minted coin.

'I tried to kiss him.'

'Ah.'

'He did not wish to be kissed by me.'

'Ah.' A pause and then: 'Stupid lad.' Esther gave a snort of laughter. Ned rested his elbows on the railings and watched the seagulls circle. 'But he is stupid, though – I mean, look at you. You're amazing.'

Esther sighed. 'You're biased.'

'True.'

She mirrored Ned's smile for a few seconds before faltering. 'I don't know why I did it. I'm such an idiot.'

'No point beating yourself up about it. Everyone's an idiot on occasion. Today was your turn. Plenty of time for all of that stuff anyway – and plenty of Toms out in the big wide world.'

Esther pictured a desert filled with Toms all wearing unsuitable desert footwear and getting themselves caught in bear traps hidden in the sand.

'How can I face him again?'

'Ah, you'll cope, trust me. If this is the most embarrassing thing you do in your entire life – you'll be lucky.' Ned rubbed at the handrail. 'But look at us …' He scraped at a bit of rust with his thumbnail and beamed at her. 'Having our first heart-to-heart. Your … I mean – your mum, she nearly took this away from us but I'm so glad I found you, I really am.'

Esther smiled too but it soon faded. Behind them a city loomed. She had expected more of a wasteland populated by grey-faced people coughing into masks, streets of boarded-up shops and a smog hanging over it all. Instead, here on the waterfront, there were jaunty red-brick and gleaming glass shopfronts. People. In the field last night, the people had seemed a harmonious backdrop, a mass of humanity moving in time like wind over grass. Here on the waterfront there were only a few and the addition of boats and walkways and bay spaced them out, made her feel safer but beyond that, in the busy city streets, it would be different … Esther traced the outline of her inhaler in her pocket.

Though there were no cars nearby, her throat felt clogged. 'I'm safe here, yeah?'

Ned gave her a thoughtful gaze. 'The air, you mean? Well, we're on the outskirts of a city so it's not as clean as back at the pub but you'll be fine. Like I said in my letter, I can't guarantee that for you – safety. That's not life in the modern world. You'll have choices you'll have to make – where you want to live, for example. There are places away from the city where you might feel more comfortable.'

Like the House, she thought. That offered a guarantee – the dark, quiet and sealed kind.

'But lots of people don't have that choice, do they? They have to live in the city. What happens to them? What happens when you live there all the time, in the worst polluted parts?'

Ned was silent. A swan glided past them, the black markings around its eyes giving it a stern expression, glaring at the boats and the ripples on the water.

'Your mother is ill, you know? What she told you … it's the product of a sick mind.'

Esther thought for a minute or so. 'She isn't crazy. I know you think she is, but she's not – or at least, she wasn't before Tom turned up. We were happy, in our way, in a quiet way. I haven't had a bad life … I want you to know that. There was cake for birthdays and treasure hunts around the House and bedtime stories and a nightlight with moons and stars on it.'

'And sedatives and lies and bear traps waiting outside.' It was Esther's turn to be silent for a while. Tom must have told him about those things. It felt strange, the two of them talking about her when she wasn't there. 'But she did it all to protect you. I try to remember that, despite the pain she's caused. She just wanted to see you safe and that became an obsession to her; it made her unwell.' The swan stretched out its wings in warning at something Esther could not see whilst Ned continued speaking: 'It's okay if you want to go back to the house, y'know – if this is all a bit …'

Go back. Esther thought about it, watching the tired glint of a watery sun bounce from the shiny hulls of the boats. Yes. That was exactly what she wanted. She wanted to go back.

Chapter 47

Hannah

Present

'You're setting the doors off, Mrs Connor.'

The man in front of Hannah was a familiar face, from what she could see of it under the stubble, the sideburns and the ratty black baseball cap.

'Hmm?' There was a soft thunking sound and then a whoosh, a rhythmic beat, which, she thought in a vague way, was really quite soothing.

'Mrs C? Would you mind taking a step away from the entrance? You're setting the doors off ...'

Ah, that was the sound. Hannah shuffled over to the side and the door came to rest with a sigh. The man, whose badge proclaimed him to be "Bob", which was accurate, and also "Happy to help" which was less so. Over the last sixteen years Bob had always been a bit put out that he would be expected to guide or give advice to any of the store's customers. However, over the years, he had rather enjoyed the challenge of sourcing some of the rarer bits of equipment that Hannah had needed. A grudging respect had settled between them.

'Mrs C? You come in, same day, same month, once a year like clockwork. Saw you day before yesterday. What's the special occasion?'

It was midday. Hannah had driven for hours and hours, not needing to stop and sleep because she had done more than enough of that after Tom's drugged tea. The van was well equipped with its own Bug-Out Bag, an idea Hannah had first heard of when researching building the House. There was a whole industry around the end of the world ... of course. Anything, even the end of civilisation, could be commercialised. Hannah had found a company who sold these bags, designed to be the kind of thing you'd grab as the nuclear bomb went off (provided you weren't ash by then, or terminally radioactive), filled with everything an intrepid end-of-days fugitive could possibly want. She had driven and driven and driven and hadn't even turned the radio on because there was already a radio station playing in her head and it was filled with all the ways Esther could be in danger whilst Hannah sat behind the wheel.

'Mrs C?' Bob's face loomed at her. Of course, she hadn't used her real name. Grudging respect did not mean trust.

'A map.' Hannah noticed that her hands were shaking.

'You want a map?'

'Yes.'

She had got this far. Only five minutes ago she had turned the van into the familiar road that led to this small out-of-town retail park: a garden centre, a coffee shop, a discount food store and this DIY shop. This place she knew. But Esther wasn't going to be sat on a bench here drinking a weird coffee with cream swirled on the top of it.

Hannah now noted that her jaw was trembling too.

Bob lifted his cap, scratched at a spot and frowned. 'We don't sell maps, not our thing, really. But Mrs C, no one really sells maps anymore, y'know? We've got 'em on our phones, or we've got sat nav.'

Hannah had a phone back at the House, something Esther had never needed to know about but needs must when the devil drives and sometimes the devil tended to turn up unexpectedly and, on that occasion, a phone could be useful. But the phone she had was a hefty chunk of black plastic and did not have any maps in it, only a pointless game involving a computer-drawn snake.

The radio station in her head added a few extra hits, all involving her daughter dying blue-faced and gasping on the floor. She noted that her knees had now joined in the shaking that had begun with her hands.

'You all right, Mrs C? You look a bit pale – do you need to sit down?'

But that was a stupid question, Hannah thought, because she already *was* sitting down – there was cold, smooth floor underneath her all of a sudden. Her heart began to pound but then that pounding seemed to come from all around her and the edges of her vision began to blacken like mould creeping in. Then came voices and a hand on her arm, helping her up, and she wanted to say that she was fine, fine, fine; she wanted to tell them that she just felt a bit light-headed because she hadn't had anything to eat; she wanted to ask them how to get to the nearest town or city and where she could buy one of those phones with maps in it. When she looked up and saw about four faces peering at her and more people hovering nearby, that pounding felt like it would crush her as easily as a person could pop overripe fruit.

Yanking her arm free she staggered from the shop, made it to the van and locked the door behind her. With her hand on the gearstick a great unknown world yawned at her, so wide she could see its tonsils and smell its rotten breath. Esther and Tom could have gone in any direction and the road she knew could split into one with different line markings and then split again, into a dual carriageway, which in turn could flow into a motorway that would carry her miles, past any number of destinations. Hannah could not search all of them.

She thumped the steering wheel.

Because the worst part was not finally understanding that Esther was unreachable, speeding towards a sky that looked the same as the one she saw but was really a bell jar for all sorts of invisible poison – the worst part was understanding that she could not follow her.

It had been sixteen years.

She did not know where to start in a world beyond the retail park, no longer knew how it all worked, what was safe, what wasn't, what lies to tell, what was needed to navigate the place. There was no way she would be able to find her daughter there and no map would help. She didn't even know where the two of them had gone.

She screamed then, sat in the van, a long guttural cry of frustration accompanied by more thumps on the steering wheel. That aching black void that had opened up for her all those years ago in the back of an ambulance was once again swirling at her heels and clouding around her little girl.

Hannah wasn't sure how long she sat in the van before it hit her.

Esther would come back. If she hadn't already succumbed to one of the many dangers her horror story radio station had been playing in her head this whole time, then she would come back. She knew her girl. Esther would not leave her with just a note and that note reinforced it – she had said she would return. In fact, she could be on her way right at this minute whilst Hannah was wasting time here in this car park, screaming into the air.

The engine roared into life and the House, her welcome ink blot on the picturesque hillside painting, was waiting for her, for them both, as it always was.

This place she knew. And this place had one last secret.

Chapter 48

Esther

Esther found that the monster under the bed was no longer there.

'It's really gone,' she said.

The three of them sat in Tom's car and surveyed the blank hole in the skyline where the dragon steelworks had once puffed and wheezed. Back at the waterfront Ned had obviously meant the House when he had spoken to Esther about 'going back' but for her it had always meant this – the house *without* a capital letter where she had lived when she was a child.

At the end of the row of terraced houses there should have been the hulking black monster that had ruled over the town for so long. Esther felt she needed to see it, to understand her mother a little more and the fear that had been struck in some lizard part of her brain. A fear that had sent her running from here to that hillside and the concrete beneath it.

Instead there was muddy ground, chain-link fences and a crane reaching into the sky on its giraffe neck.

Tom explained, 'Eco homes development. A new way of

building. I saw one of their leaflets and it says they're trying to live in harmony with nature, or some such rubbish.'

Esther got out of the car. There should have been an outline left: a pencil sketch of where the place had been, etched onto the sky so she could have been able to picture it. Her mother's past couldn't just be wiped away like that, so easily – swoosh and there it went.

A car drove by, then another, and another. Esther was all too aware of the brick and concrete around her, the roads and buildings, the cars and lorries and motorbikes. Exhaust fumes lodged in her throat, an acrid bitter taste that made her chest demon stir. As her windpipe tightened, she shook her inhaler and took a quick puff.

'Okay?' Tom glanced at the inhaler in her hand. Esther nodded.

'I can't do it.' Ned remained in his seat. 'I can't go back to that house again. This street. I'll stay with the car.' There was something flickering in his eyes, some kind of emotion Esther could not place, his one hand turning his phone over and over like the kind of meditation exercises Mother had occasionally made her try.

As Esther headed off in the direction of the houses she heard Tom shout, 'Wait, wait, wait …' He grabbed at her arm. 'Wait a sec, about earlier—'

Esther focused on his left shoulder. It was incredibly interesting. She had never really taken the time to notice before. The stitching on his jacket. The clever way a machine somewhere had tucked the material under and then closed it up along the seam. She should study things like that more often; in fact she would from now on because she was never going to be able to look him in the face anymore, was she?

'I don't know what I was thinking. I'm sorry.' Her voice was firm.

'No, I'm sorry. I mean, I shouldn't have just – or well, yes I should but … shit …'

'It's okay. I don't know what I was thinking.' It was the only phrase she could come up with but it was a good one – she could use it many more times. Every time she had to speak to him:

'*Good morning, Esther.*'

'*I don't know what I was thinking.*'

'*Tea or coffee, Esther?*'

'*I don't know what I was thinking.*'

'*How are you today, Esther?*'

'*I don't know what I was thinking.*'

Yes, that would work.

'It's just …' Tom clasped his hands behind his neck, moving that incredibly interesting shoulder stitching out of view. 'I'm the only person you've met apart from your dad and well, there's lots of people out there and I don't think it was me you were really kissing …'

No, Esther was pretty sure it had been him. She hadn't thrown herself at the fish. She had thrown herself at the man who had danced in the field with her and given the stars stupid names. So what did that even mean? In the back of her mind, a cool little voice tried to explain.

'It's okay.' Off she strode, though as she drew nearer she realised she didn't know which number she was headed for. The correct house should have simply revealed itself in a warm, welcoming glow as she got nearer, sensing her presence. She stopped.

'It's number six,' Tom said.

Try as she might, she could recall very little about this place. She remembered the inside of the house to some extent, her bedroom most of all with its toys and books and fish-patterned duvet. In front of the houses was a small children's playground and this she could remember a little, though it was staring at the turret at the end of the monkey bars that jolted her into her childhood. As she stood there the calm cool feel of its small darkness came back to her, her hands on a dusty floor as she knelt, feeling the thud of some other child's footsteps climbing the ladder up to her. In the intervening years, the equipment had been given a bit of a makeover: bright paint and a spongy black floor beneath.

But without the steelworks this place seemed like a set stage without the main actor, though she could feel the ghost of its grit against her teeth and her throat ached in memory of its smoking chimneys.

Number six.

There was a white plastic door with a swirled glass pattern in the middle, a window to the right with blinds and a dog-shaped candle holder on the windowsill. A big metal butterfly was pinned to the wall near the upstairs window as if the brick was sugar-drenched and the insect could not drag itself away.

'We could ask to see inside, if you'd like?' Tom asked.

Maybe seeing inside would trigger something, some kind of feeling, a gut recognition of this place somewhere in her soul because right now this street was no different to the village from yesterday, or the waterfront this morning. Strange. New.

She nodded. 'You explain.'

Tom rang the doorbell and Esther ground her heels into the pavement to stop herself from running off.

The door remained closed.

Maybe there was an old lady in there who lived alone and she was struggling up from one of those chairs that tilted her partway onto her feet, her shuffling slippers making their slow, painful progress to the front door. Maybe there was a young man whose child was having a temper tantrum on the floor, kicking out their legs and he couldn't even hear the bell. Maybe there was a family who were out in their back garden, or upstairs, or in the bathroom.

Tom pressed the doorbell again.

They waited. Above them the metal butterfly scraped against the brick as the breeze lifted it up and then knocked it back down again, its pin slightly loose. It looked like it was trying to escape, to flutter away and find its other metal butterfly brethren where they could flit through the skies together on slightly creaky wings.

The door did not open.

'Looks like no one's in,' Tom said. 'I guess we should—'

But Esther never got to find out what Tom guessed they should do because a door three houses down flung open and instead there came a yell of, 'Tomeeee-e-e-e-e-e!'

Chapter 49

A blur of pink, green and yellow came flying down the street towards them, its braids flapping as it launched itself at Tom and clung to him, limpet-like.

'Oof! Maisie!' Tom staggered a few paces back, the little girl hugging his neck in a fierce embrace.

'Maisie Jane Lawson!' a voice called from the open doorway. 'How many times do I have to tell you that you do *not* run outside in your slippers?'

'I have dino slippers.' Maisie waggled a foot at Esther. She also had a dino T-shirt that said "Dinos rule" on it, leggings that had a lizard-skin pattern on them and a baby dinosaur hair clip. 'But, Mum!' she yelled, leaning backwards and reaching towards the door. 'It's Tommy!'

The doorway fell silent for a second.

'What?' A head poked out. 'Tom!'

In her bare feet, the woman ran towards him and Esther knew this had to be his wife. That explained everything about this morning – he was married and had a dinosaur-obsessed child who did not call him dad because they were the kind of family where each member was an equal—

'Esther, this is my little sister Maisie,' Tom interrupted her thoughts. 'And this is my mum, Olivia.'

The woman did not look old enough to be the mother of a son in his early twenties. Mothers had salt and pepper hair, shapeless cardigans, clipboard checklists and slippers with soles that flapped loose. They did not wear colourful headscarves, a lot of brightly printed cotton skirts and metal bangles that rattled harmoniously every time their arms moved.

'Oh my!' Olivia came close to her, her hands crossed over her chest like the effigy of a saint. 'This is Esther? You found her? Oh, what you've been through … I can't even … Let me look at you, my love.' And she did, very intensely, staring into Esther's eyes so hard that Esther felt it would be rude to look away, or blink.

'Mum, no, don't read her—'

'Oh but I can't help it, sweetpea. Her aura speaks to me – it shouts.'

Olivia shifted her gaze to a spot just above Esther's head. Esther didn't know what an aura was and it sounded a bit like a disease, which was alarming, though Olivia didn't seem too worried. She had closed her eyes and raised her hands to Esther's face like a blind person feeling their way through the world, a vague smile on her lips. Esther sneaked a peek upwards in case something odd had materialised on her head, but there were simply the fat, rain-swollen clouds.

'Your gorgeous yellow, I love it. I'm bathing in it, but there are smudges of … of grey, yes and that is a shame … such a shame but, oh the grey, it's … it's darkening. I don't think it's grey, I think it's—'

'Time to go inside and have a cup of tea, yes?' Tom took his mother by the shoulders and turned her around to face her doorway.

She blinked and gave Esther a wavering smile. 'Yes, yes, tea. Time for tea.'

'And you have no shoes on. You have a go at Maisie for being in her slippers and your own toes are turning blue.'

'Dino slippers,' Maisie corrected.

'Yeah, sorry, Maiz – dino slippers.'

'Ah, well, anyway I've got hobbit feet – indestructible,' Olivia said.

Esther knew this reference. She had read the book many times and knew Bilbo with his big tough, shoeless feet. She was so pleased that she understood the joke she laughed a fraction longer than everyone else. Then blushed.

They headed towards Olivia's house, Esther wondering what an aura was and what her grey had been darkening into and why her yellow couldn't have just stayed yellow. Yellow was a good colour, the colour of the sun and daffodils and baby chicks.

'Is your father coming in?' Olivia asked as they walked past the car.

'He says he'll stay in the car. It's a bit much for him, being back here, he says.'

'Oh no, that's silly.' She turned, went back to the car and rapped on the glass with her knuckles. 'Ned Allbright – get out of that car and come drink tea with us like a civilised human being.'

'Mum!'

'Ah, he knows me – I told him to go find you, didn't I? When he came here before?' She rapped again but Ned had begun to slide the window down and so she ended up tapping him on the cheek like he was a piece of glass. 'Come on you, in you come.'

'I'm—'

'Coming in. Having a cup of tea with your daughter and me – the woman who helped you find her, yes? No time for a discussion. I'm losing the feeling in my feet and my child is in her slippers.'

'*Dino* slippers.'

'Yes, Maiz,' Tom and Olivia said in unison.

Ned got out of the car, glancing around him as if he was searching for the best exit route in case he needed to run. Esther watched him frown. Once he must have loved this place – his new job, his new home – but it had all turned sour. His expression suggested he could taste that sourness in the air.

213

'What's with the headscarf?' Tom said to Olivia as she took Maisie from him, hoisting her onto her hip.

'Ah – shaved my head. Couldn't stand the grey.' She cast a glance at Maisie. 'Though as a free-thinking woman being grey is not something to try to hide and is a beautiful part of the ageing process that every woman should embrace, right, Maiz?' She tapped the little girl on her nose. 'And I will embrace my grey hair – just as soon as it gets its act together and turns a colour that doesn't make me look like death. Anyway, my head gets a bit cold so – scarf ...'

'Is this Tommy's girlfriend?' Maisie interrupted, staring at Esther with a frown.

'No!'

'No!'

Tom and Esther spoke at the same time, both making a sound that approximated laughter if you didn't listen too closely.

'Maisie!' Olivia swung her down into the hallway. 'That's none of your beeswax.'

The little girl disappeared and Esther pulled on her fingers, hearing the small bones pop and crackle, imagining something very much like a cloud darkening to storm-black above her head. Before she went in she gave one last look at the blank space where the steelworks had once been. The monster really was gone now, not even an outline left of its lair. Another car drove past and this time she could see the fumes from its exhaust. There were trees, she reassured herself – the new eco-development had already begun its planting but those trees were spindly saplings, bolstered by supports, too weak and young to make any difference to the air.

Ned smoothed at his hair and motioned for Esther to go first, which she did because it was fine and there was no fluttering in her chest.

It was fine, fine, fine.

The door closed behind her.

Chapter 50

'These are cakes, right?' Tom picked one from the plate and studied it, then gave it a sniff.

'No, they're sausage rolls – what do you think they are?' Olivia rolled her eyes at Esther, smiled and offered the plate to her.

'No – I mean, I know what you bake into these sometimes.'

Esther's hand hovered over the cake. It looked harmless enough, some kind of muffin with raisins but little pills immediately sprang to mind. Pills that could be crushed and added to flour.

'Tom! Would I serve those kinds of cakes now?'

'Well, you did send me into school that one time with a batch of brownies that no eight-year-old should offer for a bake sale …'

'That was a mistake!'

Tom sniffed the cake again and then took a bite, his voice muffled by muffin. 'Yeah okay, these are safe.'

Olivia noticed Esther's frozen hand. 'He means hash, love. I bake hash cakes sometimes, but these aren't them. Go on.'

'Hash?'

'Marijuana.'

'Oh.'

Esther knew of marijuana as well. Characters in films smoked

215

it, or ate it, and it made them giggle a lot and then get very hungry.

The room in which they sat had purple walls, though not that much of the paint could be seen because the walls were full of prints and art. There were little things etched in brass and masks painted with flowers and sweeping curls, two china hands reaching out from the wall holding a candle each as if someone in the next room had slid their arms through the plaster. A tapestry of elephants trooped in a line, each one holding another's tail.

'Welcome to the madhouse,' Tom said.

Mother would have approved of the tea, Esther thought, looking into the small ceramic tea bowl she had been handed. It was the colour of old ponds and tasted similar. There was a sweet smoky smell in the air, which came from an incense stick in the corner. Esther liked the smell but her demon liked it more so she put her hand in her jeans pocket, touched her inhaler and took a few measured breaths.

'Debs! Tom's here!' Olivia yelled behind her, putting down the plate of cakes. A woman came in, wiping her hands on a rag, her overalls powdered in sawdust. She gave a little wave and ate a muffin whole in one bite. Maisie squeezed herself on the sofa between Esther and Ned, waggling her dino feet happily.

She tugged on Esther's arm and stage-whispered, 'I don't mind if you're Tom's new girlfriend, actually. You seem nice. Meet Mittens.'

Mittens was a toy lion whose tail was currently held on by sheer will.

'Hi, Mittens.' Esther shook his paw.

Maisie put the lion to her ear. 'He says hello. And that he likes your red boots.'

'A lion of good taste.'

Maisie squeezed Mittens by the neck and rubbed her cheek against his and, as Esther watched her, she thought of the wonky-eyed cuddly whale in her bag in the car. A silent whale now, since this morning. No wonder he'd stopped speaking – he'd been trapped underground for too long with her, tired of her questions and wheezy breathing.

'I can't believe you actually found her, Ned.' Olivia stirred her own tea.

'I can't believe it myself.' Ned sipped at his drink, managed to keep the grimace from his face, and then put the cup down.

'When you knocked on my door – when would it have been – a good year or so ago now, wouldn't it? I hardly recognised you. It seemed like such a long shot that it'd ever happen. God, this must all be so weird for you, love.' Olivia smiled at Esther.

'That's a bloody understatement, girlie,' Mr Wiffles would have said.

'You know, your mum – I think I can remember her a little from all those years ago. Your dad here, I barely saw, he worked night shifts a lot in those days. Not a good time for me. I was married to The Git and Tommy was practically feral so I didn't feel much like talking to the neighbours.'

'I wasn't born then, was I?' Maisie fiddled with one of her plaits.

'God no, you were way in the future, you and Debs.' Here Olivia squeezed Debs' hand, realised she still had sawdust on them and made a face before wiping her palm on her skirt. 'Even if it means the house is always covered in wood shavings …'

'My mum and Debs are married – they're a couple,' Tom explained to Esther. 'I don't know if—'

'Mother liked bunkers, not bigots,' Esther snapped. Across the room from her that incense stick trailed out a thin line of smoke and she could feel it rasp against the back of her throat.

'Sensible woman.' Olivia fiddled with her bangles. 'Y'know – I don't blame her, for what she did. You can't imagine it now maybe with the steelworks gone but I can see why your mum would have worried for you. It's not as if anything's got much better, has it?'

'Mum—' Tom interrupted.

'Well, it's true, isn't it? I'd move to the country in a heartbeat, maybe not in a bunker. I mean, that's a bit … but the country, yeah. Cleaner air, trees, little woodland creatures coming to do your washing-up – that's how it is, isn't it, love?' Olivia gave Esther a nudge.

Once again, Esther proudly understood this reference. 'Pretty much. I couldn't move for deer polishing the silverware …' Olivia scrunched up her nose and laughed and Esther added this to her list of accomplishments: she was funny. Intentionally. She would have laughed too but the demon bit on her throat and she settled for a shallow breath.

'But, y'know – you play the hand you're dealt. We can't just up sticks and move. I've got work. Maiz has school.'

'I could miss school,' Masie offered hopefully.

She was ignored.

That thin trail of smoke from the incense stick lingered in the air and the walls seemed much closer than they had a minute or so ago. It was such a small room, smaller than the circular living space and kitchen in the House and there was no comforting whispering from an air filtration system, nowhere for that scented smoke to go except straight into her lungs. Esther fidgeted, wanting to be back in the car, back in the village with its pub, which had been green, green, green. Green for trees. Green for go. Safe.

Her chest demon snorted awake and she gripped the edge of her chair, willing it to back down, to snuffle and snort and settle into a dozy slumber. One breath, two but then all the breaths wanted to come at once and suddenly none of them could; instead they balled up in her throat and Esther knew what to do. She had spent her life knowing what to do in this situation but she also needed out of this incense-filled room in the middle of this fume-choked town …

She headed for the door.

Chapter 51

Esther could not remember how she got into the turret.

She knew she had lurched to her feet, voices and arms around her, but she had twisted free and then there had been the street and a sky above her so big it could have been a hand about to crush her flat.

The car had been locked and she had urgently needed a roof above her so … the turret.

The ladder climb into it was a blur and then she huddled, breathing shallowly, the little peaked roof of it keeping the sky at bay. Around her, the children's playground was empty.

When Tom had first told her about the Out There he had made it sound as if Mother had been wrong, paranoid, obsessed, crazy. But she hadn't been, had she? In the time since Mother had taken them both to hide in the hill the world had carried on and done little to stop the fumes that filled the air. Esther knew that because she could feel the scratch of that pollution in her chest right now.

Her breath hitched.

She knew what was coming.

Who.

The demon who lived in her chest. This is what Mother had

warned her about, the thing would grip hold of her windpipe and squeeze until her vision blurred and blackened, its foul tongue licking up the poisoned air. She would die, gasping for breath in a turret in a children's playground.

She wheezed, sobbed, wheezed again.

However, her breathing did something unexpected, something marvellous, miraculous, something almost completely unaided … It slowed. Esther hugged her knees and waited but her demon had not even bothered to stir. Maybe it was biding its time until she climbed down the ladder, ready to catch her on the middle rung and would come roaring out so she would gasp and also fall headfirst, her neck breaking with a click like snapping fingers.

She breathed.

There were voices below her.

'Esther, it's okay—'

'Was it that damned joss stick? I swear I forgot I'd lit it earlier—'

'Come down!'

For a few seconds, her cheeks burning, she considered staying in this musty space because clearly she could never face any of them ever again. But her shaking legs found the rungs of the ladder. Her breath remained smooth, and this was her chance to get away whilst her demon lay sleeping, because that was now all she wanted. She should never have come here; she should never have gone further than that village with the pub in it. She should never have gone from green to amber to red.

She reached the final rung.

'I want to go home,' she said and she did not know what she meant by that.

'Oh, honey – you're okay.' Olivia's face swam into focus, a slash of purple lipstick below big sad eyes.

Behind everything was a gentle shushing sound that could have been the sea but Esther knew it wasn't. It was the motorway they had driven on to get here, the cars swerving around each other as if preprogrammed. All of those cars with their exhausts and the fumes that came from them, despite electric cars and eco-friendly deadlines to hit, despite legislation and politics and protests and all the rest of it.

A little warm hand slipped into hers.

'Would you like to hold Mittens?' Maisie gazed up at her, offering the toy lion by its ear.

Esther wanted to scream. She was a stupid girl, a baby with her own cuddly toy she still carried around with her. She had no idea what she should be doing, who she should believe or what would happen to her next.

'I want to go home.' Had she not made it clear? She slipped her hand from Maisie's and headed to the car, the susurration of a motor vehicle river loud in her ears, watching her own feet, red like a warning flash as they marched over the grass to the cold grey of the pavement.

In the back of the car she hugged her rucksack tight as Ned and Tom said hasty goodbyes. They drove away. In her head she moved through the traffic light colours:

Red.

Blocks of houses and parked cars went by, front doors the colour of sludge, litter at the edge of the roads. Esther stared at the tarmac as it rushed by underneath the car and this time it really was a river, black and oil-sheened, and they were sailing on top of it.

Amber.

The houses thinned out and the trees stepped forward to line the road they drove along, politely pushing back the houses and streets and curiously bending towards the car as if to have a good look at the crazy girl inside. Old stone walls, cracked and crumbling, were the boundary lines of unseen estates that no longer even existed.

Green.

Esther sighed. Soon enough there was the pub again with its moat of gravel and thatched roof. Her hair smelled of incense and she longed for a bath and to wash herself free of the pollution she could almost feel as a greasy coating.

'Esther?'

She couldn't look at them so she stared at the top of her rucksack as she clambered out of the car and then straight in, all the way to her room in the eaves with its sloping ceiling and cupboard kettle, a safe little space. From the window she imagined she could see it, across the hills and valleys, an ink blot that hid secrets, a place she was not done with yet, lodged deep in her like a broken bone shard.

The House.

* * *

She woke to a voice outside her window.

Next to her, a little red clock display told her it was only eight in the evening. After having a shower, she had flopped onto the bed where she had thought her racing mind would never drift into sleep. But here she was, two hours later.

She rubbed her neck, realising the voice was Ned's. Her mouth was dry. The last drink she had had was Olivia's bitter tea, which she hadn't finished, so she got herself out of bed and headed for the cupboard kettle with its tiny plastic pots of never-curdled magic milk and mugs that held a mouthful of liquid at best.

It was a coincidence that the cupboard was right by the window.

When she had got back from Olivia's, she had noticed it was open and her instinct would have been to close it but she had been too concerned with getting in the shower. It had taken all of her energy to get from the bathroom to her bed where she had hardly pulled the cover back before the darkness claimed her.

Her window looked out onto the side of the pub, a view of the car park and the flat porch roof of the side entrance, its covering beginning to curl at the edges. Not particularly scenic unless you liked your scenes to involve a massive rectangular bin and a variety of cars but it was the perfect place for someone to wander whilst on the phone, trying to avoid the general background noise of the outdoor seating at the back.

Esther heard her name and her hand froze holding the kettle. She leant closer to the window.

'... yeah, she found it tricky ... That's to be expected, of course ...'

Below her Ned paced: five steps from the porch nearer to the car park and then a turn and five paces back again, his voice getting fainter each time he got furthest away from the window.

The kettle was hot, but Esther's cheeks flared hotter. He was talking about her. She knew what this was – it was eavesdropping, though she had never had a chance to do it before. Who exactly would she have heard Mother talking to, except herself?

Ned chuckled. 'Ah, she's lovely but, y'know, what you would expect ...'

What did people expect of her? A wild-haired hermit, who would stumble in the daylight, confused by the modern world? A pale-faced grub, a mole?

'Timid ...'

The word stung like water up her nose. That wasn't how she saw herself at all. Timidity did not allow you to successfully live with one other person in a concrete house under a hill for sixteen years. That took will. It took a determination to not go mad and sit burbling in a corner somewhere.

Timid did not get you out of that House.

'... but amazing too ... I mean, what she's lived through, anyone would be ... a bit odd ...'

Another shot of water up her nose. Until perhaps this afternoon, she had really done her best there. She hadn't spoken to Mr Wiffles, she hadn't openly stared too long at anyone or anything, she had stood under that flat palm of the open sky and she hadn't cringed.

'Yeah, I know, love, there's not been the right moment ...'

Love. Esther snagged on that word like a nail run across wool. Love. Who was the love he was talking to? When he'd spoken about himself, he'd said he lived alone, though Esther supposed you could say that and still have a partner somewhere, someone you did not live with. Or he could be speaking to his mother, her grandmother, she thought with a jump in her stomach, though it was an odd endearment for a mother. She had never called her mother 'love'.

'... yeah ... uh-huh ... no, don't put him on the phone. It's past his bedtime. Tell him Daddy loves him very much' – the kettle clunked against the side table as Esther stood, slack-jawed – 'and tell him I'll be home soon ...'

Esther retreated from the window, clutching the kettle.

She remembered the conversation over dinner, the dim room in the pub, the glint of brass decorations on dark-wood-panelled walls and her father saying that he hadn't had any more children.

He had lied.

Chapter 52

At breakfast the next morning, Esther tried to balance two bananas, a bowl, two peaches, an orange and too many pots of yoghurt.

She had not slept. A nightmare of a sigh, a shuffling sound and a dry, earthy hand on her shoulder had kept her awake as well as imagining what her half-brother was like …

… and why her father had not told her about him. Why he had lied to her and said he had no new wife, no children.

It made no sense. Even if she was too *odd*, too *timid* to meet him, too *embarrassing* in social situations, there was no reason she could think of why she shouldn't know about him. It was not as if she would know how to find him.

Why had her father lied to her?

Tom was already ahead of her and about to sit at Ned's table but Ned stood, took him lightly by the arm and leant in, intent on whatever he was saying, his eyes serious. Esther paused, not because she could hear what they said but because of the look on Tom's face.

She hadn't seen an expression like that on his face since he'd been trapped by the leg outside the House, the frown, the set of his jaw. She actually saw him angle away briefly as if Ned had bad breath that he wished to avoid. Then he brushed the older man's hand away and shook his head, walking over to Esther.

'Getting your five a day, I see.' He tried a smile on for size but quickly discarded it.

'Is everything okay?'

'Hmm?'

'You seemed a bit annoyed?'

'Oh. No. I mean, yes. Everything's fine. Haven't had my coffee yet, that's all.' But he didn't pour himself a cup; instead he stood by the table, tapping his fingers on the back of a chair.

'Esther!' Ned came towards her, arms outstretched. As he crushed her in a side hug, she caught a scent of lemons. After being in the House for so long, all these new smells gave her a perpetual headache. 'I've already had breakfast, so I thought we—'

'No. We haven't had breakfast yet. We will let Esther sit here and enjoy her …' Tom gave her plate a glance. 'Fruit, mostly fruit.'

His words were normal but he was speaking in the kind of clipped tone Mother had always used when Esther had done something thoughtless.

Ned's hand was light upon her shoulder and it reminded her of that other nightmare hand, the one that crumbled to dirt. 'Of course, Tom. My mistake. Us early birds forget that the rest of you need sustenance too.'

Esther slid out from his hug. Tom got his coffee and enough croissants for three people. Esther seriously considered getting some more fruit, possibly to put in her pockets for later, and swirled her spoon in her yoghurt as the table fell silent. She tried to work out what she could say to get her father to tell her the truth, because admitting she had been listening in on a private conversation was not going to be the best place to start.

Ned fiddled with a napkin whilst she cut up her second peach, the flesh decadently juicy. This morning, he was dressed in the same beige trousers but had changed into a striped top that made him look a bit like a barcode. Staring at it for too long made

226

Esther's vision waver. Ned opened his mouth to say something, but at that moment Tom interrupted, 'Good coffee, yes? Good coffee.'

Strictly speaking Esther didn't know the difference between good and bad coffee, though she was beginning to suspect that the powdered stuff she had been drinking with Mother was perhaps not what Tom would consider "good". That stuff had had a burnt edge to it that she realised now was not part of the experience.

They fell silent again, though Esther had a feeling that Tom and Ned were still communicating via a complicated system of eyebrow raises and pointed glances.

'What's going on?' she asked.

Tom clattered his spoon into the saucer.

'Everything is fine,' Ned said in a tone that would have been easily used on a six-year-old. It was a tone Esther had thought she'd escaped.

'So, I was thinking, right, about what you do next?' Tom pushed his cup out of the way and put his elbows on the table. 'And it's up to you, right? You do what you want to do. But I think your mother needs help, and I think you could do with some time away from her.'

She didn't want to think of next; she just wanted to enjoy now: peaches and dinky pots of yoghurt and chubby mini milk jugs.

Ned made a little huffing noise and scrunched up the napkin he had been messing with. 'What—'

'No. Wait. Let Esther talk. Esther, what do you want to do now? I mean, we can stay out longer, see something else today if you want, maybe a film, a modern film, not one from the Nineties …'

Peaches and pots and mini milk jugs.

She opened her mouth and then closed it again. Like a fish. Like a whale – she thought of Mr Wiffles in her rucksack and wished he'd say something.

'Don't hector the poor girl. I thought you wanted her to eat her breakfast in peace?' Ned sat back in his chair and pushed his plate away, a lone piece of bacon rind left on it like a white worm.

Thinking of worms made the peach in her mouth suddenly sour. 'Look, I'll be straight with you,' Ned said, as Esther wondered if she could just spit out the bit of peach that didn't want to be swallowed, 'Tom doesn't want me to broach it but, well, we're just treading water here at the moment, aren't we? Putting off the inevitable. So, I'm going this morning even if you two don't want to come.'

'Going?'

'Back to the house. I've got unfinished business with your mother.'

Chapter 53

Hannah

Present

Hannah did not like the way the wooden bear was staring at her.

Accusatory. It was a stare that said, 'Get off that sofa and do something. You have chores, you have the Checklist to get through, you have a million things to do before Esther gets back.'

Because Esther would come back, she would, even though it had been two whole nights now.

Hannah couldn't seem to make herself move.

She remembered carving that bear. It had started out as a hippo but, well, she was still honing her whittling skills and the hippo had soon turned bear-like ... or as bear-like as she'd been able to manage. His cross-eyed stare judged her from his position on the coffee table.

It was morning. Morning should have been preparing breakfast and finishing the air filtration checks and today should have been towel wash day so she should have had a pile of fluffy cotton to fold. The thing was, without Esther here, none of that seemed important enough to do anymore. Two nights gone.

The only important thing had already been done, as soon as she'd got back from the van.

There were clouds in the sky she could see in the round window above her, and she let her head fall back so she could watch them. Under that same sky was her daughter and she had no idea where she was staying, whether she had her inhaler with her, had had enough to eat, was happy. If she was in danger.

Happiness. Strange old concept – and clearly one that Hannah had not taken enough time to consider. When she'd been a child, happy for Esther had been measured in colouring pens and snacks, the proximity of Mr Wiffles and the prospect of a Disney film as the evening's entertainment.

And for Hannah happy had been easy. Happy centred around 'Was Esther safe?' and, if she was, then there was nothing else to ask for.

She wasn't stupid. She had known that, for Esther, what happiness meant would change as she grew. That's why she had stuffed that wonky-eyed bear in front of her full of sedatives. Because the inevitable side effect of growing up in the House was that Esther had never really had a chance to become an adult. Sure, she got taller and she thought she was grown-up with her wish to go on the Yearly and her stuffed toy cull – the only survivor of that massacre being Mr Wiffles. But that was playing at being adult. The House had protected her from having her heart broken, from failing in her exams, a best friend giving her the silent treatment, her first Saturday job … all the things that forged a person. That had been the price Hannah had been willing to pay. Safe was worth it. Safe was worth everything.

The problem was Esther had stopped agreeing with her about that.

And now she was Out There, under those cold stars, still a child really, masquerading as a woman, and Hannah now realised there were all sorts of things she hadn't adequately kept her safe from.

Men like Tom.

Men with floppy brown hair and eyes that looked kind, wearing poor-quality hiking boots and making themselves vulnerable by getting their legs caught in traps. Esther had needed protecting from him.

Hannah had failed at that. She was not used to failing.

It would not happen again.

When she gave the cross-eyed wooden bear a kick with the heel of her shoe, he spun and rolled off the table, thumping onto the concrete floor below, hopefully breaking into pieces, his stupid stare cracked in two. She did not bother to check the damage.

The clouds bored her; they were just shapes in the sky. She told her leg muscles that it was time to stand, that she couldn't just sit here until Esther came home.

It would happen. She had to believe that. Esther would return because the alternative, an empty House and the knowledge that she had not been able to protect her daughter, was something she couldn't look at face-on. Esther would come back. She had said she would. It was written in the note Hannah gripped in one hand. In the other hand she held something else.

For sixteen years it had been the two of them and the House; Esther would not up and leave all of that with only a note as goodbye. Hannah knew her daughter. The only thing that would keep her from returning would be if the air got to her before she could make it back, but Hannah would not think of that yet. Could not.

This was a test. Of her as a parent, of the House. Tom had turned her head with foolish stories of an Out There full of glamour and opportunity and she had to be shown the reality; she had to be guided back to the safe path. Because that was the only test that mattered, wasn't it? As a parent, the only test you had to ace was keeping your child safe. Hannah had no intention of flunking after all these years.

There was a small crack in the skylight, Hannah could see that from this angle, one she had never noticed before. The concrete around it looked darker in colour as if damp had got in, a black bruise forming around the eye of the House. Yesterday, that would have stirred her to action, to traipsing outside and inspecting the damage, plans churning on how to fix it. The glass was toughened, storm-proof, attack-proof apparently but not time-proof. Not sixteen years of time. Bloody thing. She'd never wanted it anyway.

Somewhere there was a faint dripping noise, again something that yesterday would have sent her into a frenzy of activity to locate and fix in an effort to keep the House going, to maintain their life hidden away here in the hills.

She told her leg muscles to stand. They ignored her.

The dripping sound became something different as she sat there, slumped on the sofa. It wasn't a dripping anymore – it was a ticking.

A clock.

A countdown.

Each tick brought her nearer to the time when Esther would walk back through that door, with Tom.

And this time, Hannah would be prepared.

Chapter 54

Esther

There were words at the breakfast table.

Tom waved one hand as he spoke as if he could magic Ned away with a flick of the wrist. Meanwhile, Ned crossed his arms, his mouth a thin line. Esther tried to keep up with what they were saying but it was all so fast, sentences flung at each other, and she wished for subtitles, the ability to pause and read the text properly, to understand all the nuances and body language that went with them.

Her thoughts snagged on the nightmare whilst they argued, a shuffling sound in the darkness, her nose pressed against a cold metal door, and that shuffling was also a language she could not understand – it was trying to tell her something that she couldn't work out yet.

'I want to go,' she said, interrupting them.

Tom stopped mid-word. Ned smiled. 'You see? She knows her own mind.'

Esther wouldn't have gone that far.

But it felt right, even if this was clearly something that hadn't been agreed between Ned and Tom beforehand. The House was always there, in the back of her mind, in her DNA, and she had to go back. Mother had to see what she had done – the hurt she had caused. She had to be made to understand what she had taken from Esther.

That was the reason she told herself anyway.

'This is just stupid,' Tom said in the pub car park before they set off, limping towards her. 'The woman tried to shoot me. She set bloody bear traps in her own bloody drive. This wasn't part of the plan, okay?' He stopped and fixed her with a glare. 'When your father first got in contact with me, this wasn't the plan. Well, there wasn't really a plan, if I'm honest. I came to scope out the house with my stupid made-up story and then – well, there was that bear trap … and you. I had to help get you out. *Out*. Not back in again.'

'I don't mind.' They were the words on the tip of her tongue, but she swallowed them down. Too timid. She wanted this. She had to go back. 'This is my family. And it's probably a strange kind of family and this all seems odd to someone outside it, but I don't want to leave Mother in that house and never see her again and, well, I guess Ned has the right to want to confront her. She took his child. Me.'

Still a child.

Ned had already gone to stand by the car, driver door open and waiting. Esther looked around at the pub car park, the unkempt grass nearby held back by a chain-link fence, hopefully without the lurking bear traps. But her life hadn't always been bear traps and pills and broken legs; that had only been a very small part. Before that it had been quiet hours and Mother whittling and the flash of her smile or the drawing together of her brows; it had been breakfast, lunch, dinner and the day sectioned off neatly like portions on a plate.

The world rushed past her once again as she sat in the front passenger seat.

'I could have driven,' Ned said.

Tom checked his rear-view mirror. 'Nope. Automatic. I can drive fine, even with a dodgy leg ...'

In the back seat, Ned tried to take her mind off the racing world by pointing out some of the plants and flowers. He used their Latin names, the list of them sounding like a magic spell, or a priest's incantation, as if just by speaking he was weaving protection around the car hurtling far too fast along the road.

But whatever spell he wove was useless, merely dust and some broken twigs because she could not trust his words. He had lied to her. A wife and a child, hidden away. Her family.

When he wasn't speaking, Esther could see him in the wing mirror, chewing at his lip, teeth worrying at a flaking bit of skin. She pulled her rucksack closer, feeling the outline of her inhaler and the soft belly of Mr Wiffles.

Suddenly the car swerved to a halt and Esther was thrown against the door. With a thump of the wheel, Tom shoved the door open and got out of the car.

'What are you doing?' Ned scrambled after him, quicker than Esther with her door handle.

She stepped into their argument.

'Look, what do you want from this?' Tom demanded, keys in hand.

'What?' Ned slammed his door and stomped up to him.

'We should call the police, or social services, get some help sent over to the woman. Why do you need to go there?'

Tom had stopped the car on a lonely stretch of road, the land falling away beside them, scrub and bushes and the tallest trees Esther had seen so far. Branches rubbed together in the wind and there was birdsong. A piece of shiny plastic fluttered, speared by a bush, its flash, flash, flash as it caught the sun a Morse code she could not decipher.

'I get it, she needs help. And we'll call for help, I promise, but I don't want to scare her into doing something stupid. Sirens and flashing lights are not the way to go with this. We need to talk to her first.' Ned's eyes flashed something Esther could not work out.

'*I* need to talk to her first,' Esther corrected.

'Look, Tom, if you don't want to come with us, fine. Take us back and we'll use my car. This is a family affair now anyway. It's probably best you don't come. In fact, keep Esther with you if you want. But I'm going back.'

Keep Esther with you if you want. She did not like the tone of that. It made her sound like Mr Wiffles, something to be left on the back seat until needed again.

'No, I'm going too,' she said.

'We don't know what she will be like when we get there. What she'll do,' Tom said, acknowledging Esther's presence for the first time.

'And that's why I should be there. Who knows her better out of us? Who's lived with her for their whole life?'

'A life built on a lie,' Ned snapped.

You are hardly the person to be talking about lies, Esther thought as she glared at him, but she didn't say it and she couldn't quite work out why. It needed to be said, after all. But once those words were out there then they would bring other words with them, explanations she might not want to hear, the reason why he had kept his family from her: that she was too strange and odd to be introduced to siblings.

'I think there should be some rules,' she said instead. 'When we get back to the house, Tom and I will go in first and you don't follow until I say—'

'That's—'

'My decision,' she said firmly. Ned made an exasperated sound. All she really knew about him was that he preferred white wine over red and saved his roast potatoes until last. And that he lied too. She wanted to know much more, so much more, but first she had to help her mother because she deserved that from her, despite everything.

The world moved again, Tom once more at the wheel.

The trees became denser, the road narrower, the midday light brighter and harder.

Esther thought she would be able to know when they neared it, that living there for so long would give her an innate sense of the place, despite never really seeing any further than the drive. She was wrong.

The road cracked and broke and turned into a track that the car could no longer cope with. They got out and she steeled herself for that long walk through the trees, one she had not prepared for because she was still wearing the stupid boots from the day before and they gnawed at her heels.

There it was, a dark blood clot on the landscape, squat and black.

And waiting.

Chapter 55

The door was open.

Tom looked at her.

'Unusual?' he asked.

'Understatement.'

Leaving the door open flew against everything Mother believed in, but Esther could immediately see why she had done it. Mother was expecting her return and had anticipated a problem: the keypad, one Esther remembered spotting on her first attempt at leaving the house to help the bird. She didn't know the code as Mother had never given it to her, never expecting her to be on this side of the door.

For the first time Esther realised that she might be returning to a tomb, not a house. In her imagination she would climb the stairs, the familiar chill of the handrail on her skin, to find glazed eyes and vomit-caked lips, or a body kneeling and slumped, a kitchen knife substituting for a samurai sword.

She took a step back.

If someone had to find her mother's body, then that someone had to be her. She had left her mother, alone, with her paranoia and obsessions, a woman who had ripped apart her own life because she thought she had been protecting her daughter's.

Tom waved the stick he had been carrying through the door, just like he'd waved it in front of them as they had walked up to the House, protection against mechanical alligator teeth snapping up through the gravel.

'Seems safe enough but I'm taking no chances,' he said. 'Wait here.'

Limping off, he returned dragging the defeated bear trap that had chewed his leg a few days ago.

'What are you doing with that thing?' Esther asked.

'Escape route,' he said, jamming the rusted metal against the door frame so it would block the door from closing behind them.

They walked inside.

The inner porch door was also open and through it Esther found a familiar scene. There was the gym room with its faithful treadmill, the running tongue patched and mended in so many places; there was the washing machine and the airers, the basket of clothes she had left on top still exactly where she had placed it.

And there were the shelves.

They stretched off into the shadows. She knew Mother hadn't put windows into this floor because of the worry that someone could break in and try to steal their supplies. Though no one knew they were there. And their supplies were the kinds of dried food most people in their right mind would want to avoid.

Esther wanted to wander amongst the shelves, run her hand over the boxes and labels, the tins and packets, and keep wandering until she got to the end.

Where the tunnel began. Colder air, concrete walls, the worms waiting to wriggle out from the floor and a dream of a dry earth hand on her shoulder. A sigh, a shuffle.

'Esther?' she heard Tom whisper.

Her steps took her away from the stairs, into the tunnel gloom, past each alcove with its supplies: boxes and bags and metal things she could not identify, as well as tyres and tools and dried food and canisters.

The end.

She did not want to look in the final alcove. In her mind she walked the last few paces and there, crouched in the bottom of one of them was the body of her mother, head bowed into her knees, her skin already waxy and blue.

In reality it was an empty waiting space.

A sigh. A shuffle. Her nightmare.

'Up?' Tom nudged her elbow.

'Up.'

They climbed the stairs and Esther had to check that Tom was still beside her, that she hadn't been sucked back a week to a time when she had never seen him. The time when pills in wooden bear's stomachs and undead fathers and air that was safe to breathe were unknown. Before she found out her mother's lies. And her father's.

She adjusted the rucksack on her shoulder. There was no way she was going to leave Mr Wiffles in the car, though there was also no way she was going back into the House clutching him to her chest like a five-year-old, so the whole bag it was. It didn't matter if he was silent as long as he was still there.

They climbed into light. Sunshine streamed in through the skylight. Esther had always liked bright days like these, blue sky above her head when even the tint on the windows couldn't dampen the vibrancy. It gave a gleam to their shabby belongings.

All of those belongings were exactly as she had left them, she noted. Even the kitchen looked barely touched, though Mother surely must have used it at some point. The blanket was neatly folded on the back of the sofa, now in a spotlight of its own thanks to the circle of sunlight above.

That wasn't the only thing in the spotlight of sun, however. Slumped on that sofa, her head in her hands, was Mother.

Chapter 56

Mother smiled.

It was not a smile Esther was used to. Smiles, when she had got them from Mother, were quick, serious things, like cloud shadows over a field. But this one was a parasite clinging to her face.

From her position on the sofa in that patch of sunlight Mother had taken up watch, looking at the view through the open door of her bedroom to the window, which gave her a slice of their grassy moat and the trees beyond that, leafy troops waiting to attack. At the sight of Esther, however, she did not stay on the sofa but rushed to her. Up close Esther could see the grease in her hair and the paleness of her skin.

'You came back! I knew it! But, oh God – are you okay?' Mother started patting her in a weird way, as if checking for broken bones. 'Have you had any attacks? Did you have to go to hospital? Your inhaler – did it work?'

'Mrs Allbright, I—' Esther touched Tom's arm to make him stop. Mother twitched as if a fly had buzzed into her face by accident, but she did not even glance at Tom. She stared at Esther as she moved closer.

'Mother, we've come to help you. You have to let us.'

'You are okay? Dear God, you've been lucky! We … we've

been lucky … I knew you would come back,' she continued as if Esther hadn't spoken. 'I knew I was right. I was right about it all from the start. And now you've seen it for yourself. Just like I said.' She shifted and Esther thought she saw a flash of something metal in the pocket of her cardigan. A pocket that would fit a small gun. 'You'll stay now.'

'Just tell her,' Tom whispered.

Father.

'No,' Esther whispered back.

'You'll stay now, yes? I can see it in your eyes, you know. I'm your mother; you can't hide it from me.' Mother's gaze bored into Esther. 'You've seen what it's like. It's safe they say, no one needs to hide away, they say, you're paranoid, they say. But it's not safe, is it? None of it is. The seas, the earth – all poisoned – and the air, the air is the worst …'

Esther remembered the stench of exhaust fumes, the roads, the cars, the relief she had felt when returning to the pub from visiting Olivia and her old street. Tom began to speak but Mother talked over him as if he didn't exist, never taking her eyes from Esther.

'So you'll stay. This is your home. It is where you feel comfortable – I'm right, aren't I? After all … here, sit down, sit down. You need a glass of water. Have you got your inhaler?' Esther resisted being pushed into the nearest chair.

'I'm fine.'

'My God. So lucky. So, so lucky,' There was a pause and Esther was fixed by Mother's wild eyes, the sourness of her breath. 'To what do we give thanks?' Esther pressed her lips together, but she didn't look away. Mother sighed. 'To what do we give thanks, Pips?'

And Esther couldn't stop the answer. Call and response, every morning since she had been a five-year-old. 'The House.'

'What protects the air we breathe?'

'The House.' Her voice less than a whisper, a ghost.

'What gives us plants and water and power and comfort?' Those eyes kept hold of Esther's.

242

'The House.'

'What keeps us safe?'

Silence.

'What keeps us safe?'

'The House.'

The House, the House, the House. The air filtration system seemed to sigh in relief at her answer as Mother leant back with a small smile, moving her hand to her cardigan pocket, the one that was the perfect size for a gun. And for a second Esther was convinced that was what it would be, that really, now she thought about it, it was the only logical thing Mother would do; after all, she had brandished it before …

But in her hand was no gun, merely the television remote control. Esther felt laughter gurgle in her throat.

'You'll stay.' Not even a question anymore.

Except what was gurgling in her throat was not laughter now, Esther understood. It was something wilder than that, something fiercer, something that – if she let it – would roar out of her mouth in words that she would never be able to take back. So she only allowed one word to escape, but that one was the most important of all: 'No.'

The House held its breath.

Mother's smile disappeared.

'I don't like this.' Tom pulled on her arm.

Now she was here she realised how hard this would be, to puncture the steel self-belief her mother had built up around her, as thick as bunker walls.

Suddenly they heard footsteps downstairs and a cautious, 'Hello?'

Tom went to the stairwell and looked down. 'I knew it. I knew he wouldn't be able to stay away.'

Mother sprung up. 'Who—?'

Esther needed more time to explain. Just as one drip of water could, over years, gouge out a hole in stone, so could a gentle drip of information beat its way into the concrete of Mother's brain. 'We know. We know what you did.'

She slumped back, her eyes wide, one hand to her throat as if she was physically holding back the words. 'You know? What … what do you know?'

'About Father. What you did to him.'

Footsteps on the stairs.

'You … I didn't do anything! Nothing happened. You …'

'That's why I left, Mother. I couldn't tell you at the time because I don't think you'd have understood, but you understand now, don't you?'

Mother continued to clutch at her throat, her other hand gripping the remote, pointing it towards them as if it were a weapon.

'No, I— You can't—'

A hand came into view on the stairwell.

'You see, Father found me. And you can't hide from this anymore – you have to face him, face what you've done.'

'Your father …?'

Now the top of his head came into view. And with that, there it was – his face. He climbed the last few stairs, sure-footed, neatly dressed, eyes blazing so much they could have set fire to the room.

'Hannah,' he said, his hand trembling on the handrail.

And Mother laughed. A quick, short, choking kind of laugh.

'Mother?'

One hand over her mouth, Mother shook her head in disbelief. 'That man … that man is many things – but … but … he is not your father.'

Chapter 57

Lies.

They were like the air – Esther moved through them without noticing, she breathed them in, sucked them deep within her lungs where they lodged like shards of glass.

When would they stop? Who was she meant to believe?

Mother laughed again, the kind of laugh that had been dragged out into the desert and left for the flies. 'That's not your father.'

'Mrs Allbright,' Tom began, 'I know that—'

Ned interrupted, 'She's right.'

His words fell like dead birds – thud, thud in Esther's brain. She could only stand and stare.

'Esther – meet your uncle.' Mother got up from the sofa and wrapped her cardigan tight around her.

'I have an uncle?' Esther asked.

'You didn't even tell her I existed?' Not-Ned took a few paces closer to Mother.

Mother stood firm. 'You don't. Not here.'

'So – who exactly are you?' Tom shot the question to him.

But it was Mother who answered. 'Adam.' Not-Ned gave a slight nod. 'Always had to stick your nose in where it wasn't wanted. I haven't seen you since ...'

'Since you stole my niece.'

'*My* daughter. I didn't steal anything.'

'I'm sorry.' Here Adam turned to Esther, moving a step to her, his hands outstretched but she backed away from him. 'I am so, so sorry that I lied. You didn't deserve that but I would never have got in here, otherwise. And I have been looking for so long. My brother … it took him a few years, but it was his mission and he found you, on his own, with very little help. I discovered that letter you read – it was really from him. He must have written it once he thought he'd unearthed you but then, I guess, decided not to send it, couldn't wait and came here, not telling anyone. Because he did come here, didn't he, Hannah?'

Mother's face didn't flicker.

'And he never came home.'

Mother remained tight-lipped but she didn't drop her gaze.

'He …? My father … came here?' Esther walked closer to the circle of light coming from the sky window and tried to understand what she had just been told.

'It took me so many years,' Adam continued. 'All of those years to find out what took him only a couple. And, as every year went past, it seemed the answer got further and further away from me.'

'Until I appeared,' Tom said bitterly.

'Yes and I'm sorry I told you that I was Ned, but, well, as I'd learnt the hard way – no one really takes much notice of the uncle. But the father? The father is a different story.' Adam took some more steps into the middle of the room, walking straight to Mother, chin high, hands formed into fists at his sides. Stranger, father, uncle.

'How could you lie to *me*, though?' Esther's voice made him turn.

'I—'

Until a few minutes ago this man had been her father, a man who had shaken the grave dirt off his cadaver and sprung back to life. He had been the man who was going to help her build

246

a new life in the Out There, guide and support her like a father should and now he was as bad as Mother, both of them riddled with deceit that clung to them like moss on old trees.

'You lied to me, over and over. You gave me my father back and then you took him away again. How could you do that to me?'

'I know. I tried to tell you – you have to believe me. So many times ... but there was never the right moment and then you were so happy and, God forgive me ... I couldn't do it. I'm sorry. I shouldn't have let it come to this.'

'Get out of my house, Adam. You're not wanted.' Mother stepped between him and Esther.

'Look, I don't care about a confession, I don't care about explanations. I only want one thing. I want to know what you did to my brother.'

Mother did not move. 'I don't know what you're talking about.'

'Really? After all these years? Isn't it time to tell the truth? To me. To her?'

'Nothing happened.'

'Nothing ...' Adam's words tailed off and he gave a tight smile, moving closer again, into the middle of the room, centre stage full spotlight with Mother. 'Nothing happened. Let me walk you through what I think was the *nothing* that happened. Ned came here. Maybe you let him in, maybe you didn't. But he never returned and I can only think ... mad though it sounds ... that you killed him.'

'No.'

Adam raised his hands as if he wanted to hit Mother, but then he clenched his fists and let his arms fall back to his sides, an oddly defeated gesture. 'I just want to know. It's been so long, Hannah, I just want to know what happened to him. Please.'

Mother flinched a little at that, a quick narrowing of the eyes. Esther backed away from them both until the wall stopped her and then she didn't try to move again, wasn't sure she was able to, her head felt strangely light and the rest of her body numb, as if her skull had decided to float away, a meat and gristle bubble.

Could she believe that her mother was capable of murder? She couldn't. She *shouldn't*. She knew her mother: Checklist obsessed, maker of dubious wooden figures, shuffling about in her old slippers and terrible cardigans. She couldn't have lived with her all of this time and never suspected something as huge as that, something that was currently squeezing her backwards, pressing her up against a wall that kept her upright.

But then there was the memory of her mother crying in her sleep, and the nightmare of an earthy hand on her young shoulder as she stood with her face pressed to the door, listening to the shuffling behind her. Not a nightmare, a memory …

When she spoke, the words rushed from her, so ready was her body to give up this piece of information. 'I think I know where he's buried.'

Chapter 58

Hannah

Fourteen years earlier

As she sat huddled in the corner Hannah decided the night had never happened.

Yes. That was it.

Never. Happened.

Something wet seeped over her little finger. She moved it away. So, the night had never happened. It couldn't have happened, could it? They had had two safe, dark, underground years, her and Esther. The House worked perfectly. The days slid by. Esther was happy, playing with her toys and at their homemade school, her father becoming more of a memory and less of a person. Hannah had told her he was dead. In the end that fateful night when the steelworks had exploded had been a blessing: it had given her the chance to run whilst he had been busy. She'd done him a favour: she had made him a hero. A sacrifice, one last brave act, saving others from the explosion.

The dead cannot arrive by night at the front door, slamming

their fist against the metal. So, it couldn't have happened. She had not run down to open it, only thinking of ending the noise that could wake Esther and break her carefully constructed little world. That would have been a stupid thing to do – so she could not have done it.

He had not come in, a blazing fire of a man, the anger coming from him threatening to sweep her to ash, shouting and trying to push past her. It was unthinkable that he would ever have made it to the stairs. He did not exist. He should have been dead in an explosion in a town she never thought of anymore, and her and Esther, they were safe.

They had to *stay* safe.

It hadn't happened. Before she had opened the door, she had not scrambled to the storeroom shelves, grabbing the first thing that looked like it would stop him, a bar or wrench of some sort. Metal had not thudded against flesh – against bone.

He had not toppled. He had not slumped on his knees at the bottom of the stairs, his head bowed as if in shame. He had not slurred something and reached out a hand to her as if she could help him, a look of puzzlement on his face as blood dripped into his eye.

She had not struck him again.

It hadn't happened. Hannah was not a woman capable of doing that.

Hannah's leg began to numb and she hauled herself to her feet, wiping her hand on her pyjama top, using the wall as a support, gazing at the spot at the bottom of the stairs.

That was not his body.

It was easier then, once she understood this. Because if it was not his body then it was merely a problem that had to be dealt with – and she was good at dealing with problems. She was capable. She could do this.

First, an old sheet. She had lots of those. It was hard to roll the problem onto it because it was surprisingly heavier than she had expected and by the time it was on the sheet she was sweating.

Then – drag. She had options. Through the door and out, past the front of the House and to a spot with soft earth that could be easily dug. But that was a lot of dragging she realised and her wrists were sore from just hauling the problem a few short steps. Over uneven ground, in the darkness, alone at night? She supposed she could haul it out and then leave it somewhere, perhaps do the burying in stages once it was out of the House, but the animals would get to it and make an unholy mess she didn't want to have to look at. She just wanted it sorted. Dealt with. Now.

The tunnel.

Her solution was already there. A short drag to the last few alcoves, ones that she had deliberately left empty so they could grow into them – space for more storage that would eventually be needed. They were prepared for a lifetime after all. For the first time she blessed the fact that she had decided not to concrete the floor in this part. The digging would take her all night. But if she dug deep, wrapped carefully and carted the earth away, there would not be a problem any longer.

The dragging began.

It was fine. Nothing had happened and she had put another sheet over the problem so that it was a long, heavy, dirty-white lump, nothing more.

She did not get very far.

There came the sound of footsteps made by small bare feet.

Esther was at the last step before Hannah could stumble around the big, shrouded lump of nothing and rush towards her.

'Esther! Go and stand by the door! Face the door and stand there. Do not turn your head.' She grabbed her by the elbow, her flannel pyjama top soft against her grimy fingers and they left a mark as she hustled her to the door and nearly pressed her face into its metal. 'You stay there, d'you hear me? Why are you out of bed?'

251

'I thought I heard—'

'I'm digging in one of the alcoves and it's dangerous – you will get hurt. Stay where you are!' Esther's shoulders wobbled and Hannah softened her grip.

'But … but it's night … Why are you doing it now?'

'I – I couldn't sleep. Needed something to do.'

'I'll go back to bed,' Esther sniffed.

'No!' If she crossed back to the stairs she would look as she passed the tunnel and she would see. No – she would have to stay where she was until Hannah got the problem stuffed into the alcove. 'No,' she said, forcing the manic edge out of her voice. 'It's too dangerous to get back to the stairs. Let me make it safe – do not move an inch – and then I'll take you back to bed. Get you some warm milk, hmm?'

Esther nodded. Her good girl, her good, obedient girl. Safe. She put an earthy hand on her shoulder.

Back to the dragging whilst her seven-year-old stood with her face to the door as if Hannah had put her in the naughty corner.

And so, five minutes later she was upstairs watching powdered milk heat in a pan – the watery thin stuff tasted nothing like actual milk, but Esther did not remember the difference anymore.

Beneath their feet a problem waited.

Hannah only had one night. There was no way she could leave something like that half-finished with a seven-year-old tearing around the place. Even a good, obedient seven-year-old.

There was a simple solution. Hannah knew what she was doing and the milk was gritty anyway. There was no way Esther would be able to tell that there was extra powder in it. She didn't even have to hide it in the milk anyway. If Hannah told Esther that she had some medicine to take before bed then Esther would dutifully open her mouth. No questions asked.

Hannah needed a whole, undisturbed night.

As she cracked the pills and stirred them in, she noticed flecks of red on the cuff of her pyjama shirt. For a moment her hand paused, trembling. She took two deep breaths, thinking only about them, the way air was sucked into her lungs and then blown out again.

It was another problem. She'd been thinking about changing her clothes for the dig, but her pyjamas were grubby now anyway so she would wear them and then bleach-wash the whole outfit afterwards. Or set fire to it.

How easy it was to find a solution.

She would find the solutions to all the other issues too – the car, for example. There had to be his car parked somewhere on the main road, a car which she would be able to recognise. Take off the number plates, drive it somewhere even more remote and roll it into a convenient lake.

Esther back in bed, Hannah picked up the shovel and walked down the stairs. Nothing had happened. Nothing at all. She was merely going to dig in the alcove.

As she shovelled, she let the tears run down her face.

Chapter 59

Esther

Esther had lived a life built on bones. Somewhere down there, beneath their feet, a body rotted in the earth.

'No ... I—' Mother looked aghast, eyes fixed on Esther.

She opened her mouth but there were no words. The air filtration system seemed a lot louder than it had been moments ago, a thrumming in her brain that wouldn't let her think. Around her she could see the three of them, their eyes flitting from one to the other, jaws working, but she could no longer hear what they said. An invisible pair of hands had clapped them sharply against her head and there was now just an echoing tinny sound.

Esther closed her eyes and let herself think in the cool darkness.

She had been there that night her father had been killed; she had stood with her face pressed to the front door, seven years old, pyjama-clad, as her mother had dragged the dead body away behind her, had buried it. How could a person do that? How could they then live with that for years and years, their day-to-day life going on above the body of the man they once loved?

Esther opened her eyes. Adam moved to stand at the kitchen

counter, shoulders hunched as he took deep breaths. With him standing in it, the space looked utterly different – the kettle not their own, the knife block an alien thing. Mother didn't even look at him.

She stared at Esther.

'She buried my brother in a tunnel?' Adam said, his voice choked.

'I … that's what I think I remember. I think … I interrupted her doing it, when I was little …'

'No!' But there was no need for Mother to speak, no need for her to deny it again. Esther knew; she could see it in her eyes. Her mother was lying to them – to herself probably.

She had killed her father and buried the body in the tunnel.

No matter how many times she said it to herself though, her brain couldn't find a grip on the thought. They were sentences coated in oil.

'Nothing happened, Esther.' Mother stepped closer to her and Esther tried to take a step back, forgetting she was already up against the wall. Mother paused. 'It didn't happen.'

That was different, wasn't it? *Nothing happened* was a blank space, nothing there, nothing to see. *It didn't happen* gave a suggestion of space filled, even if the eyes did not want to see it. Her father was her uncle, her father was dead, her mother a killer. They were all things Esther had to see; she had to face them.

'You killed him.'

'No, no – no, I didn't. I didn't do anything.' She moved closer again. 'Why would you believe him over me, your mother?'

There was nowhere else for Esther to go. Her mother had her backed up against the wall and she could see the cracked red lines in her eyes and the flaking skin on her lips. Why would she not believe her mother? There were many valid reasons but going into them now was not the time. Esther realised she was meant to be the one defusing the situation, calming everyone down, getting her mother the help she needed, but all she could do was stand open-mouthed and feel the concrete against her spine.

Her mother sniffed, edging her face even closer to Esther's as if she was a wild animal sensing fresh meat. 'I can almost smell it on you …'

'What?'

'The dirt. The pollution, the bits of microscopic plastic stuck in your skin, the fumes in your hair, the black under your finger-nails … You'll have to scrub and scrub to get that off …'

'Hannah!' Adam's voice seemed to come from afar and all Esther could see was her mother's face as she got closer still. There was a bitterness to her breath.

'All that time I spent.' Her mother's voice was acid, alien to Esther with its corrosive slice. 'All that worry. The sacrifices I made, the things I did. For you … and you didn't appreciate it. You didn't listen. You had to go and see it for yourself. And now look at you.'

Esther almost did; she almost glanced down expecting to see the black dust on her hands and clothes, to shake her hair and watch the grit float away. Her mother's face was the most familiar in the world, the one she would know from only a quick glance. It was a face she had loved and looked up to and believed and trusted all these years.

It was utterly terrifying.

'Fuck this.' Adam's voice came from behind. 'I'm going down to the tunnel and I'm calling the police.'

Mother snapped her gaze to him. 'No!'

'I'll bloody well dig him up myself' – here his voice broke – 'and you're not stopping me …'

Adam crossed to the stairwell but Mother moved faster and then what happened next happened faster still, *too* fast. A tussle ensued and Esther could see her mother trying to stop him from going down the stairs. It took only a moment for her to cling on to Adam but Esther couldn't see what was happening until

Adam tried to twist free, backing onto the top step of the stairs and then her mother raised her arms.

It took only a moment.

For a spilt second Hannah looked bemused by what to do next.

'No!' Esther shouted, not sure who the word was aimed at: her uncle, about to step backwards onto thin air, or her mother who could so easily jab her arm out and topple him.

There was a yell, and then Mother pushed, one great thrust that sent Adam reeling backwards, his foot not meeting concrete but blank space so that he swayed at the top of the stairs, wobbled and tried to clutch the handrail. There was time, at that point, one or two seconds, enough to hold his arm, his jumper, to pull him back to safety. But those seconds ticked by and Mother no longer looked bemused as she reached out to him in a way that Esther told herself was surely to help, to grab him and keep him steady.

Esther was wrong.

Mother gave Adam a final hard shove.

Chapter 60

Silence.

The House sighed.

'Oh my God.' Tom, ashen-faced, steadied himself against the handrail. 'Oh my God.'

At the bottom of the stairs, Adam lay, splayed and lifeless. He hadn't fallen all the way to the bottom of the stairs but had ended up sprawled along the last three steps, eyes closed, face pale.

Beside her, Mother staggered back. Esther tried to remember the moment he had fallen, to convince herself that her mother was not to blame. But she had been too busy trying to pick up the pieces of her shattered world and all she recalled was a scuffle, a blur of arms – Adam trying to move down the stairs and Mother ... well, there was no getting round what Mother had done.

'Is he dead?' Mother asked in a toneless voice. No shock, no fear, no sadness.

'Oh my God, oh my God, oh my God ...' Tom knelt in a crouch, one hand over his face. It looked as if he was going to be sick. Esther wondered if she should be kneeling too, but her bubble head felt far too light for that kind of thing; it wouldn't let her look down. 'Oh my God.'

More silence.

Below them, Adam lay on his back with his arms flung out, one leg dangling in a horribly floppy-looking way, the foot bent back too far.

'What do we do?' Esther asked, moving down the steps.

'Esther – no! Don't go down there,' Mother said, leaning heavily against the handrail, but Tom shoved past her and raced to Adam.

'She pushed him. She fucking pushed him!'

'No,' Mother said. This word 'No' had been spoken with such conviction up until this point, all of these little 'nos' a scaffold around her that was now juddering, about to crack and break and tumble to the ground.

Esther swerved away from her mother and ran down the steps to where Tom knelt next to Adam.

'Is he dead?' she asked.

'I don't know. I'm too scared to touch him. We shouldn't move him, should we? I remember once, a first-aid thing where someone took a motorcyclist's helmet off after he'd been in an accident and it severed his spinal cord.' Esther blinked, imagining a decapitated head stuck in its helmet. 'She pushed him. I saw her.'

They stared at each other. Behind them a cool breeze from the porch ran its fingers under the neck of her jumper. The front door remained open behind them, the bear trap jammed across it and Tom's eyes slid to it.

'Is he dead?' Mother called down.

Esther stared at Adam. There was a little blood coming from a scrape on his forehead where he must have hit it on a step as he fell and his left leg looked … wrong, the shin bone sickeningly loose, like a smashed chocolate bar still tightly bound by its wrapper.

She couldn't remember her uncle.

They must have spent time together. He sounded close to his brother. There was no way he wouldn't have visited, brought her gifts and taken her to the park, maybe that one where she had had a panic attack in a turret the day before. But there was nothing of him left in her memory.

She didn't even know what job he did, or the name of his child, not her half-brother, but her cousin.

And now he was dead. Twisted and broken on the floor before her.

'Let's go,' Tom whispered to her.

'Hmm?'

'The door's open. Let's go. Run to the road, drive away.'

'I don't think you're up to running, Tom.' It was only a few days ago that she had been helping him out of a bear trap and he still limped. There was no way they would outrun Mother. 'And she has the gun. Two actually, her handgun and our old shotgun.'

'I bloody know that! That's why we should go before she shoots us – me. Before she shoots me.'

'No one is going to shoot anyone else.'

'She tried to shoot me before, remember?'

Esther did.

'We should call the police.' Tom fumbled in his jacket pocket.

'Is he breathing?' Esther put her cheek close to Adam's mouth to try to feel his breath on her skin, staring at his chest to work out if it was moving ever so slightly or if that was her eyesight tricking her. It was about time her body started lying to her, after all – everyone else had.

Tom had lied when they first met. About why he was at the House.

Adam had lied. To find the body of his brother.

And Mother. When had she ever stopped?

'Is he dead?' Mother called again from the top of the stairs in that same toneless voice.

'Shit!' Tom's hands shook as he swiped at that slim rectangle he seemed to think could solve all of his problems. Esther had noticed that, in all the time they'd been together Out There he had hardly put it down but now when he needed it, it didn't seem to be helping. 'The signal's too bloody weak, bloody basement walls. Shit! What do we do?'

We. It wasn't about we, Esther realised – it wasn't about Tom at all – none of this. There was no we. For Mother, it was only, and had only ever been about her – Esther. Tom wasn't important to her, which was the danger. Something unimportant could be got rid of far too easily so what Esther did in the next few moments had to be carefully considered.

'Esther – come away. Come back here, come away! Please!' Mother said, clutching the handrail.

'I'll go back up to her.'

'What?'

'If I'm with her, you can go. Mother won't care about you. Find a signal, get help. If you stay ... well, I don't know what she'll do. She wants me, Tom – she will be fine if I'm here with her. Go. Get help. Come back for me.'

'No!'

Between them, Adam groaned. Esther's heart lurched in relief. At least this was not another body at Mother's feet – not yet. Behind Tom the tunnel stretched out and Esther knew what waited for her there. A dry sigh.

'See? You've got to help him. Get him out. Phone the police. Come back for me. I'll be safe – that's what she wants, after all. Me. Safe.'

'No, we both go—'

'She won't let you leave if I go with you! Do you not see that? This is our only chance!'

Because it would be fine. Her mother loved her – a fierce, grasping, frightening kind of love she now understood ... but love all the same. She would calm her mother down and wait for the police and the other people who would know what to do better than she did.

'Esther, no! Wait!' Tom shouted but Adam groaned again and weakly reached for him.

Meanwhile Mother had staggered down to them, slow, halting steps and – as Esther hesitated between her and Tom – she swayed and then crumpled, falling to her knees.

'Mother?'

Esther moved before Tom had a chance to stop her.

Chapter 61

The woman in front of Esther was many things.

Liar.

Murderer.

Mother.

She was the person who had held the back of Esther's bicycle as she had ridden it around the House for the first time without stabilisers, who had shown her how to calculate equations, pencil behind her ear, the woman who had put plasters on her cuts, laughed with her at old comedies, always let the pasta pot overboil.

Her face was clammy white. 'No, no, no, no.'

'Mother?' Esther searched for signs of injury, perhaps her mother had wrenched or twisted something in the fight with Adam, but she could see nothing.

'No, no, no, no – I didn't do anything ...'

'You pushed him down the stairs – I saw you!' Tom shouted to her.

'No, no, no, no, no. I wouldn't do something like that ...' Mother hunched over herself at the bottom of the stairs, Tom and Adam a few feet away from her in the porch. She buried her face in her knees.

'We have to get him to the hospital.' Tom sat back from Adam's body and tapped on his phone again. 'I can't even call a bloody ambulance! I'll have to go outside.' He touched her chin and made her turn her face so it was only him who filled her vision for a blessed second, not blood, or madness, or grief. 'He needs help now, Esther. We can't wait.' Adam groaned once more and Tom squeezed her shoulder before turning back to him. 'We should get out of here.'

Mother struggled an arm out and sat up straighter at those words. 'No …'

Esther put her face closer, still trying to see cuts or bruises, the bags under her eyes and the wrinkles on her skin a familiar map. Her mother's mouth opened and closed a few more times, like a robot whose wiring had frazzled.

'Mother? Get up. We're leaving.'

'No!'

Tom began to drag Adam out into the daylight, through the porch and then past the bear trap holding the door open. Mother shifted and staggered upright, digging into her cardigan pocket with one hand whilst the other gripped Esther's arm. Where before she had seemed blank, now a light flickered behind her bloodshot eyes and Esther grasped her chance to reason with her. 'Mother? We're leaving. You can come with us, or you can stay here and wait for the police because they will be on their way. I …' But here Esther faltered because she did not know how to articulate the rest of what she felt towards this woman in front of her.

'No.'

But it didn't matter how many times Mother said 'No'. She could say it until there was no breath left in her lungs and it would not change the facts; one small word could not protect her from the consequences of what she had done. Esther tried to wrench her arm free and, as she did so, she saw what was in Mother's hand.

The remote control from earlier.

For a second she had thought it would be the gun again: Mother's age-old solution to problems, when she wasn't hitting them with rocks, trapping them in metal jaws or pushing them down stairs.

What did she think she was going to do? Put them all on pause for the rest of their lives ... It felt like she had done that to Esther anyway ...

But the remote control was not the one for their television, neither was it the one that worked their DVD player. This was a squat grey thing that looked like someone had hastily chucked it together from leftover bits of plastic. It had only one button.

Esther frowned. 'Mother – what is that?' she asked, still not realising, still stupid to the very end. Her chest demon was wily though, and sensed what was about to happen before her, making her chest wheeze.

One last time, Mother said, 'No.'

It was then that Esther understood, a warning light in her brain switching to red, and she reached for it, but Mother's grip was surprisingly strong. It wasn't just her grip either – with a sudden jolting movement she moved through the porch to the threshold and, for a wild moment, Esther thought she was going to run, to leave them all behind with the dead and dying bodies. But she should have known better than that, she should have known that Out There was not a place her mother wanted to be. As Tom struggled a few feet outside, dragging Adam out, Mother kicked at the bear trap that blocked the door.

Two kicks, deliberate and strong, and then Mother hauled the door across with a swift, practised push. Esther saw Tom make a dash for the door from the outside and she ran as well, but she knew they would both be too late. She was right – metal closed over before her outstretched hand could even touch it, her last sight of Tom his wide-eyed face and his mouth open in a shocked "O".

But there was no need to panic, Esther thought, Mother

couldn't trap her just by closing the door because all she had to do was open it again. There was no lock on the inside.

However, the House she thought she knew had one more betrayal left.

Mother pressed the button on the remote control.

Chapter 62

With a noise of grinding metal from mechanisms that hadn't moved for a very long time, a shutter began to come down.

Several seconds were wasted as Esther simply watched this brand-new thing the House could do. If the whole place suddenly juddered and wrenched itself free of the floor, slid out metal wings and took to the sky, Esther would no longer be surprised.

But then she tried. She yanked on the door handle, but nothing happened and then she grabbed the edge of the shutter as it came down, convinced she was slowing it until the metal nearly bit through her fingers before clanking onto the floor.

One button on that remote control. One purpose.

Mother let it fall to the floor.

Around her it felt as if the whole House shuddered, waking up and yawning from its long sleep, stretching out creaking bones. Esther snatched the remote control, expecting her mother to kick out at her, or wrestle it from her hand. It was a small, grey thing with one raised circle that now, no matter how hard Esther pressed, did nothing to stop the curtain call going on around her.

Racing upstairs to the sound of the window shutters ratcheting into place, blocking the view from outside, Esther saw the skylight begin to dim and she suddenly found herself in the middle of her own personal eclipse. A metal moon began its screeching orbit over their skylight sun. All she could do was watch as it slowly ate up the daytime and the emergency lights flickered on, casting the room in a hellish red glow.

With mounting horror, she finally grasped that Mother's idea was to seal off the entire House – the door, the shutters at the windows and the skylight. No escape.

There was nothing she could do.

The demon in her chest raked its claws over her lungs and then squeezed a hand over her windpipe. She tried to take a few deep breaths.

She was locked in.

How could she live in a place for sixteen years and never know that it did this – that it shuttered itself down like a prison at the press of a button?

She tried to breathe. Adrenaline sent tingling shocks of pain to her fingers and toes as she heard footsteps on the stairs.

Slow, measured. In no hurry.

'There,' came Mother's voice. 'There you are. You're safe now.'

'Open the door!'

Mother sighed and then shrugged as she got to the top of the staircase. 'I can't. It's a failsafe, last resort kind of thing.'

'You can't just keep me in here! I don't want to stay!'

'Look, you've had a busy few days and you're overtired—'

'Oh my God!' The hot anger burst from her and she wanted it to scald her mother. 'I'm not six! I don't need a fucking nap! I'm twenty-fucking-one and I don't want to stay in this bunker with you, a … a … a *murderer*, a minute longer!'

Silence. Mother pressed her lips together and belted her cardigan. Esther had never sworn at her mother before, had never sworn at all. She felt a wild urge to both apologise and also keep saying all the expletives she could think of, throwing them at her mother until one of them hit a spot that would magically switch on her sanity.

'This is where you're safe.'

'No, it's not! I'm safe Out There! I have been for days. And tell me, exactly how would I be safe living with you? I mean … the things you've done …'

Words were useless, Esther knew. Words were not going to get her out of this. She moved to the window shutters and ran her fingers around the edge, trying to find a weak spot, as if she had the strength to haul the metal up. Mother watched her and then turned to the kitchen. 'Tea. That's what we need. We could have a sit-down, catch our breath.' Her voice was all forced lightness, brittle as old bones.

'Tom will call the police and they will come,' Esther said, more to herself than to the figure arranging mugs across the room. 'They'll cut us out of this place anyway. All I've got to do is wait. There's no point to all of this.'

'Here.' Mother held out a cup to her, the same strong fingers Esther had always known, the ones that had spent their evenings deftly whittling those little wooden figures, or had plaited Esther's hair, or kneaded the bread they ate. Her eyes were distant but the lines around them were testament to all the times she had smiled at Esther, the mother she had known behind them somewhere, looking at her.

The House sighed.

Esther swiped the mug from Mother's hand and sent it crashing to the ground, sending a spray of brackish liquid to splatter the wall and then who knew what she would have been capable of doing next? This anger that simmered in her, she had never realised she had it, never realised its power. The way she felt she could do much more than merely knock that mug out of her mother's hands.

This is where her demon would normally come roaring in, to take her breath and render her useless until the piece of plastic in her rucksack saved the day yet again. That was how her life had gone, weak, pathetic little Esther who couldn't even trust her own body to do the simple thing that kept it alive: breathe.

But that did not happen.

Instead, Esther clenched her hands into fists and paced around the room, looking for a way out and, eventually, she stopped at the sofa, her mother's voice nothing more than insect-like in her ear. So many minutes, hours, days, years she had sat in that spot, now tinged red from the emergency light. She flopped onto it, letting her head loll back, willing herself to think up a way out of this. It was true that all she had to do was wait for rescue, for the emergency services to arrive with huge cutting things that would slice through the door, but in the time it would take them to appear – what desperate, violent act could her mother perform?

There was something wrong with the skylight.

The metal covering had stuck halfway across. How many times had she heard her mother complain about it, how she had never wanted it, how it let in the damp? This damp was Esther's saviour because it had rusted the mechanism of the shutter meant to clang across it, which was now stuck in the middle. The glass dome above was clearly visible, and also visible, even from where Esther sat, was the crack across it, a crack that could perhaps be made to split.

She needed to smash it.

Chapter 63

The laughter surprised Esther because she certainly didn't feel happy but there it was, burbling out of her just the same.

'Esther? Are you okay? You need to rest. I think—'

But the laughter interrupted Mother and Esther let the ragged gulps that passed for laughs jerk something free deep inside her, something that took over her arms and legs, that gave her the strength to stand and then to stagger and then to steady herself and look around the room.

Search.

There was no more laughing then.

'I don't know—' Mother tried to get in front of her, block her off.

'Be quiet! I don't need to hear anymore. I've heard enough from you.' Her throat was croaky and rough, not her voice, but then she welcomed that. Her voice had spent too many years agreeing and saying 'Please' and 'Thank you' and 'May I?' and she was sick of it all. She didn't want her old reedy, timid voice back.

Options for smashing the skylight flicked through her mind, each one more ridiculous than the last. She could throw something at it, a rock or something, a chair perhaps, except there was that damned light tunnel before you reached the glass so a chair would be too big and a rock, if she found one, probably wouldn't make it. She had hardly spent her years as a mole perfecting a knock-out baseball throw.

Forcing her legs to work, she began to search for a throwable object anyway, though the room tilted alarmingly and remained weirdly … *untethered*, as if it could float right out of her vision with one mistimed blink. And then it dawned on her, she may not have spent the years practising that baseball throw but there was something else she had spent that time perfecting.

'Esther, sit down. You need to rest.' Then suspicion sharpened Mother's voice. 'What are you doing?'

Going back down there was not something Esther wanted to do, not back to where a body lay under the ground and there was Adam's fresh blood by the door but, to use Mother's saying: Needs must when the devil drives.

It wasn't there in its usual spot by the doorway.

Esther gave a half-scream, half-yell and raced back up the stairs knowing she had one more chance and she couldn't blow it.

'Calm down! You'll make yourself ill—' But then Mother had the breath winded from her as Esther bowled into her, no time for coaxing, or tricks, no time for schemes and plots and plans. She wanted out of the House with its walls that seemed to inch closer every time she took her eyes away from them.

Both off-balance they wobbled in a strange embrace, Mother clutching on to Esther's shoulders, which actually helped as that left Esther's hands free, and she wasted no time in slipping one into her mother's huge, fleece-lined cardigan pocket.

'What do you think you're …' Mother trailed off when she saw what Esther now held.

'What keeps us safe?' This time it was Esther doing the asking.

'The … the House?'

'And …?' Silence. '*And?*'

Mother hesitated and then said, in a quiet voice, 'And the bloody gun.'

272

Just like the handgun Esther now held.

All those years of target practice in the tunnel, the loading and reloading, the learning to sight and breathe and then let out that breath so you could shoot precisely. All of it had trained her for this moment. Granted, this was not the shotgun, but it couldn't be that different, a gun was a gun – with all of them, you simply had to point and fire.

It wasn't until Mother raised her hands a little in surrender that Esther understood her mother thought she might actually shoot her. She supposed, from her mother's point of view, it was the sensible thing to do. This woman in front of her had done terrible things and her genes were swimming in Esther's gene pool, happily strangling any other softer-hearted brethren. Like mother, like daughter. For a few seconds there was a dizzying power to it, holding the gun, no, not holding it, pointing it, flicking off the trigger and watching her mother stiffen.

A dry sigh at her shoulder urged her on. She could almost feel the cold breath on her cheek, the ghost of a man she couldn't even remember, her father, whispering vengeance in her ear. That anger that had earlier burst from her was still there, blackened now to a slow ooze but ready to crack and spill out once again.

Like mother, like daughter.

She gripped the gun harder, not even bothering to check for bullets because Mother wouldn't have carried around an unloaded weapon, and then squared her shoulders.

Gunshot rang out three times.

Chapter 64

The window fractured into a spiderweb of cracking, a few blunt hailstones of safety glass raining down.

Not enough. Despite the damage, the fractured glass held. She needed to break it, except it was on the roof and there was no way to reach it unless she suddenly developed wings in the next few minutes.

She needed the table.

After flicking the safety catch on, she tucked the gun into the waistband of her jeans like she had seen countless heroes do in the action films she had watched. The cold metal shocked her skin, the handle digging into her flesh.

Lurching towards the kitchen table on a storm-tossed ship floor, the room darkened at the edges, a photograph curling up in the fire.

'You won't be able to do it.' Mother retreated to a corner, a dark shape watching in the shadows but her voice wavered. 'I can see what you're trying to do. It won't work.'

Luckily the table was a light, self-assembled piece of furniture and easy to move, even for a person struggling to breathe and trying not to throw up. Esther dragged it to the skylight, as close to directly under it as she could get. But the table would only get her so far. She needed something else, something to jab at the glass and she cast her gaze around, her eyes landing on a mop propped up in the corner by the bin, glad for Mother's lack of ostentation, no high, unreachable, vaulted ceilings for her.

She grabbed her rucksack, shouldered it and clambered onto the table, the floor below stretching away from her like chewed gum. Carefully straightening, she swayed, and thought for a second that she was going to fall but instead she hunkered down, resting her head on the top of the mop handle.

'Stop it! Stop it! Please – stop!'

Esther had never heard her mother plead before. Inform, admonish, joke, explain … but never that.

The House wheeled around her, the walls, sofa, kitchen, all the places she had ever known. If she focused, she could probably see herself, standing in that corner there, or at the stove, or in the doorway of her bedroom, so many versions of herself, all looking at her, waiting for her to do something …

She shook her head and stood.

The mop handle crunched through the spiderweb glass and she jabbed again and again, opening up a hole as more blunted glass hailstones fell around her. She wanted to keep stabbing until she brought the whole roof down and she might have done, if in between the sobbing and the wheezing, she had had any breath left to try.

She could almost smell the fresh air rushing in but when she tried to take a lungful she coughed hard enough to hurt.

'You won't be able to reach! It doesn't matter if you smash the glass out, you won't be able to climb through – it's too high!'

Above her there was sky, blue and streaked with cloud, and Esther could tell it was still daytime but had no idea how long she had spent trapped in the House. All she had to do was climb into that circle of blue. But Mother was right: it wasn't that easy. First, she had to pile more things onto the table to reach. The metal shutter had stuck halfway and could be used as a handhold to haul herself up but, each time she tried, her arms wobbled with the effort and she had to let go.

She screamed.

'You can't do it.' Mother was a voice from the shadows but then she stepped into view, standing below Esther perched on her precarious makeshift escape route. It was almost a different woman standing in front of her. Sagged, slumped, twisting her hands together, a wild look in her eyes. 'Please don't do it. Pips, please. What will I do if you leave?'

The House sighed.

'Don't you see though?' Esther sank onto the table and put her hands between her knees, mostly to stop them shaking. Her arms were trembling too, partly from the effort, partly from the adrenaline still flooding her body. 'It's over. Whether I leave or not, it's all over. You killed Dad and you can't just hide away from that. You won't be able to.'

For the first time she saw something like comprehension on Mother's face. Not denial this time, not the usual 'No' forming on her lips. Her face seemed hollowed out, dark half-moons under her eyes and her voice when it came was even softer than before. 'I … I only ever wanted to protect you.'

Esther sighed. 'I know.'

'Everything I did … I did for you. Everything …'

'I know.'

'And it was worth it, for you, for my beautiful daughter … and I would do it again in a heartbeat.' Tears stung Esther's eyes. She had always thought of her days in the House as so peaceful, so calm, hours slipping by like rosary prayers but look where it had led her – to this moment, to destruction and darkness and secrets and lies. 'Please don't leave me.' The words, so broken, so beaten, so hopeless.

It was almost an instinctive movement, to go and hug her mother, and she nearly did it but the walls crept just that little bit closer and the dark got that little bit darker and she didn't want to step down into it again. She could see it above her head, the world was there, with its people and space and weird tiny kettles and it was only a few damn metres away but she couldn't get to it.

Above her were fluffy clouds and sunlight and ...

... rather surprisingly, Tom's face.

Chapter 65

'Give me your hand,' he said, reaching down through the narrow tunnel that formed the light shaft. 'If I lean in and you stretch up, we can get you out.'

Above Esther was freedom; below her was Mother.

'I don't understand. Why would you want to go out there?' Mother didn't whine – it wasn't in her nature – but this was the closest she was ever going to get. 'You were happy here, weren't you?'

And Esther did not think of shutters and knives and the locked door and a body buried nearby. She thought of the afternoons once chores had been done when she had been a child still. She thought of the way her mother used to carefully write little clues on coloured card and then hide them around the House on a treasure hunt for Esther, the end being a bit of chocolate, or a wonky-eyed wooden creature. And Esther would scramble under chairs and peer into jars, search through drawers and under pillows, Mr Wiffles her sidekick. How, sometimes, because Esther begged, her mother would do it all again for her once the first hunt had finished even though she had probably been tired and had a million other things to do.

For a moment it was just the two of them. And Esther knew

all that her mother had done. She knew she had killed. She knew that her obsession and paranoia had led them here, trapped in a place built on secrets. She knew all of that but she couldn't quite get it to square with the woman in front of her. It was like trying to trace her through paper too thick to see an outline.

'It's not how you think, Out There. You're right, it's not completely safe, but not in the way you mean. There's all the things you warned me about – the traffic fumes and pollution and litter and all of that – and I know you worry about me, I get it, but I can't stay here in the darkness anymore when there is so much I've realised I could see and do ...'

She hadn't explained it properly. Below them, on the ground floor, was their garden, the hydroponic tubs filled with vegetables. It was like being a plant, Esther thought. It stayed safe under the soil as a seed, which got bigger and bigger until eventually it burst green leaves through the earth and reached for the sun, no matter that it might get stomped on, or picked, or eaten. The plant accepted that those things might happen because getting to grow in the sunlight was worth the risk.

'But ... but ...' Mother twisted at the belt of her cardigan.

Black amoebas swirled lazily through her sight, but Esther stretched upwards, one hand grabbing Tom's and the other flailing for the stuck metal sheet that had failed to make it all the way across the skylight, its edge sharp under her palm. Her plan was to balance on that metal disc first and then stand on it to haul herself out of the hole.

Tom's face turned red as he yanked on Esther's arm, his grip twisting her wrist hard. Another thing the films had got wrong – she had quite a list of them now. If this had been an action scene, then Tom perhaps would have strained and grimaced but he would have slowly dragged her upward, hardly breaking a sweat, before the two of them rolled out onto the grass above for the obligatory end-of-film kiss.

The reality was a lot more ungainly.

Despite the wheezing in her chest and her churning vision she pushed down on her hands, trying to hoist herself so she could get a knee onto the metal and he could get another arm under her armpit and across her back.

She felt her wrist bones grind under Tom's fierce grip.

Scraping one knee over the edge of the metal disc she paused and took another breath, her chest tight, before beginning to move the leg that was dangling. Nudging her knee into position, her muscles complained but they did their job, limbs moved and the disc stayed steady. Her second knee was about to join the other and soon, she told herself, she would be crouched on the shutter, safe. From there she would be able to stand and then climb out of the skylight.

'Come on!' he yelled through gritted teeth, as if she was in labour and he was the midwife. But no, Esther thought madly, as she heaved herself upwards, that was wrong – the House was the one in labour, forcing her out, a bruised and battered newborn into a chill fresh world.

Success. She had done it. Despite demons and shutters and poisoned air, she was going to make it out – the House would not have her. She stretched upwards to grasp Tom's hand, sweat, or maybe tears, making her eyes sting, ready for warm sunlight on her skin and the feel of grass under her hands. Blinded a little by the bright sky above her, she smiled and Tom's face was a faithful planet always in her orbit.

But at that moment, as she put more weight onto her knee, she felt the metal underneath shift and throw her off balance. She wobbled and slid out of Tom's grip with a painful wrench, slipping off the edge of the disc until she hung on by her upper arms, her hands clawing for purchase, the sharp edge digging into her chest, legs dangling into the room below where she heard Mother gasp.

A familiar sound made her stomach dip.

Metal began to grind.

Chapter 66

Esther counted her blessings. It didn't take long as there was just one: the skylight shutter only moved a few inches and stopped short of crushing her against the wall.

Stillness.

Esther froze. If the metal moved again and then carried on moving it would squeeze whatever air was left right out of her lungs as it tried to carve a path through her torso.

The metal vibrated.

'Give me your hand!' Tom yelled.

Stupid idea, she thought. She needed both hands to grip on, most of her weight being taken by her upper arms. From below her mother screamed and the metal trembled as if in response.

'I can't!' she whispered, not sure why she felt she had to lower her voice – as if the House was listening in on her. She glanced down, past her red boots that she had been so proud of in the shop, thinking this was the new her, the kind of her that wouldn't be dangling from a skylight in the home that now wanted to kill her.

'Drop the bag!' Tom shouted. 'It will give you more room!'

At first she didn't know what he meant because she wasn't carrying a bag, didn't have the hands for it, both of them busy helping her not get crushed by a vicious-looking metal edge. But she realised he meant her rucksack, which wasn't a bag – it was a part of her. She had taken it everywhere in the Out There and it was filled with the things she had hoped would keep her safe.

Mr Wiffles was in it.

She tried moving an arm and the metal squeaked. Below her the stairwell gaped. She wondered, if she dropped and fell, whether she would keep falling straight through that hole as well, arms and legs flailing, a frightened Alice definitely not going to Wonderland.

'Get rid of the bag!'

Careful not to make any sudden movements she shrugged out of the rucksack's straps and it swung down one arm, coming to rest in the crook of her elbow. She waited for Mr Wiffles to say, *'Don't even think about it, girlie,'* but he didn't. A breath, a flailing with one arm and she watched it fall into the gloom.

Esther looked around her.

The pressure on her chest eased and now she had enough room to wriggle and haul herself up by the arms until she was once more kneeling on the disc. Her muscles trembled as she began and each movement brought with it the fear that she would set the metal sliding again.

Slow.

Slower.

Slowest.

'Reach for my hand!'

'I know! I'm trying!'

'Come on!' Tom shouted.

She tried to move her foot. It felt as if her stupid boot with its even stupider heel had partly unzipped and had now wedged itself tight, not that she could see properly, though she twisted to get a look as Tom pulled on her arm.

But her boot was not stuck – it was being held by Mother.

Esther didn't know if her mother planned to drag her down again, into the darkness, but she knew that even if she did Esther

282

would crawl up here, again and again. No matter how many times she was pulled back, she would clamber and drag and sweat and even if the shutter closed, she would prise it open, not caring if it made her fingers bleed.

The metal disc that she was precariously balancing upon jolted …

… Jerked …

… And then began moving.

Esther gave a half-strangled scream and lunged for Tom's hand as the moving shutter pushed her away from it. Her one foot was trapped by Mother's hand and her ankle was right in the path of the inexorably grinding piece of metal that would soon slice flesh and splinter bone until her foot became a sinewy pulp.

'Quick!' Tom tried to keep a grip on her arm.

Mother's muffled voice came from below.

The House would not give her up. Even at the very end, even as she could feel the wind on her face, its teeth held her back, caught onto her in a death choke, which would not let go.

But she was wrong, as she had been wrong about so many things in the past. Her mother was not trying to tow her back into the darkness, she realised as she felt her foot rise, a blessed lightness as, underneath her, Mother supported her weight, giving her a boost.

There was no time to say anything because then she was moving, wiggling her foot through a rapidly closing hole as Tom yanked her upwards, through the skylight window and there was hardly time to turn and watch the metal disc close with a final clang over Mother's face.

But Esther had heard it. That whisper, that murmur, what her mother had said to her as she pushed on her foot and those two words brought tears to her eyes as she collapsed with Tom onto the roof in the fresh air.

Her mother had said, 'I'm sorry.'

Tom and Esther both knelt in silence, chests heaving, Esther's lungs burning as she took big cooling breaths of air and flopped onto her back where her world became sky. Stretched out and sweat-drenched, she realised there was something missing: the hard weight of the handgun that had been tucked in her waistband. She put a hand to her spine to check. It could not have fallen by accident during her escape – she had wedged it in too tightly for that.

It was only when she heard the noise from below that she understood.

From the House came the sound of a single gunshot.

Chapter 67

Esther always knew that she would end up back in the tunnels, standing on the bare earth floor amongst the shelving, the concrete, the shadows.

After all, she was the only one who knew where the body was buried.

It was a few hours after she and Tom had escaped, staggered down from the roof, sat with Adam, found a signal. Phoned for help.

The next thing Esther remembered was the rustle of the foil blanket over her shoulders. She stared at the warning red of her boots, which were now scratched and muddy. Behind her was the ambulance and she didn't look up because there were too many people scurrying about the place. The House.

Red and blue lights flashed. Sirens blared then stopped. Footsteps, crackle of radio, shout.

Too much noise, too much colour.

Tom came to sit with her as the body was carried out. She had been given tea in a strange squishy plastic cup that spilled most of the stuff on her and she felt exactly like that cup – one squeeze a tiny bit too hard and everything would just overflow, a hot torrent of emotion and words that would break her apart as easily as the plastic cup snapped in her hand.

Tom didn't say anything.

The sound of metal cutters set her teeth on edge.

A shape in a body bag. It didn't matter that Esther couldn't see her face because that face would always be there, in her head. Her voice would always be in her ears.

'What keeps us safe?'

'The House.'

There she was, breathing in her brain once more. No one would ever know why her mother had done what she had done at the end. Perhaps she had killed herself rather than face the consequences of her actions, or perhaps, with Esther gone, she had thought there was nothing left for her; whatever the reason she had, at least, let Esther go, had even helped at the end. Esther remembered that ghost touch of a hand on her ankle, boosting her up.

Adam had already been taken to a hospital. Pale and bloodied on the stretcher, he had not met her gaze but had turned his head away instead.

'Take your time.'

The policewoman next to her was just a low voice, the soft tone meant to be soothing, but, of course, the woman did not understand that time didn't work here, standing at the open door. It never had. The House had always gulped hours and spat out stretchy saliva minutes.

She stepped into the darkness.

The footprints were the first things she noticed. Mud on the floor and the imprint of all the people who had trooped in and out over the past few hours, scuffing earth across the concrete.

'What day is it?' She turned to the policewoman.

'Wednesday.'

Wednesday. On the chores rota, her tasks for the day would have included cleaning the kitchen and swapping the cushions around on the sofa, giving them a bang together that made a satisfying thumping sound. If Mother had seen the state in which the emergency services had left the floor, then mopping would have been added to that list.

Except Esther had dismantled the mop to use in her escape.

'Just take your time …' the policewoman whispered.

One foot in front of the other. That was all. It was easy when you reduced it to that. One foot moving, then the other. Taking her time. Except her time had already been taken, the minutes and hours and days, all sixteen years of them gone.

There were the shelves. Esther had a wild impulse to try to hide amongst them, hunker down amid the tins and first aid and wait for everyone to leave: her personal maze. Maybe in the silence she would have been able to think.

One foot in front of the other. There was Mother's clipboard, the Checklist never to be checked again. As she walked past she tucked the pen back into its holder, her hand lingering over the rows of neat ticks.

Though the round wall lights were switched on, it remained gloomy and, in the murk, she could have been six, ten, sixteen. She half expected to hear Mother's voice one more time, to see her come from the laundry room, or the gym, her glasses on her head, the belt of her cardigan hanging loose …

'Do you need a break?' The policewoman once more.

Esther shook her head.

One foot in front of the other.

Through the storeroom and into the tunnels with its alcoves.

Her father should have died in a warm place, near a window, at a ripe old age, with someone's hand in his, even if he no longer knew who that person was. Instead he had died in the dark, cold and terrified, and had been buried next to machinery and dried food.

One foot in front of the other.

Mother had died in the dark too, alone, the cold barrel of the handgun pressed against her skin.

The tunnel widened out and now the shelving was set back

into the walls themselves, some stubby branches ending in alcoves of their own, each one packed high with tools, machinery, sacks, boxes, crates, barrels and a thousand other things.

Except for one.

The one that had always been empty.

She got there too quickly.

All she had to do was confirm, a nod of her head. A dark archway.

Final resting place.

She couldn't really cry for a man she couldn't remember, who she thought had died years ago and had only briefly been resurrected only to fall to bone again. So she cried for her mother, for the only love she had ever had, even if that love was a darker and more twisted thing than it should have been. She cried because it was gone and the hole it left in her was raw and open and she didn't know how to fill it.

In the swinging beam of her torchlight, there, high in the corner, hidden so you had to go right into the room and then turn, in a little niche above the entrance, dug out especially for that purpose was a very familiar type of object.

A little wooden figure in the shape of a man. Hand-whittled. Grave marker.

Esther turned and made her way back out into the light.

Chapter 68

Another door.

It seemed that Esther was doomed to always be stuck on a threshold, not knowing if she should go through. A week had passed after she had climbed, half choked, out of a skylight window and collapsed in a heap on the roof of the House with Tom.

The week had been dizzying. She had been assessed and checked over, left waiting in overheated hospital corridors, and there had been a police station and bitter coffee in disposable cups. She could not remember much of either. Toxicity reports told her what she already knew: that there were traces of sedatives in her system but, other than that, she was fit and well, even with the asthma.

And then there were no more corridors or cups. She was spun into the Out There, no other family left apart from her uncle, no friends, no money, a home that was a crime scene.

When she stopped spinning, there was Tom.

He was waiting in the car. The awkwardness of that day at the aquarium had faded like breath on glass. Too much had been survived and there was too much to do, a web of paperwork and requirements to start a life in this Out There, that without him, she would not have known how to build.

She had spent a few nights in the spare room in his small flat in the city but soon there would be money from a fund her father had left her and some from her mother too, hidden in the House. That money would allow her to decide where she wanted to live ... and not have to share a bathroom with a man she had tried to snog. She had thought that she would like the city apartment block where he lived in the bay, big windows with a view of the boats, giving the illusion that the polluted streets and roads behind them were not there.

At night though, when she tried to sleep, she could hear people moving in the upstairs flat – footsteps on tiles, blurred voices, snatches of music. It made her feel haunted and she slept badly, the voices and footsteps and music leaking into her dreams. Those big windows let in too much light so it gave her a headache, and she might not have been able to see the roads and the traffic and the litter and smoke, but they were there all the same.

She stayed inside a lot.

Esther peered through the window of the door where she currently stood. It reminded her a bit of the door in the House with its metal trims and the heaviness of it. Inside was a room with a hospital bed and a side table under a window where there was a vase of tulips, their heads already drooping in the warmth.

In the bed was Adam.

Visiting had felt like the thing to do. He was her uncle. He had spent years trying to find his brother, her father, and he had succeeded.

He had broken apart her crab-shell world.

She could only see the back of his head, that silver hair, the bulk of him under a blue blanket and white hospital sheet. The smell of bleach was overpowering in the corridor but only barely concealed a hint of something rotten underneath.

He turned.

Esther gasped as he gazed at her. She had to go in now, she thought, her hand flat against the door, except she made no move to push on it, unable to drag her eyes away from him. She couldn't read his expression – probably there was no expression for this moment, nothing that could completely convey the pain and guilt and anger and sadness. Facial muscles weren't up to the job. Perhaps he wasn't even seeing her, too drugged up on painkillers to realise that she was really there and not a figment of his imagination.

Esther willed herself to push her hand and open the door.

He stared at her some more and though the expression was difficult to read she could see it wasn't pleasure to see her washing over his face. Maybe that would never come, even if they did manage to forge some kind of relationship. Every time they saw each other, the pain would needle first and they would have to grit their teeth to get through it before any other emotion could nudge in.

Esther turned from the door.

She could almost hear the sigh that breathed softly against her neck and she shook her head as she walked to the main entrance. No. Not her today either. Ever since she had left her mother's body cooling in the darkness she had had a tingling feeling in her head that she was only a step behind her – that if she turned fast enough then she would see her standing there, arms crossed, shabby cardigan, fierce stare.

A woman and a little boy hurried past her and Esther didn't know what made her stop and watch them. The woman had long glossy brown hair that she wound up in one hand and flicked over her shoulder in an irritated fashion, her other hand dragging the little boy who was in turn dragging his feet. There was nothing in his face that Esther recognised, no hint in the tilt of his head or the shape of his jaw, nothing that called out to her. His was just another face in the hundreds she walked past every day.

They headed into Adam's room and Esther did not follow them. Not today.

Chapter 69

Another door.

Further down the street was a sugar-coated house with metal butterflies feeding from it. But she no longer wanted to see inside what had once been her childhood home. She was here for a different house.

The door opened.

'Tomeeee!' A shape launched itself at Tom, stood next to her.

'Oof!' He staggered backwards as Maisie gave him a death-choke hug, wrapping her arms around his neck. Today she had added a knitted hat with dinosaur scales on it to match her slippers and T-shirt.

'Maisie Jane Lawson! How many times do I have to tell you? Do not open the front door without—' Olivia's scolding came to an abrupt stop when she saw Esther on her doorstep.

'Umm ... I have something for Maisie, if that's okay?' Esther faltered. 'And, umm ... sorry for, well, for the last time—' But she didn't get to finish as Olivia had already enveloped her in a hug.

'Lovely girl, come in, come in! No apology needed.'

'What's my present?' Maisie twisted in Tom's arms and pushed her face into Esther's. 'What is it? What is it? What is it?'

'At this rate, missy, it'll be a lump of coal – in!' Olivia stood back to allow them to enter, Maisie jumping down from Tom's arms and whispering very loudly to herself as she walked past her mother that she liked coal a lot and it would be a brilliant present.

There was the room with its walls hung with prints and pictures and brass things that tinkled softly. There were the brightly patterned throws and rugs with edges beginning to fray. There was tea and that sweet, smoky smell, though Olivia pinched out the incense stick, whipped it away and opened a window.

'Tea party!' Maisie ordered, dragging Esther by the hand through the living room and out into the back garden where a tent had been set up on the grass. Calling it a tent was probably an ambitious word for it – it was a blanket fixed by hope and two broom handles. Underneath was a tea set and an arrangement of dolls and toys, each one with a cup next to them, Mittens the toy lion in pride of place at the centre.

'Tea.' Maisie pushed a cup into Esther's hand. It was full of a liquid that certainly looked like a kind of green tea, with some added bits of lawn in it. A bear toppled into his drink, nose first. 'Are you going to run off again?'

'I don't think so.' Esther fished out a blade of grass from her tea and took a pretend sip, not willing to trust Maisie's tea-making skills just yet.

'Mummy says that your mummy died and I'm not to talk about it.'

A sigh. A breath on her neck. 'That's right.'

'You must be sad.' Maisie straightened the drunken bear.

That word "sad" would do for now because there wasn't an actual word for the maelstrom of emotions that gut-punched her at the oddest of times. 'I am.' Maisie nodded and poured more tea. 'I'd like you to meet someone.' Esther fished into her bag, not the rucksack from before but a proper handbag – the kind she had seen women carrying on that first visit to the village, smaller and sleek with a gold clasp. It had been hard to stuff him into the space. 'This is Mr Wiffles.'

Maisie stroked him. 'Hello, Mr Wiffles.'

'You see, Mr Wiffles is mine. I had him when I was little like you and I've kept him for a very long time, but I don't think I should keep him forever. I think he'd like to join your toys.'

Once more, the bear slid into his cup of tea.

'I'd keep him?' Maisie stared at her, wide-eyed.

'Yes. I think he'd like to swim here from now on.'

'But he's yours.'

Esther smoothed the velvet nap along his fin. 'I'm too old for him.'

Maisie sat back on her heels and frowned. 'Mummy has a teddy with one ear that she's had since she was little and she loves him. She wouldn't give him away.'

How to explain it? Doing this wasn't even about Mr Wiffles, not really – doing this was a line in the sand, a symbol, a ceremony. A jumping-off point. She didn't know what it was, but she needed to do it.

'How about a holiday then? Can Mr Wiffles stay for a bit?'

'A holiday … like sandcastles and ice lollies? Mummy could knit him a swimsuit.'

If Mr Wiffles was ever going to talk to her again, it would have been now. She could imagine what he'd say about sporting a knitted one-piece. And that was the thing – she could imagine it, but she couldn't hear it. Not anymore.

'Yes, like that.'

'I guess so.' Maisie pushed the teddy bear into a seated position, sounding more convinced. 'A holiday would be fun. And you could come back and get him when you miss him too much.'

'Yes.'

'Mummy!' Maisie jumped to her feet and raced inside. 'Tom's girlfriend has given me a whale!'

Esther smiled. Then she gave Mr Wiffles the cup she had been drinking from and propped him next to Mittens, who was sporting bows in his mane, 'Goodbye, Mr Wiffles,' she said, smoothing his nose. What she meant was goodbye, rosary days; goodbye, Checklist; goodbye, the sighing of the air-conditioning system.

What she hadn't been able to say yet: goodbye, Mother.

She waited for a response.

In the silence she got up and had actual tea inside with Olivia and Tom whilst Maisie ran about with a cardboard dinosaur tail strapped around her waist and all the while, during every sip and in the pauses between conversation topics, she waited for a familiar gruff voice in her ear.

It never came.

* * *

On the way back to Tom's flat they passed the pub they had first stayed in when she had left the House, the one where they had sat in the darkness with the stars wheeling above them.

Stopping seemed the right thing to do.

There was the same beer garden bench except now there were couples and families around them and it was just warm enough to remember what summer felt like. There were no stars this time, but they sat with their backs to the table so they could lean and watch the clouds.

'Fat dog's nose.' Esther pointed at a tattered cloud.

'Weird eagle with fish tail.' Tom pointed at another.

They sat in silence for a while and considered the sky. The stars were there, Esther thought, they just couldn't see them. It was only because of the earth's atmosphere that the daytime sky was blue, without it the sky would be black and the sun would shine down like a massive spotlight, turning the world into one huge amateur theatre production.

'Can I drive the rest of the way home?' she asked.

'Oh God. I'm going to need a stronger drink.'

Learning to drive felt important – the ability to escape if she needed to, to go far away. Though going anywhere further than a mile or so would take a while as she currently did not like using anything over second gear.

Her chest tightened but her demon would always be with her, inside her. She couldn't reach in and rip it out of her body. The rattle of her inhaler was a comforting sound. So far she had not had a bad attack but she knew one would be coming at some point and she couldn't hide from it. More importantly, she didn't want to.

She sat up and bent over as she took drags from the little plastic lifesaver always in her pocket. At once, Tom was by her side.

'Okay?'

'Okay.'

But he didn't move back to his original seat. The blue sky above them was not the blue of aquarium water, however, and no fish swum around them. Esther could feel his shoulder next to hers and it would take hardly any movement to lean in to him. It felt like she knew him, the way his hair curled at the nape of his neck when it got too long, the ready smile, the way he bit his lip when thinking. It felt like he knew her. But the thing was – *she* didn't know her yet – not this her, the one who walked around Out Here and bought takeaway coffee after getting off a bus. She could not let herself lean on anyone's shoulder just yet because she had done far too much of that in her life up until now. Time to do the heavy lifting herself.

'Ready?' he asked.

But she wanted a bit more time in the sun. She wanted his hand next to hers and his shoulder close to her own. She wanted invisible stars and a sky that was the colour of the sea.

She knew there was one more door left.

Chapter 70

The final door.

The only one that had mattered to her for sixteen years.

Esther was alone. It had been a few months since she had moved out of Tom's flat. She needed to be on her own, so that if her washing machine broke, she would be the one who would have to fix it, so that she would buy her own shopping and work out how to set up broadband. By herself. She would have to go into the Out Here to get those things done.

No more apartments with their thin walls and ghost noises. No. She had chosen to rent a tiny end-of-terrace house in a village that was never going to be big enough to be a town and where the nearest city was a forty-minute car ride away. Old habits died hard.

Road, to dirt track, to path, to gravel, to … House.

One last time.

She got there before the rest of them. She had been up so early that the sky was still deciding what colour it would be and the trees hadn't yet shaken night from their branches. That was okay. She was happy to sit and wait.

She had had the option to sell the land and everything on it. That was what had been expected. Who would want to keep such a place? You couldn't have a fresh start with a whiff of rot following you everywhere you went. You had to get rid, move on.

Except.

As much as she liked her end-of-terrace rented house in the village that would never be a town, so far away from the city, every time one of her neighbours had a bonfire or barbecue, or she saw exhaust fumes in the air, she wanted to hide in the house all day. The sound of her neighbours' cars out in the street were animals growling warning snarls, snouts pointed to the sky, sensing the poison in the air.

She read a lot, about eco technologies and super plants that could filter out noxious traffic fumes and deadlines and agreements and treaties and breakthroughs.

But they were only words.

The diggers rumbled in first along a dirt track now widened enough to use. They had known Esther was going to be there and the lead driver touched his cap in what looked almost like a salute.

She gazed at her narrow bedroom window, realising with a jolt that she was right back at the beginning. Tom had stood here, where she was, such a short and also achingly long time ago and she had watched him from that window, a willing captive, sometimes imagining an Other Her out there living a different life.

Here she was.

Not Other, just Her.

The hairdresser's appointment had been one of the first things she had done. Textbook apparently, for people like her, people who'd been through some kind of trauma, to hack and dye their way to a different person. Except that wasn't what she was doing – she was whittling, shaving away the curls of wood until she could see her true shape in the block.

Someone sighed at her shoulder.

If she let her eyes wander a little, she could almost kid herself that she could see a flicker at that window, a pale face gazing out, trapped in her slice of glass: a scruffy figure in a baggy cardigan with a clipboard in her hand.

More machinery rumbled into the clearing.

She planned to sit through the whole thing, however long it took – though she had learnt that destruction was quick. Years to build and maintain, gone in minutes, the time it takes to open a door and allow someone in.

The man who had saluted her earlier, paunch straining the T-shirt he wore under his hi-vis jacket, raised his hand to her again, waiting.

Esther felt like a Roman emperor at a gladiator game. Thumb up, or thumb down: one movement from her hand holding the power to bring down what had once been her world.

She did not believe in ghosts. But, if there were any attached to this building, she meant for the diggers and trucks in front of her to so completely turn the place to rubble there would be nothing for them to haunt.

She raised her hand.

The man nodded and swung back into his seat.

The first digger chugged into movement, its arm lifted in front of it as it wobbled forward. Giant metal teeth met concrete and bit down hard, tugging and shoving until the stone began to crumble and then crack.

Esther settled in.

Her hand instinctively went to her pocket, her fingers finding the shape of the inhaler, tracing over it like a talisman. The camping chair was comfortable enough. She had a flask of coffee with her and a warm jacket. She could sit here all day.

The metal teeth continued to chew.

Earlier that month there had been a graveyard with two glossy black headstones, their gold lettering shining in the sun. A father she had never known, a mother she thought she had. People came to speak to the dead, she knew. They brought flowers and told them about children and grandchildren, about their feelings and what the weather was doing. Esther had not known what to say. It would take a while before she worked that out, if she ever did.

She would build a different home on this land. A home with big windows and a garden ... a driveway in block paving that invited visitors up to a normal-sized door, not made of metal. This, here, amongst the trees and the whispering grass was where she felt safe, but it was no longer where she wanted to hide. This new home would sit *on* the hill, not *under* it, it would be visible from the path – a glint of glass and soft cream stone. Esther could see it in her mind.

It occurred to her that once again, she was sitting and watching as the action went on around her. But this time, once the last wall had fallen, once the window frames had buckled and twisted and the rubble as it fell sent clouds of dust into the air, she would get up from her spot on the ground and she would turn to that dirt path, free to keep walking for as long as she wished into a world where the sky had finally settled on a startling bright blue.

She took a deep breath.

Acknowledgements

It is only fitting that I should liken the whole process of writing *The Safe House* to ... well, a house; a house very much under construction for the most part of the writing process but luckily surrounded by some much-needed scaffolding to keep the thing from collapsing.

Here's to my scaffolding.

My agent, the ever-supportive and best cheerleader Kate, who was one of the first to read my final-definitely-not-going-to-rip-it-up-and-start-again draft and her encouraging words meant more to me than possibly she knows.

My insightful and brilliant editor Abi, who immediately nailed what needed to be improved when I couldn't work it out anymore and who always remains unfailingly enthusiastic and kind.

Once again, to my literary fairy godmother Lisa Milton who gave me a chance in the first place and, without her, I wouldn't be in this amazing and privileged position of publishing my second book.

Everyone at HQ who has worked on the book in whatever form: the design team, publicity and marketing, Helena my copy-editor, typesetting and proofreading (especially proofreading!). They are all stars.

I have never lived in a bunker, though, some might say, growing up in a small Welsh town in the Eighties is perhaps a very similar thing. So, to answer queries and questions, I read a lot about the end-of-the-world business and doomsday preppers and I now know perhaps too much about how to grow vegetables in the dark. Particularly the book *Bunker: Building for the End Times* by Bradley Garrett and the beautifully bizarre Christopher Walken/Brendan Fraser film *Blast From The Past*. Thanks also to James Borland for explaining some legal issues to me.

To my bookish internet community, in particular Crime Cymru, my Primadonna Festival crew, the Newport Writers and The D20 authors who are all very talented but also very generous with their help and support. Book people really are the best people.

To my gym class buddies, especially the Friday Combat girls – they probably don't realise how much those times mean to me in the week where I can get away from my desk and have a laugh with them all … oh, and do push-ups too.

To my friends and family. Look, I named you all in the first book, do I have to do that again? Oh, you know too much about me and it's not a good idea to annoy you? Well, when you put it like that … Thank you my friends Em, Chris, Dennis (after all, teaching wasn't my forte!), Will, Dan, Fi and Knibbsy, Liz: evenings with you all, drinking wine and talking rubbish, are always the best evenings. My lovely family: Mart, Cath, Aidan, Ffion, Gwen. Continuing the house metaphor: thanks to my mother and sister Caroline who have always been, and still are, my foundations.

Mostly and always, to Jason who often finds me lost in another world inside my head and keeps the show on the road whilst I'm there. Despite hardly ever reading fiction, he always reads my first draft and that, folks, is true love.

Finally, to you, dear reader, who picked up this book and gave it a chance. Thank you.

Keep reading for an excerpt from *Sleepless* …

Chapter 1

There was already a gridlock of cars stretching away behind the accident. *Her* accident. Thea felt a weird ownership over it, like a cat licking at her poor dead kitten.

Her fault – no doubt.

It had to be. In total, she'd probably only slept for four hours … that week.

Behind her was the three-vehicle sandwich in which her car was the crushed metal filling. She staggered back and tried to close the mangled door.

Someone pulled at her elbow: a man, dragging her back from the road where she stood gazing into the traffic. He was uninjured but shouting something, and Thea couldn't focus, her mind slipping off him in the same way his glasses slid down his sweaty nose.

The actual moment of impact had been strangely soothing. Thea couldn't remember any sound really, so there had just been this lovely, pillowy-white cushioning as the airbag deployed and then – whoosh! – like a fairground ride, she was spun around.

She hadn't done it on purpose. She'd thought about things like that quite a few times, in those dead, red-eye hours of the night when she felt like the only person left on earth who was still awake. Ironically, as her car smashed into the one in front, she had actually been congratulating herself that she'd got through the day, that she could do this living thing, even without any sleep, with just a cold sponge for a brain and sandpaper balls for eyes.

She could do it.

But clearly, she couldn't.

How many years of sleeplessness? Too many. Too many achingly long nights that then smudged themselves into joyless, grey, listless days before lights out and another eight hours of frantic panicking. Too many nights etched into the bloodshot spiderwebs in the whites of her eyes.

There was a woman with the man now and Thea looked for blood on her, expecting broken limbs and jagged wounds, but there was nothing, not even a torn blouse. Both of them worked their mouths madly, like gulping fish, expectantly looking at her and then the cars and then back to her again. She should respond, she thought, but she didn't know what to say. The words were there, but they were busy dancing in her brain, enjoying themselves – shaken loose by the impact and free to partner up however they chose.

Her car was concertinaed. It was a shock, how impressively the whole thing could crumple, yet keep her whole as a seed inside its tattered fruit.

But, if she was fruit, then she was the rotten kind, she realized with a gulp that turned into a choking gasp. She could have hurt that man and woman staring at her now. She could have *killed* them. Up until that point, the only damage her insomnia had done had been to herself – her social life, her concentration, mood, skin, memory and general joy in living. It had never affected someone else, never nearly crushed them in a smoking metal box.

There was pain now. Her nose a tender, pulsating blob, her knees suddenly shakier than they had been, blood on her collarbone where her seatbelt had taken a bite.

Abruptly, she sank to the cold ground at the roadside. Soon there would be flaring emergency lights and sirens; there would be gentle fingers prodding at her and questions asked and, dimly, she realized she would have to get herself together for all of that. More people gathered, but from her viewpoint sat on the ground, they were just feet, their voices so far above her they may as well have been stars.

There would be so much to do after something like this, Thea thought: the forms and phone calls, appointments and claims. The effort. She didn't have it in her. She felt so light there was nothing left of her and dealing with all of this needed solidity; it needed heft, a person who felt like they left a footprint when they walked. If someone blew on her she would simply dissipate, like dust on the wind.

Idly, she watched liquid seep from under her car and with the same blankness with which she'd thought of everything else, she wondered if the liquid was flammable, or if it was merely water.

She should have cared, one way or the other.

At that moment her hand buzzed. She blinked. Maybe it was an injury of some kind, she thought slowly. She would probably need to get it checked out, once she got up from this really rather comfortable bit of damp ground. It buzzed again and this time her eyes managed to get the message over to her brain that she was still clutching her phone. Looking down at it, a notification flashed up, some advert from one of her apps, something she'd probably seen a thousand times before. At first, she thought it was the universe's idea of a cruel joke. But then, as she sat there amongst the twisted metal and shattered glass, she came to think of it more as salvation:

Morpheus. Dream your way to a better you – one sleep at a time.

Chapter 2

Thea stared at the frog.

She had successfully risen from the dead for yet another day.

It was one week after the car crash. Thea had removed all clocks from her bedroom to prevent feeling anxious at night about the hours passing. However, this now meant she spent the time feeling anxious about *not knowing* how many hours were passing, which she wasn't sure was an improvement. Last night she had certainly spent many hours in bed, a lot of them with her eyes shut kidding herself she was dozing. The sky had been a watery blue when she finally did drop off.

Waking to the alarm was like dragging herself out of a deep grave.

She did the usual estimation again: an hour or so of sleep, tops. That was pretty much classed as sleep deprivation, wasn't it? Some dictatorships used that as torture. By rights, after years of sleeping like this, she shouldn't have been walking, talking, working ... driving. She should have been huddled in a corner, hollow-eyed and drooling.

Mornings were finely tuned. As adrenaline kicked at brain cells that only wanted sleep, she had discovered that mornings were not a time for decision-making. She washed, dressed in the clothes laid out ready the night before, grabbed her preprepared breakfast and lunch and got out of the door, her head beginning to pound.

She was a bruise and the rest of the world was a poking finger.

The frog looked at her.

Instead of work, this morning Thea found herself at the Car Recovery Centre, picking her way through the graveyard of other people's vehicles with an overly cheerful assistant. She clutched a cardboard box to her chest. It was filled with the belongings that had been rescued from her car. The bright green frog sprawled on top, a present from her mother when she had bought her first car. He had a red kerchief around his neck and a button in his middle that, when pressed, played a selection of children's songs. His green was clean, his kerchief still tied neatly, his button still working. It was as if the crash had never happened. She, on the other hand, felt as if her own stuffing was showing.

'We clear out the cars ourselves, but just wanna check that there's nothing we missed.' The man edged his stomach past the hulk of an estate car.

'Umm … I'm okay. You seem to have it all here. I don't need to see the—'

'There you go.' He pointed.

The thing in front of her still had some of the essential features of a car, but they were in all the wrong places: wheels squashed too close together, windscreen crumpled, half the bonnet missing. Suddenly, the car park around her shifted and fell away and she was back in the driver's seat, the airbags a cushion around her, smoke in her hair.

She took a deep breath.

Someone else could have ended up as twisted and shattered as the lump of metal and glass in front of her.

And then, within twenty minutes, she really was back in the driver's seat. A different car provided by her insurance, the inside smelling of polish and air freshener.

All she had to do was turn the ignition key.

A woman with a clipboard stood expectantly by the car, waiting for her to drive away, smile frozen.

It was now 10 a.m. and the world had come into pulsing, throbbing focus. Thea popped a paracetamol for her eternal headache, stared at the dashboard and blinked a few times, hoping that would make her eyelids lighter.

The woman waited expectantly.

All she had to do was turn the key.

Her hand hovered near the ignition, but, in her head, she could hear the grinding squeal of metal against metal and the noise was so loud it made her fingers shake.

People as twisted and shattered as that lump of metal and glass.

She fumbled for the door handle and lurched out of the car, grabbing her box of belongings.

'Umm … Miss Mackenzie?' She heard the woman call out after her, but the voice was an echo and Thea walked fast, away, out of the car park, not looking back.

'I'm sorry!' She shouted behind her. 'Can you just—? Look, I'll pick it up later …'

And she kept walking until the whole place was out of sight and she was out of breath, her eyes stinging with tears she hadn't realized she'd cried. The frog stared at her as she got out her phone to call a taxi, and, once again, the notification popped up on her screen:

Morpheus. Dream your way to a better you – one sleep at a time.

Thea blamed the frog and the broken carcass of her car as the reasons why she found herself that evening in the local pub, squashed between her desk-mate, Lisa, and a man from a different department with a thin face and thinner hair.

The office where she spent her days moving numbers from one spreadsheet to another was a grey, open-plan box. It always smelled of microwave-ready meals from the encrusted kitchen in the corner, had carpet the consistency of Velcro and an air-conditioning system that had a poor grasp of the seasons. She didn't even have a desk of her own but shared one with Lisa, a middle-aged woman who filled her workspace with so many photographs, paperweights and cute figures that they often made attempts to colonize Thea's territory. She spent probably too much of her day pushing back googly-eyed unicorns with a pencil. One cuddly car-frog was more than enough for her.

But, this time, when Lisa had asked her to the pub for after-work drinks, Thea had said yes.

She deserved a night out. She deserved the kind of night other people had regularly. One without worrying about how late it could get and that she wouldn't have time for her wind-down routine and it was Thursday and she had work the next morning and she couldn't get up late but she wouldn't get any sleep at all and that car crash would be nothing compared to the mistakes she could make if she was utterly, utterly sleepless—

'See? Aren't you glad you came out? You should do it more often.' Lisa's nails had tiny daisies painted on them.

It was Margaret's leaving drinks. Thea hadn't really known that Margaret had ever arrived in the first place.

'Too good for the likes of us, eh?' The thin man smiled.

Thea thought about trying to explain it. She didn't feel like she was better than them at all; in fact they were all quite clearly better than her – better at being human and sociable and remembering each other's birthdays and the ages of their children. Thea didn't have the energy for any of that. She tried sleeping later at the weekends in the hope that would tide her over for the coming week, but it never did. Sleep debt, it was called, and her debt was the kind that got loan sharks circling. She would never be able to repay it.

But that was going to stop, Thea thought, taking a swig of her wine. She couldn't let insomnia continue to ruin her days as well as her nights. A life – that's what she was going to have. Starting now.

'Cheers, Mark,' she said, raising her glass with a hand that continued to shake.

'It's Mike.'

Luckily, her 7 p.m. boost of brief energy kicked in and she listened, laughed in the right places, bought drinks, admired photos of holidays and children and did it all despite the fact that her brain began to whirl and the noise and heat of the pub began to close in on her.

'And so, Mark, what do you like to do in your free time?'

He had a weak chin and there was a strange smell to him, as if he'd been out in the rain and left to dry too slowly, but he seemed pleasant enough. Thea smiled.

'It's Mike.'

More photos, more drinks, more laughing, more brain swirling, more noise and heat. But the noise was welcome; it drowned out the sound of grinding metal that she couldn't get out of her head. Lisa's perfume masked the acrid smell of burnt rubber.

People as twisted and shattered as that lump of metal and glass.

'Another, Mark?' She forced the corners of her mouth back up into a smile and motioned with her empty wine glass.

'Mike.'

'Shit! Sorry! Really, I'm—'

But he had already turned away to the woman on his other side. She couldn't blame him. It seemed that she could do everything except remember this man's name. It slipped out of her grasp every time she opened her mouth. The wine churned in her empty stomach and suddenly she wanted to leave, before Mark – Mike! – told everyone how stupid she was, before she threw up the wine, before her exhausted brain refused to tell her equally exhausted body what to do and she had to be carried out of the pub like an invalid.

Using every last bit of willpower, she heaved herself up from her seat and shuffled past Lisa who tried to grab her hand and slur something incomprehensible. Then she was out of the door, the air hitting her like an open palm. She wasn't sure if it was alcohol or exhaustion that made her steps wobble.

Of course, back at home, after a bath and a ready meal, she was wide awake. This state continued until early the next morning, and, at some point during one of those red-eyed hours, she looked once more at the notifications on her phone, emboldened by the wine still fizzing in her blood.

Morpheus. Dream your way to a better you – one sleep at a time. She clicked on it.

Chapter 3

'Well, it's probably a cult, isn't it, darling?'

It was a week after Thea's unsuccessful trip to the pub and her mother was eating haloumi salad, her silk scarf nearly trailing in the food. Luckily, you had to get really close to see that the scarf was printed with tiny little vaginas.

'You'll get there and then, give it a few weeks, you'll be having orgies and giving blow jobs. Constantly. Mark my words. Cult.'

Sometimes Thea wished she didn't have a mother who said things like "orgies" and "blow jobs" in the middle of a crowded restaurant where the tables were so close you could practically breathe on someone else's food.

'A cult might be good for you.' Vivian speared an asparagus tip thoughtfully. 'More sex.'

Thea could feel her face burning. She wasn't sure how much more of this she could stand.

Vivian lowered her voice to a dramatic stage whisper, but couldn't hide the glint in her eyes: '*I think I have more sex than you!*'

She probably did. Thea had to admit it.

'Mum! I swear I will leave if you carry on!' Thea tried to keep her voice stern as Vivian smiled at the few furtive glances she was getting, like a queen amongst her courtiers.

'Sorry, teapot. Can't help myself. Winding you up is too much fun. Will be good.'

Thea hated being called "teapot" too. Her mother had started it when she was little because, 'You had such a sweet little rounded tummy and these skinny arms and legs.' Vivian thought it cute. Thea disagreed.

'Right. It's not a cult. It's a trial for a new sleep app and they'll pay for me to be a part of it. All I have to do is apply for an interview. Thing is, it'll last for six weeks, and obviously the office won't give me leave for that long so' – Thea momentarily found her ham panini fascinating – 'umm … if I'm accepted, I'll just leave my job.'

That was all it had ever been – a job. Not a career, not a vocation, not a calling. Hers was one desk among many in an office with strip lighting that buzzed. It paid the bills. Of course, those bills would still need to be paid, even if she left that desk …

Unhinged, that's how she felt. It was as if the car accident had snapped a vital part of her and it was now flapping wildly in the wind, loose from its fixings, hanging in there by not very much at all.

Vivian stopped eating and reached across the table, laying her hand over Thea's. She stared intensely into her daughter's eyes and, when she spoke, it was with a deliberate solemnity. 'That, my love, is the best news I've heard this year. I'm delighted! You're wasted in … whatever it is that you do in that little office. Come help us out at HQ. We always need someone to paint the placards.'

HQ was a living room. The Menopausal Army ('Probably best to call us Post-Menopausal now, darling!') had had many names over the years but always the same goal: change. Vivian Mackenzie had spent nearly thirty fervent, bright-eyed years protesting, marching, arguing and educating on anything and everything that needed it. A lot of things needed it. They still did, but Vivian had, over the last few years, taken a step back from leading it all. Thea was banned from calling this retirement.

'You are a creative soul, anyway – I've always thought it,' Vivian continued. 'We can find you another job.' She gripped Thea's hand tighter. 'I blame myself, you know, for this inability of yours to sleep properly. We moved around so much when you were little, there was no routine, no stability. You were so well behaved, but it's left its mark. I see that now.' She emphasized the next words. '*I own it.*'

There it was. There was the pause, which Thea was meant to fill with the reassurance that Vivian's chaotic lifestyle when she was little had not irrevocably scarred her in any way. Old age was making her mother sentimental.

'Mum, it's not your fault—'

'Is it dangerous? How does it work? You hear such stories these days. These big companies, they have no morals, no sense of responsibility …'

'I don't know. I'm being sent an introductory pack. I can back out if it doesn't sound right. There are loads of these kinds of sleep apps around. It'll probably turn out to be crap and I'll be back at square one.'

Vivian sighed, frowned and fiddled with the huge turquoise bangle on her wrist. Today she was dressed in a bright red tunic top and a necklace in the shape of bats joined together at the wing, even though Hallowe'en was weeks away. Thea wished she'd worn better-fitting jeans, and that maybe she hadn't decided to cut her own fringe this month. But both jeans and hair were clean, and on some bleak mornings, after only an hour's sleep, that was all she could manage.

'I don't like it,' Vivian finally proclaimed. 'But I raised you to know your own mind. So do it if you want to. But you call me the minute anything feels off and I will come and get you wherever you are. And, darling … remember the keys.'

Ah yes, the old key trick: Vivian's idea of teaching Thea self-defence when she turned thirteen. 'When out late at night, teapot, hold your keys in your hand like this … yes, that's it, with the points sticking out between your fingers, like a knuckleduster. Okay, then if any man makes a grab at you, just swipe ... yes, like that ... mind the cat, teapot ... swipe up and nearly blind the bugger.' She hadn't yet had a chance to try it out.

'Okay, Mum.'

Vivian unwound her scarf, shaking it out so anyone left in the café who hadn't yet seen its print got an eyeful. 'I suppose you could make some new friends at least, and anyway – you might not even get accepted for this interview, hmm?'

That was the thing, Thea thought as she avoided her mother's eye. She already had been.

Dear Reader,

We hope you enjoyed reading this book. If you did, we'd be so appreciative if you left a review. It really helps us and the author to bring more books like this to you.

Here at HQ Digital we are dedicated to publishing fiction that will keep you turning the pages into the early hours. Don't want to miss a thing? To find out more about our books, promotions, discover exclusive content and enter competitions you can keep in touch in the following ways:

JOIN OUR COMMUNITY:

Sign up to our new email newsletter:
http://smarturl.it/SignUpHQ

Read our new blog www.hqstories.co.uk

https://twitter.com/HQStories

www.facebook.com/HQStories

BUDDING WRITER?

We're also looking for authors to join the HQ Digital family!
Find out more here:

https://www.hqstories.co.uk/want-to-write-for-us/

Thanks for reading, from the HQ Digital team

HQ

If you enjoyed *The Safe House*, then why not try another gripping thriller from HQ Digital?

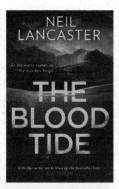

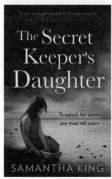

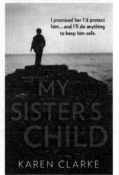